Spirit Pass

Revised and Expanded

Collection of Novellas

<u>Books by Angela Grey</u>
Missing and Murdered Indigenous Women
& Girls: A Jessica Stone Novella #2
The Lasting Echo of Lost Souls: A Jessica
Stone Novella #3
Sifting Through a Storied Past
Prologue to an Epitaph
A Childhood Lost to the Wind
Secret Whispers
Déjà vu
Of Laughter & Heartbreak
Beating Drum of a Broken Heart
Bdóte
Bedridden & Gutted to Mindful
Between Shadows and Lies
Nostalgic Tendencies, Idyllic Endeavors, &
Current Inclinations
Dreamcatcher
The Cartography of First Love

<u>Also by Angela Grey & Paige Peterson</u>
Lake of Secrets
Dancing Without Music
Echoes of the Past
Echoes at Midnight
Madness & Mayhem
Long Since Buried
Since You've Been Gone
Some Species of Outsider-ness

Spirit Pass

Revised and Expanded Collection of Novellas

Angela Ellen Grey

Printed in the United States of America.

For more information or to book an event, contact :

angelagrey@ShadyOakPress.com

http://www.ShadyOakPress.com

Cover by SelfPubBookCovers.com/FrinaArt

ISBN: 978-1-961841-56-7

CONTENTS
INTRODUCTION

To the love of my life, Robert,

and our four adult children,

Paige, Cody, Chase, & Brooke,

children-in-law

Vince and Angel,

and grandsons Logan and Luke

—AG

Introduction

Step onto a reservation near a thriving city, and the first things you'll notice are the contrasts. Casinos glitter against the night sky, drawing tourists and capital that flow back into tribal economies. Paved roads stretch smooth and lit, new schools gleam with modern design, and homes rise with the latest fixtures and finishes—high-tech, stylish, and built with the money that comes from a steady revenue stream. Here, infrastructure feels almost seamless, and some tribal communities have managed to carve out a degree of comfort and opportunity in the shadow of the metropolis.

But travel farther out beyond the edges of the interstate, past the last suburban sprawl, and the picture changes. Rural reservations, far from big cities and steady tourism, often hold a different reality. Roads fracture and fade into gravel. Homes weather into trailers, shacks, and patched roofs. The schools struggle with funding. Grocery stores are few, jobs scarcer still. Generations carry the weight of displacement, neglect, and broken promises, and with them come poverty, despair, and a lack of accessible support resources. Where one reservation builds upward, another fights simply to survive.

It is in this tension between glittering proximity and forgotten remoteness that the stories in this collection take root. These novellas are not just tales of crime, resilience, or survival; they are reflections of what it means to live between two faces of Indian Country: one pressed against the modern world with its high-tech ambitions, the other still caught in the long shadow of history and the intergenerational effects of colonialism.

ANGELA ELLEN GREY

ANGELA ELLEN GREY

1

CREEPING LIKE THE DAWN

A full moon spills its pale light across the quiet Minnesota prairie at midnight. The two-lane highway stretching from the reservation to the Twin Cities lies mostly deserted, its surface gleaming faintly as the river nearby rushes over rock and stone. For a while, that is the only sound—until headlights flare and the hum of an engine grows unsteady, breaking the stillness.

Johnny Skye, Tamryn Willow, Bethany Lufkins, and Wolfie DesJarlais—fifteen-year-old Native kids lingering at the roadside—huddle together in the shadows, sneaking one last smoke before crossing the pass to slip home past curfew.

The pickup truck ahead lurches. Brakes slam. Tires screech. Then, with a sudden roar, it accelerates, only to halt again. From the cab, a door swings open and a figure struggles to break free. Arms thrash in the dim light; the driver yanks at the passenger, fists flying, tangling in her hair. Bethany swears she sees him rip away the woman's tank top.

The truck jerks forward, stops short, and the woman's scream slices the night. For a moment, the cab light flickers, catching the chaos inside. Then, with one final wrench, the passenger tumbles out. Barely clothed, she staggers upright and flees, vanishing into the trees across the road.

The truck creeps closer, and the teens hear the rock band Indigenous blasting through its speakers. Startled, they press themselves behind a roadside tree, their view of the driver obscured. The truck whips into a wide U-turn, fishtails, and hurtles down the empty highway, its muffled music fading into the prairie silence.

A few miles farther on, light glows in a modest trailer set back from the road. Inside, twenty-three-year-old Claudia Shepherd sits at her computer desk, shoulders squared with ambition. A second-grade teacher fresh to the district, she is known for her energy and resolve. On the wall above her immaculately arranged living room hang two framed milestones: her high-school diploma and her college degree. The brand-new furniture gleams beneath the soft lamplight.

At her feet, two German shepherds lift their heads. Their low growls ripple into sharp barks as they trot into the kitchen, then return, hackles raised.

"What's up, guys?" Claudia asks, glancing over her shoulder. She reaches to turn down her stereo—Indigenous, playing loud enough to rattle the tassel dangling from her graduation cap, which tips to the floor.

She pauses, listening. Silence. Then she parts the blackout curtains just enough to peer outside. Only the walkway lights glow faintly, spilling across the gravel drive where her new car rests in perfect order. Nothing stirs.

"Raccoons again, guys," she murmurs, kneeling to stroke the dogs until they settle.

Returning to her desk, she closes the accounting program—a neat record of a limited but carefully tended income—and opens her Dakota language dictionary alongside her lesson planner. On the screen, the week's classroom notes wait, steady and precise, as if nothing outside has shifted at all.

The next morning, Claudia sits in her classroom, the glow of her monitor reflected in her glasses. She scrolls through her lesson planner, typing in last-minute notes. Outside the window, school buses exhale clouds of exhaust as children spill out in noisy clusters, darting toward the building like bright-coated sparrows.

Her focus returns to the screen just as a chat window flashes open with a sharp bell. The dating site photograph that fills the pop-up shows a white man in his thirties, his expression flat, unsmiling. The message beneath his username cuts across the quiet of the room:

AVIDHUNTER89
You're pissing me off!

Claudia's fingers hover over the keyboard. Before she can react, the classroom door bursts open and a wave of children surges inside. Their chatter drowns out the uneasy echo of the words on her screen. She bends quickly to greet them, her smile genuine, her hugs warm and steady.

Across the small reservation, in the upstairs offices of the Community Center, Claudia's grandmother, Agnes Greyeagle, pins a poster to the bulletin board in the waiting area. Sixty-five and young at heart, Agnes serves as the tribe's Volunteer Coordinator. Her gray-streaked braid swings as she smooths the edges of the announcement, its bold letters declaring:

SPRING LAUNCH
Saturday, May 9th
Drag the River & Ground Search for Missing &
Murdered Indigenous Women & Girls

Detective Sergeant Jessica Stone, thirty-two, climbs the stairs as Agnes works. With her gentle features, she could easily be mistaken for younger, but her steady eyes carry the weight of hard years. Behind her, a young mother cradles a crying baby. Stone ushers the woman toward the receptionist, then turns as a door swings open and a little

Native girl bursts out, running straight into her mother's arms.

Bernice O'Reilly, a counselor in her fifties, follows the little girl very close behind. "You made it," she says warmly.

"I had to walk," the young mother answers, bouncing her child, "but Detective Stone gave us a ride for the last stretch."

Stone pours herself a cup of coffee, watching Agnes adjust the poster. Bernice crouches to the girl's level, smiling. "I stopped by preschool downstairs and picked her up. We had a good talk—almost an hour. I'd like to see her again next week, if that's okay."

"Definitely. And I'll be on time."

"Just check in with the receptionist to schedule."

The mother nods, grateful.

Bernice rejoins Stone and Agnes at the bulletin board. "Pre-registration looking good?" she asks.

"Mostly our regulars," Agnes replies. "A handful of techies signed up for drone duty."

"It'll help, having the new search boat alongside the kayaks," Bernice offers.

"Different depths," Agnes mutters, her tone weighted.

Bernice brightens. "The casino confirmed—they'll provide food and drinks for all volunteers that day." Then, lowering her voice, she leans toward Agnes. "What's bothering you?"

"Just the same old faces," Agnes sighs.

"What does it take to make people care? The rest of the state doesn't give a damn." She glances at Stone, memory flickering across her eyes. "Jessica, I'm sorry—I know you're in this heart and soul." Her hand squeezes the detective's arm. Stone blinks hard, fighting the reaction, scanning the room to see if anyone noticed her slip. "But the FBI..." Agnes finishes bitterly, "...they're useless."

At the reception desk, a young woman—well-dressed, no more than twenty—sets down her headset and walks over. "A call came earlier," she says. "I couldn't transfer it before they hung up."

"Therapy intake? Or employee assistance?" Bernice asks.

The receptionist shakes her head. "The woman wanted someone to talk to her daughter. She claims she was abducted but escaped last night. She won't go to the police because she'd been drinking."

"Was she hurt?" Stone asks quickly.

"Scrapes and bruises from rolling out of a moving vehicle, the mother said. But the girl refuses to make a report. She doesn't want to be blamed, or made to look like it was her fault."

Agnes shakes her head. "Hazards of judgment."

"Or self-preservation," Bernice adds.

"Any caller ID?" Stone presses.

"Anonymous," the receptionist answers.

The words hang heavy in the small office, as though the walls themselves have heard them before.

Claudia's desk phone rings just as she helps a small girl wrestle her backpack over a bulky coat before sending her toward the waiting buses. Claudia waves after her, the child's braid bouncing down the lighted hallway. By the time she reaches the phone, the ringing stops. Caller ID: ANONYMOUS.

She exhales, then erases the Dakota language lesson from the whiteboard. Between swipes of the marker rag, she glances out the window to watch students clamber onto buses, their laughter spilling briefly into the fading afternoon. Engines rumble, then one by one, the buses pull away, leaving the playground still.

A sudden noise at the door makes her pause.
"Hello?" she calls. Silence.

She returns to her desk, but another sound pricks at her curiosity. "Is someone there?"

Claudia pulls open the door and finds a ball rolling lazily across the hallway. She follows it with her eyes, scanning both directions. The corridor, dim now and hushed, offers no answer.

As she bends to pick up the ball, she collides with someone hard. The young janitor stands inches from her, broom in hand.

"Oh! I'm sorry, but I didn't see you there. Hello."

He doesn't respond. He only stares, then lowers his gaze and begins sweeping. Claudia forces a small smile and retreats into her classroom, uneasy. Through the narrow pane of glass in the door, she watches him a moment as she gathers her tote. When she turns back for her keys, he has vanished.

Heart quickening, Claudia hurries into the parking lot. Only a handful of faculty cars remain, and she waves at the last vehicle leaving the drive. The lot feels cavernous, shadows pooling at its edges. She fumbles with her keys, dropping them once before snatching them up again. Finally, she slips into her car, locks the doors, and pulls out fast—tires spitting gravel as she flees toward the highway.

At tribal police headquarters, the air hangs tense. A young office clerk slides a property bag across the counter. Hunter Daniels—white, mid-thirties, tall, his frame carrying the rough swagger of the backwoods—snatches it up. His face is mottled with fresh bruises.

His eyes lock on Detective Sergeant Jessica Stone, who is bent over the printer behind the young receptionist's chunky desk. "What the hell are you staring at?" he barks.

Stone doesn't flinch. "Calm down, Hunter."

He smirks, laughter rasping in his throat. "Is that what your momma used to say to your daddy? *Calm down, honey?*"

"Watch your mouth, Hunter," the clerk snaps.

But Hunter steps closer, his voice low, venomous. "Tell me, how's it feel knowing the only reason you're here is because your daddy raped your momma in the gutter?"

Stone's back stiffens. Her eyes flick to the bulletin board, where rows of missing women's faces gaze back at her. Her breath hitches, rage burning beneath her ribs.

"Go to hell," she says.

Hunter sneers. "I'll say hi to your momma when I get there."

Stone moves before she thinks. She barrels forward, slamming him into the wall, fists knotted in his shirt. The crash echoes down the corridor. Within seconds, two tribal detectives rush from the back office, dragging her off him as Hunter spits blood and grins, satisfied.

Back on the rez, Claudia wakes on the sofa, her two German shepherds sprawled on the rug below, all three lulled by the low murmur of the television still playing in the corner.

Her gaze drifts to the wall. A map hangs there, its surface marked with photo printouts. Above one face, in thick red marker, the word *MURDERED*. Another picture is scrawled with *MISSING*.

Claudia reaches for her cell phone and dials.

"Claudia, are you okay?" her grandmother's voice answers.

"Yes, Grandma."

"It's late. Shouldn't you be asleep?"

"Shouldn't you?" Claudia teases gently. "But I know you too well."

A sigh on the line. "Genetics. We suffer the same worry."

"Are you on the crisis line again tonight?"

"Yes. And you know I have to hang up if I get a call."

"I know. It's good people have you, Grandma."

"And you know I'm always here for you, too."

"I know. Anything happen at work today?"

Her grandmother hesitates. "An anonymous call. The woman hung up before anyone could take it."

"Serious?" Claudia scribbles notes on a pad.

"An abduction. The girl got away."

"What do the police say?"

"Detective Stone came by. But she can't do much without a name."

"Why stay anonymous?"

"She'd been drinking. Afraid of being judged."

Claudia's jaw tightens. "We need to talk to Stone. There are people she should look at more closely."

"Claudia! Don't you get involved in these cases!"

"Grandma, why don't people care? The numbers are staggering."

"I have a call coming in. Go to bed. I love

you."

"I love you too."

Claudia sets the phone down and opens her laptop. Pop-up messages flood her screen. She clicks them away until one lingers:

I know who you are!

Her stomach knots. Another message flashes:

You're the teacher who lives in the pretty little trailer on Hwy. 62 with the two dogs.

She types quickly: *You're being silly. Who are you?*

The reply appears:

I met a girl last night. She reminds me of you.

Her fingers tremble as she responds: *What happened to her?*

She got away. The good ones always do.

Claudia stares at the photo of a missing girl pinned to the map. She types: *So you know who I am. Play fair—tell me who you are.*

In due time, Claudia.

The message vanishes. The dogs bristle at the door, ears sharp, bodies tense.

Claudia parts the curtains. Nothing. Only the walkway light spilling across the gravel to her car.

She grabs the phone and curls up on the sofa, twisting under the blanket, restless. The clock on the end table marks the long hours.

11:49 PM — she dozes.

01:02 AM — the dogs growl; she rolls over.

01:56 AM — she startles awake from a

nightmare, gulps water, checks the dogs, returns to bed.

02:35 AM — unseen, someone lingers in the trees, watching the lit trailer.

03:41 AM — Claudia wakes gasping, clutching the covers, fumbling for her phone.

"Chet, I need to come over right now," she pleads.

"It's late. I'm still mad at you," Chet O'Reilly replies, voice cold.

"Chet, please. I'm scared."

"I don't care. You hurt my feelings."

"Chet, I *have* to come over."

"Good night, Claudia."

The line goes dead.

Claudia bolts into the immaculate bedroom, shoving clothes into an overnight bag. In the kitchen, she pours kibble into bowls, kneeling to coax her dogs from the door with hugs and kisses. Reluctantly, they retreat.

She slips outside, locks up, and hurries down the lit walkway. The dogs bark furiously behind her, rattling the curtains. Claudia freezes, eyes scanning the trees. A rustle. A shadow. Her heart thrashes. She dashes to the car, drops into the driver's seat, and locks the doors.

As the engine turns over, she catches sight of the dogs leaping at the window. Beyond them, the trees seem to shift—something— or someone—is out there.

She throws the car into drive and peels

onto the highway, not noticing the dark puddle spreading beneath her vehicle.

In her rearview mirror, headlights flare. A truck swerves into view, bearing down fast, erratic, hungry. Claudia presses the accelerator, horn blaring at the oncoming road. Behind her, the truck looms, its silhouette monstrous against the night.

2

BEWARE THE NIGHT

Inside a sedan gliding down Highway 62, an elderly couple rides through the dark. Both are well into their seventies, the man's hands knotted with arthritis on the wheel, the woman's gaze fixed on the ribbon of road unfurling ahead. The radio hums with an overnight talk show, the host's voice animated.

"Are you certain it couldn't be anything else but Bigfoot?" he asks a caller.

The woman chuckles, reaching to switch the station off. "Why do you listen to this nonsense? You know it's just some man pretending."

But her husband doesn't answer. His eyes narrow as he points beyond a stand of trees. Headlights glow eerily in the ditch, illuminating a twisted sedan.

"Darling," he says softly. "What's that?"

She waves him off, forcing a smile. "Oh, you can't scare me."

He silences the radio, never looking away.

Her teasing falters as the night swells with sound—a horn, shrill and unrelenting, echoing across the prairie. She lowers her window, the noise growing louder, until her husband guides their car onto the shoulder and cuts the engine.

The old man steps out first, stiff but determined. His wife follows, clutching her phone, the beam of their headlights throwing stark shadows across the roadside.

"There's someone in the car!" he shouts.

Across the ditch, the wrecked sedan leans into a tree, its driver's side door hanging open. Claudia Shepherd slumps against the wheel, her face bloodied, chest pressed hard against the horn.

The man strains down the ditch, his joints protesting with each step, and climbs toward the wreck, calling for help. His wife, trembling, dials on her cell phone from the gravel shoulder. The horn blares endlessly, a single, piercing note over the silent countryside.

From the horizon, flashing police lights approach, cutting across the darkness in red and blue sweeps.

Soon, the road is alive with responders. A young tribal patrol officer—fresh to the force, his uniform still stiff with newness—questions the couple under the strobing lights.

"So, when did you first see the car?" he asks, pen poised above his notepad.

The old man wipes sweat from his brow.

"A half-mile back. I spotted the lights in the ditch. I was listening to the radio—national talk. Bigfoot night."

The officer raises an eyebrow, jotting it down but studying him carefully. "I see."

Behind them, paramedics move swiftly into the ditch, their shadows converging around Claudia's crumpled body as the horn finally sputters into silence.

The next morning, inside the Community Center's waiting room, counselor Bernice O'Reilly stands beside a thin young client in a glittering casino waitress uniform. They linger at the reception desk, chatting idly, when out of the large picture window, a black SUV pulls into the lot.

Bernice exhales sharply. "Oh, what fresh hell is this?"

"My boyfriend's cousin's girlfriend said she saw a totaled car hauled north on a flatbed," the waitress murmurs.

"Whose car?" Bernice asks quickly.

"She's new here. Doesn't know people yet."

The receptionist and both women crane their necks toward the glass. Another vehicle speeds in, a tribal police SUV, pulling up alongside the black one. Detective Sergeant Jessica Stone steps out, brisk and composed, intercepting a suited man climbing from the other. He's in his early thirties, handsome in the way of someone who knows it.

The three women lean over the stair rail

to listen as Detective Sergeant Jessica Stone addresses him.

"Upstairs."

The man arches a brow. "What does she do here?"

"She coordinates all volunteer activities. Mid-sixties, tireless. Everyone adores her," Stone replies evenly.

The women scatter back to the desk before Stone appears upstairs in the social work coordination unit at their side. "Agnes in?"

"No—cafeteria," the receptionist says.

"Basement patio," Bernice adds.

Just then, the elevator doors slide open. Agnes Greyeagle steps out, coffee in hand, startled to find Stone waiting.

"Agnes," Stone says gently, holding the door for her. "This is FBI Agent Casey Borgreve. He needs a word."

Agnes leads them into her office, setting the cup aside, her face already pale with dread.

"Please sit," Borgreve offers.

"Just tell me," Agnes answers, standing rigid behind her desk.

Stone lowers her gaze. "Your granddaughter. Claudia."

Borgreve's tone is clipped, bureaucratic. "Her vehicle struck a tree."

"She passed away," Stone adds softly.

"Dual master cylinder damage," Borgreve presses.

"Brake lines severed," Stone confirms.

Agnes grips the desk edge. "It happened in the accident?"

"She missed the puddle of brake fluid under her car before leaving home," Borgreve says flatly.

"She didn't use the emergency brake," Stone explains. "And there are signs she may have been followed."

"Tire marks suggest she was chased off the road," Stone adds, measured.

"Had she mentioned anyone tailing her?" Borgreve asks, eyes locking on Agnes.

Agnes shakes her head, fear stark in her expression.

"Could it have been a romance gone wrong?" Borgreve presses.

"She's dated Chet O'Reilly since high school," Agnes answers quickly, her voice tightening. "Bernice's boy."

Borgreve turns. "And the therapist next door? Her kid? Half Native. Same age as Claudia. Still at home."

"Thank you for your time," Borgreve says, already rising.

"Agnes, I'm sorry," Stone adds quietly.

"Yes, me too," Borgreve tosses in, perfunctory.

The two leave. Agnes collapses into her chair, hands trembling. The receptionist hurries in and closes the door.

In the office next door, Borgreve hands Bernice his card. She ignores it, facing Stone. "What is this?"

Borgreve interjects. "Where was your son

last night?"

Bernice glares past him. Stone meets her eyes. "Claudia's dead."

Bernice staggers. "Last night?"

"Car wreck," Stone confirms.

Borgreve leans forward. "Where was your son?"

"With me. All night." Bernice presses a hand to her mouth.

"What times?" Borgreve demands.

"But you said it was an accident," Bernice protests, shaken.

"The evidence suggests otherwise," Borgreve insists.

"Claudia was forced into the ditch," Stone adds.

Bernice covers her face. "Oh, Agnes..." She bolts for the door, but Stone's hand steadies her. Borgreve's pen scratches across his notebook.

"Bernice, just tell him," Stone urges gently.

"We ate late, around seven. I dozed in the living room while Chet played his game. At midnight, we shared a snack. I woke him at five-thirty for his shift at the casino."

"And he works as?" Borgreve asks.

"Warehouse manager." Bernice's voice is ice. "And no, I know of no fights with Claudia."

Her eyes blaze at Borgreve. "Stone, get him out of here."

Stone releases her shoulder. Bernice storms toward Agnes's office. Borgreve straightens, adjusting his suit.

"Where do we find her son?" he asks.

Stone nods toward the casino visible through the window. She leaves first.

In the waiting room, they find Bernice and the receptionist holding Agnes up as overwhelming grief breaks through. "Oh, God. My grandbaby!" Agnes sobs.

Stone stops, stricken. Borgreve brushes past, already signaling her to follow. She doesn't.

"Ass," Stone mutters under her breath.

She bows her head to Agnes and the women before rushing down the stairs. At the main door, she intercepts FBI Special Agent Casey Borgreve.

"What the hell is wrong with you?" she bursts.

He startles. "What the fuck?"

"She just lost her granddaughter. Show some compassion, you asshole."

"I was," he insists, incredulous.

Stone's eyes burn. "Out here, missing and murdered women aren't statistics. They're *ours*. Grandmas, aunties, daughters. Our people search every damn week. This is real." She sweeps a hand toward the beadwork and photographs lining the walls. "You might not care, but we do."

"Okay, I get it," Borgreve says tersely. "Now, can we go?"

Stone lets him pass but lingers, wiping her eyes before following. Above, she catches the quiet rustle of the women leaning over the railing, listening.

Stone and Borgreve cut across the lower delivery dock at the casino, eyes locked on Chet O'Reilly. Tall, twenty-three, with dirty-blond hair and the unkempt look of someone who just rolled out of bed, he finishes a word with a soda deliveryman before hopping down from the dock. A stocky, middle-aged casino security guard lingers behind him—clearly a friend. The truck pulls away, leaving Chet face-to-face with them.

"Hey, prison baby," Chet calls, his smirk aimed at Stone. "My mom said you were coming."

Stone's face is stone cold. Borgreve stays outwardly calm, but his eyes flicker—digesting the jab.

"I can't wrap my mind around it, that she's gone," Chet mutters.

"Where were you last night?" Borgreve asks, flashing his badge.

"Same as Mom told you. Played *World of Warcraft* till midnight. Crashed after that."

"Any arguments I should know about?" Borgreve presses. His phone buzzes. "Excuse me."

He steps aside, pacing as a semi-trailer groans into reverse, its engine drowning half his words. But Stone and Chet catch fragments.

"She did what? ... How many? ... Since when? Okay, got it."

Borgreve turns back, eyes sharp. "How long have you known about the other guys she was seeing?"

Chet blinks. "What?" His laugh is sharp, disbelieving. "No, she wasn't. Stone—Claudia wouldn't do that. Tell him!"

Borgreve cuts in. "She had an online dating account. Three other men, at least. Were you jealous?"

Chet's face drains. He can only point, stunned, to a blue Dodge Ram parked nearby.

"Popular truck on the rez," Stone says evenly. "The casino even raffles them off. You'll find them parked out here for weeks at a time."

"This one isn't moving until my guys process it. Do you understand me, Stone?" Borgreve snaps.

Stone waves to the security guard, who nods stiffly. Chet throws up his hands, defeated. His friend only shakes his head.

Borgreve storms to his SUV, tires squealing as he rips out of the lot. Stone bolts to hers, following in his wake.

Outside Claudia's trailer, FBI techs carry boxes to the mobile crime scene unit. Borgreve arrives, pausing at the dark puddle of brake fluid before heading in. A CSI tech waves him over.

"We found this email," she says. "From a publisher. Looks like the deceased was accused of plagiarizing a book."

Stone jogs up, flushed, wiping sweat from her brow, straining to hear.

"Any legal issues tied to it?" Borgreve asks.

"Not that we see. She wrote back, demanding the author's name. Something scribbled here: Marsei Abernathy."

"Marsei Abernathy," Stone interjects.

Both tech and agent glance at her.

"She's Claudia's sister," Stone says quietly.

"Then we talk to her too," Borgreve replies.

"She lives across the river. White side of town."

"Adopted?"

Stone shakes her head, moving aside for techs hauling boxes. "Half Dakota Sioux, half white. She didn't do well here. Fights. Foster care. Took off in high school. Twenty-seven, twenty-eight now."

"And?" Borgreve prompts.

"I've seen her drive through a few times. Last week she filled up at the gas station. Thought it was nostalgia."

"She still has family here?"

"Hasn't seen her mom in ten years."

"Could this be retaliation—stolen book rights?" Borgreve asks.

A tech offers a phone screen. "Here's her address."

"Send it to me. Now, about the men."

Another tech stops a colleague with a box. She pulls out a folder of newspaper clippings. "She'd been tracking unsolved murders. Missing Indigenous women. Trying to link men from the dating site with cold cases."

Borgreve flips through the clippings. A flyer and matchbook spill out—*The Copper Mule Bar & Grill.*

"So, she never met them?" he asks.

"Doesn't look like it. Still sorting files. Maps of homes, parks, bars where women were last seen."

"Read the book," Borgreve says flatly. "I'll see the sister."

Screams erupt outside. Claudia's parents—Lucy and Leonard Shepherd—push past tape.

"What are you doing to my daughter's house? Leave her things alone!" Lucy cries.

"Lucy," Stone says softly. "They have to. Claudia may have been murdered."

"My mother told me you're asking about men! Claudia wasn't like that!" Lucy protests.

"We're considering all angles," Borgreve interrupts.

A tech seals a box and walks past them, newspaper clippings tucked out of sight.

"We're wrapping here," Borgreve says, turning to Stone. "Meet me later."

He pushes out the door. Stone stays, trying to comfort the couple as CSI seals the entrance with tape. Borgreve waves a tech down, whispers an instruction, then strides to his SUV. Tires crunch over gravel as he pulls away, leaving grief hanging heavy in the air.

While Agent Borgreve crosses the river into suburbia to track down Marsei Abernathy,

Detective Sergeant Stone returns to tribal police headquarters, the lobby is unusually full for morning—four teens slouched together on the benches, their sneakers squeaking on the tile. Johnny Skye, Tamryn Willow, Bethany Lufkins, and Wolfie DesJarlais straighten as she approaches.

Stone raises an eyebrow. "To what do I owe this pleasure, ladies and gentlemen?"

Wolfie, braver than the rest, clears his throat. "Our grandmas said we had to come in. Tell you about the other night. When we were out past curfew and... saw something."

Stone crosses her arms. "What exactly did you see?"

Bethany leans forward, words spilling fast. "A dark-colored, newer pickup. The guy driving was beating up a girl and ripping part of her clothes."

"She got away, though," Tamryn adds quickly. "Ran over the hills, toward housing."

Stone's eyes sharpen. "How close were you? Where, exactly? Show me. All of you—come out to my SUV, we'll drive it out together." Her tone softens, just slightly. "And tell me, were any of you smoking or drinking at the time?"

"Just cigs," Johnny blurts. "Didn't have money for anything else."

The others glare at him, but Stone only nods, gesturing them toward the door. One by one, they file out behind her, their shoulders tense, the weight of what they've seen pressing in as the morning light spills across the steps of headquarters.

3

AS THE WIND
BENDS THE TREES

Agent Borgreve steers into the driveway of an upper-middle-class suburban home. In the front yard, Marsei Abernathy kneels by a flower bed, gloves muddied, hair a bottle-blonde halo in the sun. She stiffens when she sees him—and stiffens further when a city detective pulls up in a cruiser and joins Borgreve on the walk to a compact SUV parked neatly in the drive.

"May I help you with something?" she asks, brushing soil from her hands.

Borgreve raises his phone and snaps a picture of the SUV's tires before answering. "We'd like to speak with you inside, Mrs. Abernathy."

Her eyes flicker. "What's this about?"

"Please," Borgreve says, gesturing toward the door.

"Certainly. Let me get my husband." She ushers them into the tidy foyer, disappears upstairs, and soon returns with Michael Abernathy.

"Good afternoon, gentlemen," Michael says smoothly. "What may we do for you?"

Marsei gathers a sweater and blanket from the couch as the two men settle into the immaculate living room. "Would you like anything to drink?"

"No, thank you, Mrs. Abernathy," Borgreve replies, opening his notebook. "First—where were you last night?"

Marsei bites her lip, glancing at her husband.

"She was here. The whole night," Michael answers for her.

"Ma'am?" Borgreve fixes her with a stare.

"I was up most of the night in my office. I'm a writer."

"I could see her from across the hall," Michael adds. "Or hear her. My office is right beside hers."

"And you were awake?" Borgreve presses.

Michael nods. "Insomniac. Had the radio on with embarrassing stuff. UFOs."

"Show me," Borgreve orders.

Michael leads him upstairs. Marsei sits awkwardly on the sofa, fingers tightening in her lap. She clears her throat. "Excuse me, I'll get some water. Are you sure you don't want anything?"

The city detective shakes his head with a faint smile.

Marsei returns with a bottle in hand, but barely sits before Borgreve's voice booms down the stairs. His tone is cutting, final. "We're investigating a homicide. You know the victim. Your half-sister—Claudia Shepherd."

Marsei flinches. "I'm not close with my birth family."

"So, you don't see them at all?"

"No."

"When was the last time you were on the reservation?"

She hesitates. "I can't recall."

Borgreve leans in. "You need to tell me the truth."

Michael's jaw hardens. "My wife said she can't recall. She's not welcome there."

Marsei stammers, bewildered. "There was abuse. We chose not to live in it. I only went out there to research my book."

Michael gapes at her. "What?"

"Last week," she admits. "And again, last night. Six to nine. I needed to double-check some data."

"And the book?" Borgreve presses.

"On the unsolved murders and disappearances of women and girls from the reservation."

"Is it true your sister was writing the same book?"

"Yes. My publisher told me."

Michael's voice cracks. "Claudia?"

Marsei nods faintly.

Borgreve writes, then looks up. "Did you harm Claudia Shepherd?"

"Of course not."

"When's the last time you spoke to her?"

"Nearly ten years. I'm not welcome out

there."

"Why?"

Her voice trembles. "I was never Indian enough. And when I refused to respect my stepfather, my mother told me not to come back."

Borgreve tilts his head, eyes narrowing. "So, you carry jealousy. Anger at the sister who thrived where you could not?"

Marsei shakes her head fiercely, biting her lip, looking to her husband for strength.

Michael answers for her, firm. "My wife holds no such anger. She's always wished her family well. She just can't be part of their lives."

Borgreve's expression shutters, as though tucking something away.

Outside the run-down trailer listed on Hunter Daniel's license, Stone and Borgreve approach cautiously. A crash, then shouting—male, furious—erupts inside. Both draw their weapons.

"Open up! Tribal Police!" Stone pounds the door.

More rustling. Furniture overturned. A pause, then a faint female voice. "I'm coming. Just a second."

The door creaks open. A petite Native woman in her twenties stands there, bruises shadowing her cheekbones, a gash along her forehead. She tugs her hair forward to cover the redness.

"Everything all right, miss?" Stone asks,

eyes narrowing.

She glances back nervously. "Of course. Just had the TV too loud. What do you want?"

"We need to speak with Hunter," Stone says.

"He's not here."

"We'll wait," Borgreve answers flatly.

Behind her, the sound of heavy steps. Hunter Daniel appears, scratched, bloodied, grinning through the damage.

"We heard you've been staying here, Hunter." Stone's voice is ice. "This is Agent Borgreve, FBI. He needs a word."

Borgreve's gaze drops. "Why is your hand bleeding?"

"I punched the wall. That a crime?"

"And the scratches on your arm?" Borgreve presses.

Hunter smirks. "Cat got me. What's this about? Why the tribal cops and the feds?"

"This trailer's on the rez," Stone replies coolly.

"And murder out here is federal," Borgreve adds.

Hunter chuckles. "Who got murdered?"

"A teacher. Claudia Shepherd."

"Never heard of her."

"We pulled your dating profile—AvidHunter89."

"Not a crime to date online."

From inside, the young woman snaps, "Go to hell!" A mug sails past Hunter, smashing against the wall.

"She turned up dead the day after your

last message," Borgreve says.

"Then you know we never met." Hunter shrugs.

"Do you frequent the Copper Mule?"

"It's one of a dozen bars I go to. So does everyone else. What of it?"

"There was also an abduction. Suspect matches your description."

"Probably just ditch trash," Hunter sneers.

The woman hurls more objects. Hunter steps onto the stoop to avoid them.

Stone's hand brushes her holster. "What did you just say?"

Hunter grins. "Forgot—that's how your mom ended up."

Stone snaps. She yanks him off the stoop, knees him in the crotch, and slams him against the dirt. Hunter thrashes, swinging wildly as Borgreve merely watches.

"Where's your truck?" Stone demands.

Hunter gasps. "In the shop."

"Where?"

"Chuck Wallace's. Ask him yourself." He turns toward Borgreve. "You gonna let her do this to me?"

"I didn't see a damn thing."

From the doorway, the bruised woman shouts: "You goddamned bastard!"

Hunter smirks. "That's my call."

Later that afternoon, the Community Center grows quiet as the last client of the day schedules an appointment. Agnes and

Bernice linger by their office doors, waiting until the receptionist finishes.

"What's the next opening?" the client asks.

"May ninth. Two-forty," the receptionist replies.

"That works, thanks."

"Have a good evening." The receptionist gathers her purse and lunch bag, waves, and then disappears down the stairs.

Agnes lifts a cardboard box, clutching it tight. Bernice relieves her of the weight. Agnes presses her hand to her mouth to stifle a cry.

"The FBI doesn't know their heads from their tails," Bernice mutters. "First, they accused Chet. Now Marsei? I've never trusted them."

The two women sit in the waiting area, the box between them on the coffee table. Through the window, they watch the receptionist cross the lot.

"What did Marsei say happened?" Bernice asks gently, taking Agnes's trembling hand.

"She went willingly to the city police. Gave fingerprints and a DNA swab. They said she had an alibi for the night, but they treat Michael like he's lying for her." Agnes shakes her head. "It's all grasping at straws. Same with Chet's truck. They seized it this morning."

Bernice opens the box, spreading newspaper clippings, maps, and photos across the table. "Stone's clerk told me something. Claudia and Marsei were both digging into the murders and missing women cases, each on their own."

Agnes's tears fall. "And that's where the FBI crossed a line. Claudia wasn't sneaking around with men online. And Marsei didn't kill her sister."

"It's judgment. Nothing more," Bernice agrees.

Agnes straightens, resolute. "I'll go through these files again and coordinate volunteers for the drag-the-river search."

Bernice nods. "She must have found something. And been killed for it."

"And it wasn't Marsei. I know it in my heart." Agnes whispers.

Bernice pulls out a folded volunteer map and spreads it open. "And it wasn't my son either. He'd never hurt Claudia."

The room falls into heavy silence as the map flutters between them, the names of missing women circling back like echoes they cannot ignore.

At tribal police headquarters, Detective Sergeant Stone unfurls a copy of the same volunteer search map Bernice had shown Agnes. She tapes it to her office window, stepping back so she can study its tangle of red lines and circled names. Through the glass, she spots Borgreve at the front desk, phone pressed to his ear.

"Borgreve here."

On the other end, a CSI tech: "I've got that background on Stone."

"Go."

"Stranger rape outside an uptown bar. Jessica Stone's mother hunted the rapist down, killed him brutally, and then gave birth to Stone in prison. Stone was raised by her native grandmother. Both mother and grandmother are deceased. After her release, Stone's mom was found in a ditch. No other relatives."

Borgreve freezes, staring at nothing. He exhales, a long, heavy breath, then steadies himself. "Got it. Thanks."

He storms into Stone's office, closing the door hard behind him. "What did you find?" His eyes sweep the boxes stacked against the wall, landing on a folder of photos. He snatches them up. "These are the men she met online?"

Stone takes the prints from his hand and begins taping them around the map. "Some are family pictures."

"And the rest?"

"Possibilities."

Borgreve jabs a finger at one photo. "So why him?"

"He's a mechanic. Search volunteer."

"And him?"

"Pizza delivery. Another volunteer."

Stone rifles through another box, pulling more headshots and laying them out.

"She narrowed the field," Borgreve mutters. "Anything on the sister?"

"Claudia kept an online log tracking Marsei's movements," Stone says.

"The estranged sister, under surveillance by her own blood. Interesting. Besides plagiarism, any other motive? Something Claudia could've held over her head?"

"Nothing I've seen yet. I haven't gone through Claudia's work desk."

"The elementary school? On the way into town?"

"Yes."

Borgreve gestures toward the door. "Then what are we waiting for, Jessica?"

"After-school programs should be letting out right about now."

He holds the door for her. Stone strides past, all business. Borgreve lingers a moment, staring down at the floor, then back at her retreating figure—something unreadable flickering in his eyes, as though he's just uncovered a truth he hadn't wanted to know.

Borgreve studies the classroom walls, their bright posters and hand-lettered charts in Dakota and English. He moves toward Claudia's desk while Stone thanks a fellow teacher for unlocking the room. From his jacket, Borgreve pulls two sets of gloves, handing one to Stone.

"What language is this?" he asks, nodding toward the board.

"Dakota," Stone replies softly, tracing the words with her eyes. "She taught her kids both."

They slip on their gloves. Through the door's narrow glass, the late-twenties janitor—tall, blonde, unkempt, his expression unsettling—glances in at them before resuming his sweeping.

"Which grade?" Borgreve asks.

"Second," Stone says.

"Anyone used the desk since yesterday?"

"A sub. City sent her out."

Borgreve drops into Claudia's chair, rifling through drawers. Stone scans the shelf of binders until one labeled *FAMILY* catches her eye. She opens it, pages through photos. Three-quarters of the way in, a tab marked *MARSEI*.

"I noticed you released the boyfriend's truck," Borgreve mutters, still digging through papers.

"Similar tire tracks, nothing else. Dozens of the same trucks out here," Stone answers, eyes lingering on the photos. "Claudia tracked Marsei. Here, on the rez."

Borgreve snatches the binder from her hands, flipping through with quick, hungry eyes.

"One of my techs found clothing snagged in the hedges across from Claudia's place," he says. "Branches tore the fabric—cut whoever wore it."

Stone turns another page. "She narrowed her suspects. Mechanic. Pizza guy. Both search volunteers."

Borgreve glances toward the door. A

sound. The janitor peers in again.

"You know him?" Borgreve asks.

"Used to work maintenance at the casino," Stone replies. "Not sure if he volunteers."

Borgreve smirks faintly. "So what's that crap you wrote about UFOs?"

Stone tilts her head. "Michael Abernathy's alibi."

Stone pauses. "Hmm."

"What?"

"Nothing. Just... feels like I read it in another statement."

The janitor vanishes from the window. Borgreve lunges for the hall, sprinting one way, then the other, searching side corridors. When he rushes back, the classroom window gapes open.

Outside, Stone has the janitor pinned, cuffing him on the grass. Borgreve hurries over.

"What took you so long?" Stone quips.

"Why'd you run, buddy?" Borgreve asks, looming over the man.

Stone searches him, pulls a baggie of pills from his pocket. "Maybe this."

"They're not mine," he stammers.

"Then why run? Did you know the teacher who died?" Borgreve presses.

"She caught me once," the janitor admits.

"Doing what?"

"Smoking weed out back. After school—no kids around. I thought everyone was gone."

"You aware she's dead?"

"Everyone knows it was a car accident," he

mutters.

"Not everyone, buddy," Borgreve says coldly.

Stone hauls the janitor to her SUV. Across the intersection, Bernice's car idles at the light. She drives; Chet rides shotgun. Both watch as Stone shoves the janitor inside and Borgreve scans the street.

"With all the missing and murdered we've lost, and only now they send one idiot to half-ass his way around the rez after a car accident," Bernice mutters.

"I just hope Agnes's heart can take what he'll put her through," Chet replies, eyes narrowed.

Bernice lays a hand over his. "All this investigation so soon after Claudia's death. You holding up?"

Chet nods faintly, gaze fixed on the scene outside. He smirks when Borgreve meets his eyes through the windshield.

Borgreve stands in the lot, watching the car roll past, Stone already on the phone beside her SUV.

4

AS THE SECOND
PETAL FALLS

Later that evening, Agnes sits on her porch, a photo album resting at her side, cell phone in her hand. Her eyes follow Bernice's car as it slows at the corner, waiting for a street kickball game to scatter before easing into the driveway.

Agnes watches Bernice climb out, balancing a casserole dish from the passenger seat.

"I know you haven't eaten all day," Bernice says gently.

Agnes wipes her cheeks. "No."

"Don't tell me you're working the phone lines. You already give too many hours."

Agnes shakes her head. "No."

Bernice nods at the cell in her hand. "Tell me right now you're not on duty for crisis calls on that phone."

Agnes doesn't answer. Across the street, another car crawls past, its passengers waving cheerfully at her through rolled-down windows. She forces a faint wave back.

Bernice picks up the scrapbook, sets it on her lap, and lowers herself onto the bench beside her friend. The phone in Agnes's hand rings.

"Crisis hotline, how may I help you tonight?" Agnes answers softly.

"Hello. I'm scared," a young woman whispers on the line.

Bernice slips inside the house. Agnes rises, watching through the living room window as Bernice sets the casserole in the oven, lays bread on the table, and pours iced tea into glasses.

"Tell me what's troubling you tonight," Agnes says, her voice steady.

"It was two nights ago... no, yesterday morning. I was on the road when, out of nowhere, headlights flicked on in front of me. A truck swerved, almost pushed me off the road."

"But it didn't hit you?"

"No. He sped past. And then—at the intersection—I saw the wreck. The one where Claudia Shepherd died."

Agnes grips the phone tighter. "What?"

"I thought it was an accident. But I just heard the FBI is calling it murder. What if I saw the killer? What if he comes after me next?"

The front screen door bangs open as Agnes hurries inside, still on the phone.

"Oh, what now?" Bernice mutters from the kitchen.

"Did you see the driver?" Agnes presses.

"No. I was watching the road. Help me. I'm scared."

"Do you think he could see you?"

"Probably not. If I couldn't see him..." The girl breaks into sobs. Twenty seconds drag by before she blurts, "But if he's from the rez, he might know my car. Oh, God. He knows my car."

"You need to talk to the police," Agnes urges.

"I don't trust them."

"Not the FBI. Detective Sergeant Stone. I can connect you—just wait one second—"

"No!"

"How old are you?"

"Eighteen."

"Where were you headed so late?"

"It was early. I was on my way to work. At the casino."

"What kind of work do you—"

"Gotta go."

The line clicks dead.

"Wait!" Agnes cries into the silence. Slowly, she sinks into an armchair, the phone limp in her hand. From the stove, Bernice watches, her face lined with worry.

The next morning, Borgreve's SUV slows as a banner flaps ahead of him:

DRAG THE RIVER – Valley Bottoms Park.

Beyond the trees, small motorboats

churn the current, something heavy rising between them. He turns off the highway, following a rutted gravel road until he spots the coroner's van parked beside Stone's tribal SUV. Stone stands near Agnes and Bernice at the tree line.

As Borgreve steps out, Stone approaches.

"What are they doing here?" His voice is sharp, agitated.

"Volunteers," Stone replies evenly. "Spring Launch. They set it up weeks ago. Kayakers on the search found the body."

Through brush and saplings, the coroner leads them toward the riverbank. Borgreve pushes through branches, Stone close behind.

"How long's it been in the water?" Borgreve asks.

"A few—" the coroner begins.

"She," Stone cuts in, her tone deliberate.

Borgreve shoots her a glance, jaw tight.

"She," the coroner repeats, "has been in the water only a few hours. Cause of death occurred prior to placement."

Stone gestures. "Caught in the brush. This way."

They kneel near the girl's body, pale against the snarl of reeds. FBI crime scene techs fan out behind them.

"How old?" Borgreve murmurs, pen scratching.

"Late teens," the coroner answers.

"No ID. Kayakers didn't know her," Stone adds. Her phone rings. She rises, stepping aside. "What do you have?"

She paces, watching Agnes and Bernice hand out bottled water to weary searchers filing back through the trees.

"Where?" Stone presses into the phone. Her hand rakes through her hair, her thumb snapping the call closed. She turns to Borgreve.

"We may have the murder scene. Accident. Missing driver. Skid marks confirm another vehicle. Found a casino lanyard—female employee. She's missing."

They sprint back toward their vehicles.

"I'll follow you, Jessica," Borgreve calls.

"It's close—just down from Claudia's crash site."

Behind them, Agnes and Bernice watch the agents vanish. A crime scene tech approaches.

"Ladies, I'll need you to shut down operations here."

"Where did Stone and Borgreve go?" Bernice asks.

"Didn't say. You did great work today. Please tell your searchers to pack up." He heads back to the coroner.

Agnes and Bernice thank volunteers as they straggle in, handing out the last of the water bottles before the kayaks are loaded and cars begin to pull away.

Bernice's cell buzzes. She answers quickly. "Hi, sweetie. What's up?" Her face tightens. She turns her back, gesturing for Agnes to wait. "Where?"

Her voice cracks as she rubs her temples, cooler handle clutched in her free hand. "Okay. Just stay home till I get there. Bye."

She ends the call and hurries to Agnes.

"Chet says there's crime scene tape up," Bernice whispers, breathless. "Not far from Claudia's crash site."

Tribal police SUVs block off the road, holding back traffic in both directions. Tire marks crisscross the asphalt. A sedan sits abandoned in the ditch, its door gaping open.

Stone and Borgreve hurry down to join patrol officers at the wreck.

"Her casino ID and purse were still inside," the first officer reports. "Car doesn't look touched. Grass from the driver's side shows someone walked off."

"Across the highway," adds a second officer, "an old farm road's got fresh tracks—muddy, cut straight across."

Borgreve ducks into the car, scanning. An unopened twelve-pack. A bottle of vodka on the floor. A lanyard on the passenger seat. He lifts it with gloved fingers.

"It's her," he says.

"She's from a few towns over," the second officer adds. "Boyfriend's car. She's the only one working—casino convenience store. Couple lives with his mom."

"Who called it in?" Stone asks. "No 911?"

The first officer points to a sedan idling on the shoulder. "Old lady in the front car. First pass she thought it'd just broken down. Coming back, she saw it hadn't moved so she called us."

Borgreve rakes his hands through his hair, tugging hard. He exhales, wordless. Stone opens the trunk with him. Empty bottles. Fast food wrappers. Dirty clothes.

"Can you get more support out here?" Stone asks.

"We've got the Shepherd case stretching our team. And with alcohol in the mix, they'll call it possible DUI. Won't add anyone."

"The tire tracks," Stone presses.

"Already juggling two county searches—a school threat, missing man with Alzheimer's, and an Amber Alert. Resources are thin."

"This driver is in the river a mile from here," Stone snaps.

"Or she ran off the road, wandered in the dark, and drowned. Let's get tox screens on both bodies."

"Fuck you, Borgreve." Stone shakes her head, storming back to her SUV. "Damn it."

Patrol officers' glance at one another as she peels away, tires spitting gravel. A tow truck rumbles into place behind her.

The next morning, Borgreve sits at Stone's desk, her computer humming in the glass-walled office. She enters with a cluster of uniformed officers.

"Late start, Stone?" Borgreve needles.

"Some of us just came from Claudia Shepherd's funeral."

"Anyone stand out?"

"Just grieving family."

"Marsei and Michael Abernathy?"

"The only one who ever welcomed Marsei was her grandmother. Agnes always favored her."

"I thought the book angle might mean something. But the boyfriend—Chet—still looks better. I've been combing Claudia's texts and emails."

A commotion breaks out in the lobby. A young Native woman, disheveled and bruised, points at Stone. Patrol officers try to calm her.

Stone steps forward. Borgreve follows.

"Where'd you get the cuts and bruises?" Stone asks.

"Some guy grabbed me outside a bar a few nights ago. Hauled me to his truck before I could stop him."

"Were you drinking?" Borgreve asks.

"I was at a bar."

"Then what?"

"I went to leave, and he came out the back. Caught me in the lot."

"His name? Description?"

"Don't know. White."

"Anything else?"

"Taller. Dirty blond. Blue eyes, maybe."

"Seen him before?"

"A few times, in his truck. Engine running. First time I went inside, he followed me out."

"You don't frequent this bar?"

"No. It's mostly white. The lot's shared

with a couple of bars. He sits there sometimes."

"You live nearby?"

"A few towns over. We come to the casino. Sometimes stay with friends."

"He hit you?" Stone asks.

"I tried to get away. He punched me over and over. Nearly knocked me out. Then I saw his knife. I screamed, kicked, bit him, and fell out of the truck. Thought he'd chase me, but he waited, then drove off."

"If we bring a sketch artist, can you describe him?" Borgreve asks.

"Maybe. Only saw him dim inside. Dark outside. Always with his cap pulled low."

Borgreve straightens. "Write this up. Show her mug shots. I'll get an artist here within the hour. Stone, office?"

They close the door behind them, still watching Cally Thunderhawk slump at the desk.

"Does she have a record?" Borgreve asks.

Stone flips through a file. "DUI. Revoked license. Paraphernalia. Domestic violence victim. Dropped charges each time."

"Shit."

Stone's voice hardens. "Most women who come through here are like her. Victims. Drinking or using just to cope. No way out."

Their eyes meet across the desk. Stone sees it in him—the knowledge of her own history. She looks away.

"Shit," she whispers. Then sighs, heavy.

Out in the lobby, Thunderhawk lowers her

head to the desk, hands covering her face.

5

LOST EYES AND TREACHERY

It's nightfall, but the basement meeting room of the Community Center is stirring with life. A sheet of printer paper taped to the door reads:

DOMESTIC VIOLENCE SUPPORT GROUP ALL ARE WELCOME

Inside, Agnes sets out cookies and napkins. Bernice straightens chairs into a circle, then drops a folder onto one of the seats.

"Agnes, I can do this," Bernice murmurs. "You just buried your granddaughter. You should be home."

Agnes stiffens. "I can't sit at home, helpless, while men keep murdering our girls. Hell, Bernice—what about the possibility it's Chet, for Christ's sake?"

Bernice's hand flies to her mouth, appalled by both the words and the weight behind them.

"And the FBI isn't doing anything," Agnes

seethes.

One by one, women trickle in with battered faces, bandaged arms, voices hushed. Ages blur together: sixties, fifties, forties, thirties, twenties, and late teens. They find chairs around the circle. Agnes quietly pulls extras from the corner. Bernice rises to close the door, but just as it swings shut, a straggler slips inside. Bernice glances at Agnes, who pointedly looks away.

The next morning, inside tribal police headquarters, Borgreve bursts into Stone's office, papers in hand.

"Forensic tox screens are back," he announces. "Claudia Shepherd and the girl from the river? Clean." His voice carries an edge of triumph.

Stone doesn't look up from her desk. "I pulled profiles of the men Claudia messaged on that dating site. Most fit the description Cally Thunderhawk gave of her attempted abductor."

"As do Hunter Daniel, Chet O'Reilly, and the elementary school janitor," Borgreve cuts in. "Let's get Thunderhawk in here. Show her the headshots."

Stone finally meets his eyes. "Will do. By the way—Chet lied."

"I read it too." Borgreve's jaw tightens. "Let's talk to him."

Stone and Borgreve pull into the casino's warehouse lot in separate SUVs. On the loading dock, Chet O'Reilly chats with a delivery driver. He stiffens as he spots them. Stone raises a hand, motioning him over.

"Still focused on me while the real killer is out there?" he says, defiant but wary.

"You failed to tell us Claudia broke up with you right before she died," Borgreve counters bluntly.

"She did that all the time."

"You shoved her. Hit her," Borgreve presses.

"That was an accident. If she were here now, she'd tell you." Chet's voice wavers; he sniffs hard.

"But she's dead. Someone killed her," Borgreve snaps.

Chet turns to Stone, almost pleading. "Stone?"

She shakes her head. "Can't help you, Chet. I read the hospital report."

"You punched her so hard she hit her head. She was nauseous."

"She had a concussion," Borgreve adds.

Engines roar as one truck pulls away and another rumbles into place to unload. Chet gestures, his words tumbling out.

"I pushed her away, that's all. She tripped over one of her dogs in that cramped trailer. Smashed her head. The damn mutt nearly tore my arm off for it."

"Why didn't you tell us about the fight? About the breakup?"

"We weren't broken up. Not really. The night she died, she called me. Sounded scared—like she was coming to my place. Then she crashed."

"What did she say?"

"That she was scared of something. Needed to come over. But I told her not to. Told her to stay away."

"Do you go to the Copper Mule?" Borgreve asks.

"No. Never. I drink at parties, or here in the casino restaurants. Whatever you're getting at—I didn't do it. Pushing Claudia was an accident. I was pissed. That's it."

"Pissed about what?"

Chet spreads his arms, voice rising. "She told me I wasn't ambitious enough. Said I was lazy even though I bust my ass here every day. She wanted me to take classes, quit the games, move out of Mom's house. You're not gonna tell my mom that, are you?"

Stone and Borgreve exchange a look—half disgust, half disbelief—as the dock clatters with the sound of pallets being unloaded.

Weeks later, Highway 62 stretches before them in a summer haze, the prairie rolling with wildflowers. Bernice and Agnes scan the panoramic field as volunteers spread out a hundred feet apart, combing the grass. Sneakers crush petals underfoot. A purse lies open, its contents scattered in the weeds.

Bernice prods it with a stick. "I got something here."

Agnes glances back at the line of searchers

before stepping closer. Bernice crouches, slips on gloves, and digs carefully through the contents until she pulls an ID card free.

"It's our missing girl."

Agnes exhales. "Another one trying a shortcut through fields to get to the city?"

"I hope no harm came to her," Bernice murmurs. "We'll ask around Friday night when we do street patrol."

Twenty feet away, Agnes stops, her stick tapping something half-buried in the grass. She leans down to the bloodied underwear and shorts, balled together.

"Bloody clothes over here," she calls.

Bernice's eyes harden. "Predator?"

"The human variety," Agnes replies grimly. "I'll get the drones over here—have them trace a path down to the river."

"I'll call Stone," Bernice says, already reaching for her phone.

Outside the casino convenience store, Stone stands at the pump, topping off her SUV. A Memorial Day banner droops across the brick facade. She sits back in her driver's seat for a moment, watching a young couple argue in front of the store. The man wrestles a case of beer, the woman shoves him, then swings with her fist. Stone's phone rings.

"Stone here." She listens, shakes her head, scribbles notes on the pad, riding shotgun. "I'll be right there."

She pulls the nozzle free. Across the lot, Marsei Abernathy glides up to another pump. Baseball cap low, she steps out, shoulders tense. Stone freezes, watching her. Then, without a word, she slides back into her SUV and drives off.

Back on Highway 62, tribal officers photograph the purse and bag up the clothing. Drones hum overhead, sweeping the fields. Stone stands with Bernice and Agnes, watching silently.

"Will this get the FBI back out here?" Agnes asks.

"They've done nothing on Claudia's case in weeks," Bernice adds bitterly.

"Borgreve's working it from the office," Stone says carefully, almost as though convincing herself.

"What exactly is he working on?" Bernice shoots back. "Pinning Claudia's death on my son? Chet loved her. I bet they'd be making announcements by now if she'd lived. That's how close they were."

"Bernice, talk to your son," Stone urges.

Bernice glares, her voice sharp. "He's grief-stricken and hitting the bottle harder because you still haven't caught a killer."

The wind tugs at the prairie grass. The drones buzz overhead, circling wider, as silence drops between them.

6

MORE SOLEMN
THAN A FADING STAR

Weeks later, inside *The Copper Mule* bar and grill, Chet O'Reilly slouches over the counter, slurring at a waitress in her thirties.

"The bartender says you're cut off. Go home, Chet."

"Maybe I will," he sneers. "You wanna take me with you, pretty lady?"

The door opens, and a group of Native women in their mid-twenties filters in, sliding into a booth in the far corner. From his barstool, Chet stares at them through the haze of his last drink. Their laughter and glances, innocent as they are, draw him.

He stumbles to their table.

At the bar, the tall, blue-eyed bartender and the waitress exchange uneasy looks, watching as Chet sways over the women.

Chet leans close, fingers trailing through the hair of the nearest young woman.

"Don't touch me. Go away," she snaps.

"Get the hell out of here," another shouts, trying to catch the bartender's eye.

Chet jabs a finger at one woman's chest. "Got dressed up all pretty, for me, huh?"

"Why isn't he doing something?" one of the women hisses. "He can see this asshole."

"Watch your mouth, tramp," Chet spits.

"Go to hell, you dumb drunk," the third woman fires back, standing.

Chet snarls, yanking the first woman's hair with one hand, groping with the other.

"Don't test me, bitches! You don't know who I am."

The bartender turns away, serving new customers. The waitress fumes. "I'm not going near him till he's out of here."

Finally, the bartender raises his voice. "Chet—time's up. Go home."

Chet releases the woman, his grin twisted. "I'll see you again. Mark my words. Nobody shits on me and lives."

The bartender grips his shoulders, marches him to the door, and shoves him out.

Outside, Chet staggers across the sidewalk. He halts at an easel sign:

SPIRIT PASS CASINO GALA
Saturday, May 23rd
A Caribbean Night Theme
**ALL PROCEEDS to Families & Survivors
of MISSING & MURDERED
INDIGENOUS WOMEN & GIRLS**

Chet rips the sign down, tears it to shreds,

and tosses the pieces into the street. In the parking lot, he fumbles with his phone, leaning against his truck.

"Hey, beautiful. Heard you just got back from college. Wanna hang out tonight?" He smiles into the phone, nodding. "Great. I'll be right there, baby."

Drones hum overhead, scanning fields. One pauses, holding position over tire ruts in the mud. Agnes's handheld radio crackles.

The pilot's voice comes through: "Got tracks from a heavy-duty vehicle heading toward the river. Wet ground should give us solid casts. Also, some footprints back and forth from where the truck stopped."

Stone lifts her phone, hesitates, then nods. "Good work, ladies. I'll get the lab out here."

Later that night, under the height of the moon, Chet swerves down the road. Up ahead, floodlights blaze, casting hard shadows across the prairie. Police cruisers cluster near the riverbank where Agnes, Bernice, and Stone had stood earlier.

Chet slows, watching the scene. For minutes he sits motionless, engine idling. Then, headlights flare behind him with cars approaching fast.

Chet grips the wheel, snarls, and slams his foot down. The truck roars to life, tearing down Highway 62.

Drones sweep the sky in slow arcs. One hovers low, a hundred feet from where Stone, Agnes, and Bernice stand by the highway shoulder. Agnes's radio crackles to life.

The pilot's voice: *"Got tire tracks from a heavy-duty vehicle starting at the roadside and running toward the river. Ground was soft—casts should be clean. Looks like footprints too, back and forth from where the truck stopped."*

Stone raises her phone, hesitates, then lowers it. "As usual—good work, ladies. I'll call the lab out here."

At the height of the moon, Chet's truck lurches down the road. Through the windshield, floodlights blaze against the dark with police cruisers and scene tape clustered near the riverbank, the same place Bernice, Agnes, and Stone had stood earlier.

Chet brakes in the empty lane, engine idling. He sits there, watching the pulsing strobes. Then, the headlights flare behind him with oncoming traffic closing fast. Chet jerks the wheel, tires shrieking, and roars down the highway into the dark.

The following morning, in the community center's basement, Agnes hangs banners, strings balloons, and sets out streamers. Bernice rushes in, slightly breathless.

"This is my favorite thing," Agnes says softly. "Celebrating birthdays for the preschoolers."

"Especially knowing most of their moms sit in our domestic violence circle," Bernice murmurs.

Agnes's smile fades.

"Sorry, I'm late," Bernice adds. "Had to drag Chet off to work. He's struggling—grieving under the microscope of that FBI agent."

They leave the decorated room, closing the door as the first preschoolers shuffle across the wide hallway.

Later, upstairs in the waiting room, Agnes kneels in the kids' corner, stacking blocks with a three-year-old boy. When his mother exits Bernice's office, the child darts into her arms. Agnes waves goodbye, then leads Stone into her office.

Inside, Stone sits while Agnes drifts behind her desk, staring through the window at the distant horizon.

"The FBI hasn't found the woman?" Agnes asks.

"No. They're checking city addresses."

"For how long? A day, two, before they give up again?"

"Casts of the tracks look promising," Stone says.

Agnes leans forward, eyes hard. "And Claudia's case?"

"Borgreve's going to interview Marsei again."

Agnes slams her palm against the desk. "She didn't do this, Stone!"

"Have you seen her lately?"

"No. But I know, deep in my heart, she didn't."

"Agnes, both sisters wrote the same book. One stole from the other."

"No. Somebody's wrong. That industry's a mess."

"They're both Native. They both carry ties to this land, to these losses. More than the FBI ever will."

"Marsei's tie doesn't look that strong," Stone challenges.

"You don't know her like I do. She was abused as a child, ostracized as a teen. Her wounds run deep."

"I see her sometimes passing through," Stone admits.

Agnes leans back. "Like I said—she has ties. Mental, spiritual. She just can't face the past."

Stone softens. "Maybe it's safer for her in anonymity. Less pain."

"You're right. But remember, sometimes we wear blinders with the ones we love."

Marsei stops vacuuming when the doorbell rings. She opens it, startled to find Agent Borgreve with a female CSI tech on the stoop. Michael descends the stairs.

"Who's there, hon?" he calls. Seeing them, he forces a smile. "Sorry, bit of a surprise. Hon, offer them a drink."

"Nothing for me," Borgreve says. He gestures to the woman beside him. "This is CSI tech Ramirez. We need a favor, Marsei."

"Of course."

"Your book files. Missing and murdered Native women. Specifically, early drafts."

"I switched computers recently. Don't have files that far back."

"Anything helps. Ramirez can accompany you."

"Sure."

"What happened to the old computer?"

"Recycled. City program," Michael answers for her. "What's this about?"

"Timeline comparisons. That's all," Borgreve says smoothly.

Marsei leads Ramirez to her tidy office, lined with bookshelves. She pulls her laptop from the desk. Ramirez hands her a flash drive.

"Let me load what I have."

"Paper notes? Early drafts?"

"No. I recycle constantly. Keeps things neat."

Ramirez glances around. "No bulletin board? No whiteboard?"

Marsei shakes her head. "Post-its, index cards. I cleared them out years ago." She hands back the drive.

They return to the living room, where Borgreve studies framed photos—mostly Marsei and Michael. In one, Michael beams in front of two jet skis hitched to a gleaming new truck.

"Nice toys," Borgreve remarks.

"You know it," Michael grins. "Lake Minnetonka, mostly. Florida trips in winter."

Ramirez rejoins him, flash drive in hand. Borgreve nods. "Before we go can you just walk us through your research timeline."

Marsei stiffens, Michael squeezing her hand.

"When did the book idea first take root?" Ramirez asks, pen poised.

"A few years back. I drove through the rez. Picked up a newspaper. Saw a story about a body in the river."

"So, three years ago?"

Marsei exhales. "Yes. But I've known about the disappearances since I was a kid. Women vanish, and nobody cares off the rez."

"They'd say she was drunk, walked away," Michael mutters bitterly.

Marsei nods. "It happened so often. I thought someone needed to tell it. To make change."

"But authorship-wise, it's three years?" Borgreve presses.

Michael snaps, "Quit beating a dead horse."

"Yes," Marsei whispers.

"Research methods?"

"Exactly as in my book."

"Your book?" Borgreve corrects.

"Yes. If you'd read it, you'd know."

"I have," Ramirez says quietly.

Marsei stiffens.

"So, you tracked boyfriends, checked tribal papers," Borgreve pushes.

"Yes. Backgrounds only."

"Speak with them?"

"No. I kept to myself."

"She's introverted," Michael says, protective.

"But you did leave your comfort zone," Borgreve prods.

Marsei nods. "Bars. Frightening, but necessary."

"Which bars?"

"The Copper Mule, for one. Many times."

Michael jerks. "Jesus, Marsei! Alone?"

"Anyone recognize you?" Borgreve asks.

"I doubt it. Years ago. And I'm blonde now."

"Stone saw you. Multiple times," Borgreve says flatly.

Marsei freezes.

Michael rises abruptly. "There. Proof she was researching. A sworn officer saw her. Now you've got your files. We've been accommodating. Enough."

Borgreve lingers a beat at the photo wall, then gestures to Ramirez.

"Beautiful family," he says, voice even.

"Thank you." Marsei closes the door firmly behind them.

Borgreve waits in the sleek publishing house office, restless in his chair. Finally, NANCY WALKER, white, forties, elegant in her long hair and tailored suit, strides from the door to her desk with practiced ease.

"Sorry about that," she says, settling in.

"So, this is about Claudia Shepherd's submission?"

"Yes," Borgreve leans forward. "And the murder tied to it."

Nancy blinks. "Excuse me?"

"You know she was murdered?"

"No. How would I? We don't exactly run in the same circles."

"I assumed Marsei Abernathy told you."

"I never gave Marsei details about the other writer in question. We don't share that sort of information."

"Marsei and Claudia Shepherd were sisters. Half-sisters."

Nancy shakes her head firmly. "No. Absolutely not. I can assure you—"

"Those are my facts," Borgreve cuts in.

Nancy falters, stunned into silence.

"Now," Borgreve presses, "the timelines. What do you know about their submissions?"

Nancy composes herself with hair tucked neatly behind her ears, posture tall, voice controlled. "As you might imagine, this is a shock. I've worked with Marsei for years, even through her breakdown and regression therapy for childhood abuse. I thought we were close. To learn, she kept this from me."

"Timelines," Borgreve reminds her.

Nancy inhales sharply, then types at her keyboard. "Marsei sent us a complete manuscript fifteen months ago. Six months back, Claudia began sending inquiries—post, email, phone. Four months ago, she submitted three chapters. When we requested the full draft to confirm plagiarism, it was verbatim. Two editors compared the works. We notified Claudia of the plagiarism."

"And you still believe Claudia stole from Marsei?"

"Besides her silence about the family connection, yes. Marsei has a long history with us. Claudia was fresh out of college and a hobbyist. Marsei was established."

"I see." Borgreve exhales, long and heavy.

"Excuse me?"

"Nothing," he says quickly, softening his tone. "I'm sure you know your business. Thank you for your time." He rises, showing himself out.

Back at tribal police headquarters, Stone types at her desk when Borgreve barrels in.

"How'd it go with the editor?" she asks.

"She believes Marsei."

"I never saw the evidence before the lab got it. You sure you're not barking up the wrong tree?"

"Post-its. Legal pads. Spiral notebooks. Bulletin boards. Claudia documented everything. Thorough enough that we've already cross-matched cases. We're digging into them." Borgreve drags his fingers through his hair.

A young tribal police clerk raps on Stone's glass door. She waves her in.

"What've you got?"

"Call from the county sheriff. Disturbance

at The Copper Mule. Chet O'Reilly's drunk, aggressive. Waitresses refused to serve him—possible assault in the parking lot. Sheriff said you'd been asking about him. Wants to know if you're available."

"I'm on the way. Don't let him go," Stone orders.

"I'll follow," Borgreve adds.

Minutes later, Stone and Borgreve park behind an ambulance outside The Copper Mule. The county sheriff, white, fifties, with a belly stretching his belt and a genial face, steps over.

"This is FBI Agent Casey Borgreve," Stone introduces. They shake.

The sheriff turns back to her. "I remember you asking about him. And here he is, at the exact bar you mentioned. He's liquored up, oblivious, banged up from a scrap in the gravel. The woman in the ambulance took a beating too. Won't say it was Chet. Looks like she fought hard until passersby heard her screams and told the bartender. They didn't see the fight. Bartender found her by the dumpster with clothes torn, near shock."

"Intoxicated?" Borgreve asks.

"Couple beers, max," the sheriff replies. "You can try to get her to press charges."

Stone and Borgreve approach the ambulance. Inside, a young Native woman in her twenties sits wrapped in a blanket, cuts striping her face and neck. EMTs step aside.

"Are those bite marks on your arms?"

Stone asks gently.

The woman pulls the blanket tighter. "I don't want to press charges. You don't need my name."

"The ambulance, the hospital, they'll need your info. That head wound's bleeding. They'll have to stitch you up. Please, can you tell us what happened?" Stone says.

"I said no."

"This wasn't your fault," Stone urges.

"You think I don't know that?" The woman's voice shakes, angry. "I just don't want any part of this."

"You pressing charges might stop him from doing this to someone else," Borgreve adds.

She barks a bitter laugh. "No one stopped it from happening to me. Everyone for themselves, I guess."

"Please," Stone pleads one last time.

The victim turns away, eyes fixed on the blood dripping down her arm.

"EMTs, help her. The gash just opened up again," Borgreve calls.

The medics step in, pressing gauze to her temple as Stone and Borgreve stand grim at the door.

7

MEMORY'S MADNESS

The city after dark wore its neglect openly. Streetlamps buzzed weakly above cracked sidewalks. Narrow alleys festered with broken pallets, rusting bikes, and the damp stink of mildew. Neon signs sputtered and flickered across the rain-streaked windows of pawnshops and corner liquor stores. Sirens echoed in the distance, muffled by brick and smoke.

Agnes and Bernice moved steadily through it all, reflective jackets catching the glint of headlights. Jeans tucked into boots, hoods pulled up against the wind, they looked smaller beside the bulk of the other street patrol volunteers, Native men with shoulders broad as shadows, their faces lined by years of standing watch.

Together, the group threaded alleyways littered with soggy cardboard, collapsed shopping carts, and plastic bags tangled in chain-link. Rats skittered from trash bins as they passed.

"Hey there," Agnes called softly. Her flashlight beam caught the worn face of a homeless Native man, mid-fifties, perched on a crate under a rusted fire escape. His hands shook slightly as he clutched a blanket.

"You doing all right tonight? Want a food card for the grocery store down the street?"

"Yeah," he rasped. "Thanks."

When he reached for the card, Agnes clasped his hand warmly, refusing to let the exchange be impersonal.

"Could you look at this picture? Tell me if you've seen her around?"

She pulled a laminated, enlarged copy of a young Native girl's driver's license photo, holding her flashlight steady over the face.

The man squinted, shaking his head. "She's a young one. Haven't seen her. But the kids down at the other end might know. Just be careful. They're cranked up."

"Thank you," Agnes said gently, pressing the card into his palm. She gave his hand another squeeze before retreating.

They pushed deeper into the alley. The damp air grew heavier, carrying the reek of urine and wet brick. Shadows shifted: two figures darted into niches in the wall, wrapping themselves in rags and cardboard as the patrol passed.

"Hello," Bernice called softly, but they melted back into silence.

Further on, a trash fire burned in a rusted barrel. Around it huddled half a dozen young

Native men and women, late teens and twenties, their faces carved by hunger and smoke. The orange light glowed off hollow cheeks and wary eyes.

"Whassup?" one mumbled, flicking ash from his cigarette.

"Can anyone here use a grocery card?" Agnes asked.

Hands rose instantly. More shadows moved, two others stepping forward from the dark. Every face looked older than its years. Agnes handed out the cards, one by one, her voice steady, her flashlight beam soft so as not to blind.

Bernice held up the printout. "Have any of you seen this girl?"

The group leaned close, passing the photo carefully from hand to hand. Silence pressed in until one voice broke it:

"Serena."

"Yes." Another nodded. "Haven't seen her in a while."

"Do you know where she might be?" Bernice asked.

"She's with some white guy. Living with him, maybe. It's been three weeks or more."

"Have you tried the rez? She talked about wanting a job in housekeeping at the casino," one offered.

"We already checked out there," Bernice said.

The youngest boy jabbed a finger across the street. "Last time I saw her, she was getting into a truck. White dude. Blonde hair.

Parked right over there."

"Older truck?"

"Newer. Dark. Can't say the make."

"Seen him before?"

The boy hesitated. "Maybe. He looked familiar, but... a lot of white guys come here. Pick up girls. Over and over. You know what I mean?"

Agnes dug into her jacket pocket and pulled out a card. "Please call me if you see him again. The Native Center has phones you can use, right?"

"Yeah."

"And if you see Serena, call us, too," Agnes urged.

Bernice lowered her eyes, her voice quiet but firm. "Yes. Please."

Agnes scanned their faces, each marked with smoke, fatigue, and suspicion. "Thank you. All of you. You've been very helpful."

The group shifted back toward the fire, huddling close again, their shadows flickering against the brick as Agnes and Bernice moved on into the cold maze of the city.

The night pressed heavier the deeper they walked, as if the alleys themselves leaned closer, swallowing sound. A train whistle moaned in the distance, followed by the hollow clang of steel wheels on tracks. Agnes tugged her reflective jacket tighter, though the damp air clung stubbornly to her skin.

They turned down another corridor between two warehouses, the concrete walls weeping with condensation. Graffiti curled across every surface with angry names, crude symbols, half-faded memorials for kids gone too soon.

Bernice's flashlight beam swept over a row of pallets stacked against the wall. A figure stirred, then two more. Eyes gleamed from the shadows. Three young women, wrapped in tattered coats and thin blankets, crouched together against the cold.

"Hello," Agnes said softly, crouching down so her voice carried without looming. "We've got grocery cards. Can I give you one?"

The eldest, no older than twenty-one, reached out cautiously, her knuckles raw and red. "Yeah. Thanks."

Agnes touched her hand briefly as she gave her the card. "Do you know Serena? Have you seen her?"

The girl studied the photo, lips pressed tight. "She used to crash with us sometimes. But not lately. Heard she found a guy."

Another of the women, barely eighteen, shook her head. "He's bad news. Picks girls up, buys 'em booze. Haven't seen her since she left with him."

"Do you know his name?" Bernice asked gently.

"White. Blonde. Truck. That's all I know." The girl folded the card into her palm as if it were gold.

"Thank you," Agnes whispered.

They moved on.

Further down, the alley opened onto a

back lot where smoke curled from another barrel fire. A circle of men warmed their hands, their eyes tracking the patrol volunteers with a mix of suspicion and fatigue. The smell of cheap whiskey and damp wool carried in the breeze.

Bernice lifted her chin. "Evening."

A heavyset man muttered, "Evening," and gestured for them to approach.

"You need food cards?" Agnes asked, holding one out.

Grimy hands lifted hesitantly. One of the men stepped forward, the light catching his hollow cheeks and wiry beard. He accepted the card, then pointed to the photo Bernice held.

"Serena?"

"You know her?" Bernice asked.

"Yeah. Saw her with a blonde guy. Newer truck. She looked scared. Didn't want to get in. But he grabbed her arm." He looked away, ashamed. "Should've done something. But..." He spread his hands helplessly.

"You told us now," Agnes said, squeezing his hand. "That matters."

As they walked back toward the main street, Bernice's voice trembled with anger. "Everywhere we go, it's the same story of our girls disappearing with men who treat them like trash, and no one stops it. Not the police. Not the city. Not the FBI."

Agnes nodded grimly. "That's why we do this. Because if we don't, no one else will."

The wind picked up, carrying the sound of

sirens farther away, a reminder of how distant official help always seemed. The alleys smelled of rust, smoke, and the faint sweetness of spilled liquor.

They passed a mural painted on the side of a warehouse, faded but still visible under the grime: a Native woman's face surrounded by red handprints. *No More Stolen Sisters.* Agnes paused before it, her flashlight grazing the paint.

Bernice's voice dropped low. "How many more before someone listens?"

Agnes reached out and touched the wall, her fingers trembling. "As many as it takes. We keep walking. We keep asking. That's all we can do."

The sound of footsteps echoed ahead. A small group of teenagers, half drunk, half defiant, emerged from the shadows. Their eyes gleamed in the flashlight's sweep. Agnes and Bernice straightened, their hands steady even as the tension thickened.

"Evening," Agnes said calmly, holding out the cards. "We've got something for you."

The group of teenagers stepped into the glow of the flashlight. Hoodies pulled tight, faces half-hidden, their laughter was edged with something brittle, something sharp. The youngest of them flicked a pocketknife open and shut, open and shut, the metal clicking like teeth in the silence.

"Evening," Agnes repeated, her voice calm, the cards still visible in her hand. "We've got food cards if you need them."

One of the older boys, tall and wiry, spat onto the pavement and took a step closer. "What we need is to be left the hell alone."

Bernice moved subtly to Agnes's side; her eyes locked on the knife flashing in the dark. "We're not here to bother you. Just trying to help."

The boy with the knife smirked. "You think a five-dollar card fixes anything out here? You think it stops what happens in these alleys?" He jabbed the blade toward the picture in Bernice's hand. "That girl? I saw her. You think you're gonna find her with cards and questions?"

Agnes's heart thudded. She steadied her flashlight on his face. "Then tell us what you know."

The group stirred uneasily, their bravado cracking. One girl, maybe seventeen, tugged at the boy's sleeve. "Don't, Jason. Just let it go."

But Jason jerked his arm free, eyes glinting with something darker than teenage rebellion. "White truck. Blonde dude. Same one picks 'em up all the time. He drops bills on the ground like he's a savior. But once they're inside—" He stopped short, swallowing hard, as if he'd already said too much.

The sudden roar of an engine cut through the air. Headlights flared at the end of the alley. A dark truck idled there, just long enough for everyone to see its silhouette against the brick walls.

Bernice froze. "Agnes."

The teens scattered like smoke, vanishing into shadows. Jason snapped his knife shut and bolted with the others. The truck revved, tires spitting gravel, before it tore off down the cross street.

The alley fell silent except for Agnes's ragged breathing.

Bernice's hand tightened on her arm. "That wasn't coincidence."

Agnes raised her radio with shaking fingers, her voice steady only by force. "Stone—we've got movement. Dark truck, blonde driver, just circled us at the north end of the warehouse alley. Send a unit now."

Static hissed in reply before Stone's voice cut through. *"Copy. Hold your ground, Agnes. I'm on my way."*

Agnes lowered the radio and looked down the alley where the truck had been. The mural of the red handprints loomed in the dark, its message heavier than ever.

Bernice whispered, almost to herself, "Memory's madness. That's what this is. We're chasing ghosts and the monster's right here."

The alley lay empty now, the barrel fire crackling to itself, sparks drifting into the night. Agnes still held the photo in one hand, the edges trembling under her grip. Bernice steadied her, eyes fixed on the street where the truck had been.

The glow of its taillights was gone, but the echo of its engine still hummed in the concrete walls.

Agnes lifted her radio, her voice controlled only by sheer will. "Stone, we've got movement. Dark truck. Blonde driver. He circled us at the north end of the warehouse alley. Send a unit now."

Static. Then Stone's clipped reply: *"Copy. Hold your ground, Agnes. I'm on my way."*

Agnes lowered the radio, staring into the dark mouth of the alley. The mural of red handprints loomed behind her, the painted woman's eyes wide and sorrowful.

Bernice whispered, almost prayer-like, "Memory's madness. We chase their ghosts... while the monster circles us."

The cold wind swept the alley, carrying the smell of oil and smoke, and the night pressed closer, as if holding its breath.

8

THE NIGHT'S PRICE

The Spirit Pass Casino glittered under chandeliers strung with paper lanterns, each glowing like bottled sunsets. The grand ballroom had been transformed into a tropical dream with tables draped in turquoise and coral linens, palms in oversized pots casting playful shadows across walls painted in light. The air smelled faintly of citrus, rum punch, and lilies from the centerpieces.

Agnes and Bernice, their dresses bright as hibiscus blooms, stood shoulder to shoulder, surveying the final touches as catering staff laid out platters of shrimp skewers and frosted cupcakes adorned with pineapple slices.

"I'm thrilled we sold out of tickets," Bernice said, smoothing her dress, eyes darting over the crowd already queuing outside the ballroom doors.

"Especially with that concert at the amphitheater tonight," Agnes replied. "The younger crowds will go there. We'll get the donors."

Bernice's satisfaction curdled in an instant. Her jaw tightened. "What the hell is he doing here?"

Agnes followed her gaze. Agent Borgreve strode into the room in khaki pants and a floral shirt that looked stiff against his serious posture. At his side, Stone wore her uniform, no pretense of festivity.

Agnes lifted an eyebrow. "Is that as tropical as you get, Agent Borgreve?"

"I wanted to blend in and maybe learn a few things while I'm here." His smile was dry, his eyes anything but.

Bernice's voice sliced. "Shouldn't you be out catching a killer? This night is for families, for survivors, for raising money. Not for police parading around in costumes."

Borgreve tilted his head. "And hello to you, Mrs. O'Reilly. Will Chet be joining us this evening?"

Bernice stepped close, her words deliberate. "You. Stay. Away. From. Him."

Agnes tried to smooth the jagged air. "You'd better find your seat, Agent Borgreve. And not next to Stone, she'll give away your disguise."

"Doors are opening. Find your places, ladies," Stone advised, positioning herself by the entrance as the first wave of guests entered.

A throng poured in with sun dresses, flowered shirts, linen slacks. Laughter rose, buoyed by the cover band striking up an old sixties tune. Agnes and Bernice worked the room, polite smiles masking nerves.

Chet arrived last, in tow with Tracy who is a vivacious, sharp-eyed young woman in a short coral dress. Her energy sparkled, her laugh too loud for the somber occasion.

Bernice's breath caught. "What are you doing?" she hissed as Chet approached.

"Um, my date, Mom," Chet said, gesturing with mock pride. "Ready to party."

Bernice's face hardened. "It hasn't been long enough since Claudia died. And you, of all people, under scrutiny."

Chet slipped his arm around Tracy, grinning at the band. "I can take care of myself. Night!"

Tracy twirled under his hand, laughing as they drifted toward their table on the edge of the room.

From across the ballroom, Borgreve raised his glass in Bernice's direction, his eyes fixed not on her but on Chet. Bernice froze, then quickly turned away, retreating to Agnes's side.

"I'm sorry," she whispered.

Agnes pressed her hand. "Not tonight. Tonight, we smile. Tonight, we raise money."

Bernice exhaled shakily. "Maybe it's grief. I remember when my husband died and I couldn't sit still, not for an hour. Cleaned the house top to bottom just to keep the ghosts at bay."

"Chet's young," Agnes offered.

"And stupid," Bernice snapped.

Agnes squeezed her hand again.

On the dance floor, Tracy spun away from Chet, quickly latching onto another dancer near the stage. Chet stood awkward and alone.

At the bar, Borgreve took a call, his gaze never straying from the crowd. "I've been waiting for your call all day. What do you got?" He listened, eyes narrowing, then cut a look at Stone across the room. "Got it." He snapped his phone shut, already weaving through the tables.

He found Stone by the far door. "Chet's tires are a match for Serena, the missing girl from the field search. Exact. We can bring him in, question him, while we get warrants for his shoes and DNA."

Stone scanned the ballroom, bright gowns, jewel-colored ties, clinking glasses, laughter that seemed too loud, too oblivious.

On stage, the emcee in a flowing tropical gown announced Agnes and Bernice, applauding them as "our ground search leaders, our patrol coordinators, our hearts." The room lifted in recognition, but Agnes barely smiled.

"I'll check the bathroom," Borgreve muttered, disappearing into the corridor. Minutes later, he returned, grim. "He's gone."

They followed the trail through the corridor of casino shops and onto the gaming floor, the din of slot machines swallowing the gala's music. Borgreve's eyes locked on Hunter Daniel, leaning too close to two young waitresses. Hunter saw him, cursed under his breath, and retreated.

"Coward," Borgreve muttered, scanning the rest of the floor.

Outside, Chet skulked across the parking lot, shoulders hunched, head snapping left and right. He fumbled with his truck keys, glancing toward a dumpster near the employee entrance. From the bed of his pickup, he hauled out a black trash bag. A sneaker tumbled free with mud crusted on the sole. Chet swore, shoved it back inside, and sprinted to the dumpster. The bag hit the bottom with a muffled thud.

Headlights cut across the lot. A novice security guard in a Jeep slowed beside him.

"Hey, Chet. Headed to the amphitheater?"

"Yeah, yeah. Busy night, huh?"

"Packed. But still sober, for now." The guard laughed.

Chet forced a grin. "Well, I better get going."

"You're headed the wrong way, buddy."

"Forgot my wallet in the truck."

"Right. See you later."

Chet climbed back into his truck, slammed the door, and peeled out of the lot, tires squealing.

Back on the casino floor, Stone's radio crackled. *"Chet O'Reilly was just in Lot C at the back of the property. Left in a hurry."*

Borgreve cursed. "Damn it. He saw me in the ballroom."

Stone frowned. "Too bad he lives on county land. If he were on the rez, we'd already be at his door."

"My office will get the warrant soon enough."

Stone gave him a hard look. "I wouldn't count on it."

The music from the gala floated faintly behind them, discordant against the chase that was already slipping through their hands.

Inside Chet O'Reilly's small bedroom, drawers yanked half open, clothes strewn across the floor, he stuffed his laptop, a fistful of photographs, and women's panties and bras into a black garbage bag. His movements were frantic, jerky, as though time itself was snapping at his heels. Without looking back, he tore out the door.

Borgreve and Stone bolted from the casino floor, strobes of slot-machine light still clinging to their clothes as they hit the night air. Their SUVs fishtailed out of the lot, headlights spearing the dark, until they arrived at the O'Reilly home. Another FBI agent, younger but sharp-eyed, waited at the door.

"You got the warrant?" Borgreve barked.

The agent held up a folder. "Right here. The team's en route."

Borgreve twisted the knob. "It's unlocked."

They swept inside. The house smelled of stale cigarettes and detergent, the air too still. Borgreve's command cut the silence: "Tear this place apart."

Uniformed agents poured in, flipping cushions, bagging hard drives, turning the quiet home into a storm.

Stone's shoulder radio crackled. *"Chet O'Reilly is washing his truck at the casino convenience store."*

By the time Chet pulled around from the car wash to the vacuum station, his shirt clung with sweat. He leaned inside, jamming the nozzle against the floorboards, desperate.

That's when Borgreve, Stone, and a tribal patrol SUV shot into the lot, lights washing the night red and blue.

Chet bolted, scrambling out of the truck, cutting through a copse of trees into the dark.

Stone sprinted first, branches whipping her face as she tore through the grove. She burst into a housing development; the glow of porch lights scattered like beacons. Dogs barked and strained on their leashes, snarling at the scent of pursuit.

A metallic clang echoed. Stone spun toward a backyard shed. She yanked the door open just as Chet exploded outward, slamming her onto the ground. They wrestled in the dirt, her breath crushed from her lungs until she twisted, hooked his arm, and drove him down. The cuffs clicked home as Borgreve skidded up behind them, panting.

At tribal police headquarters, Chet sat across the metal table, wrists cuffed, eyes red but defiant.

Borgreve leaned forward. "What do you have to tell us? Because we're going to find it anyway. We're collecting the vacuum contents right now. We've got a warrant on your house."

Chet's voice cracked. "Don't tear apart my mom's place. She'll kill me."

"Speaking of murder." Borgreve's tone cut like glass.

"I never killed anyone!"

"Then what were you dumping at the casino? We'll comb every trash can in that lot."

Chet sagged back. "I was with Serena. We were in the field out on 62. Things got rough."

"What happened to her?" Stone's voice was low, steady.

"Nothing. She took off. Crazy bitch—she was tweaking."

"Was?"

"When I last saw her," he muttered.

"She's missing."

"I don't know where she is."

Borgreve leaned in. "We found her purse.

Bloodied clothes. DNA's being tested against yours."

"You can't charge me without a body. For all you know she's shacked up with some guy on the rez. All you can prove is we had sex."

"And bloodied clothes," Stone countered. "Something happened."

"She happened to herself. Kicking, punching, crawling toward the river. I tried to cover her up, tried to help, and she went wild."

Borgreve let the silence hang until Chet squirmed, then said flatly, "You're lying."

Chet snapped. "You're pinning this on me. I want a lawyer. Now."

Stone and Borgreve rose. Outside, Stone's voice was low. "We don't have a body. As much as I want it to be him—I'm not getting that sense."

Borgreve pinched the bridge of his nose. "At least we've got him on fleeing and assaulting an officer."

Back in the casino's grand ballroom, the music had faded to a gentle hum. The cover band packed their gear as the last donors slipped away. Kitchen staff cleared platters and folded linens.

By the exit doors, Agnes and Bernice clasped hands with an affluent donor couple. The wife, elegant in a coral gown, pressed a check into Agnes's palm.

"This work matters. People need to know it's happening here, not just in Canada, but right here."

Agnes's smile shone through her exhaustion. "You don't know how much this means to us."

Bernice echoed warmly, "Your generosity will carry us forward."

When the last guest had gone, Bernice closed the ballroom doors. She twirled in giddy relief, laughter bubbling out. Agnes, still glowing, swayed to the echo of the band's last notes.

"We surpassed our goal," Bernice whispered, almost reverent.

Agnes took her hand and danced with her, two weary women refusing to let grief rob them of this single victory.

The ballroom had grown quiet, its energy exhaled like the last candle flickering low after a feast. Chairs stood askew, tables bare except for the shimmer of glassware waiting to be cleared. The cover band's laughter echoed faintly as they packed up their instruments, the hollow thump of drum cases carrying across the empty space.

Agnes and Bernice stood together beneath the chandeliers, the check still folded in Agnes's hand. The paper felt heavier than its weight—like proof that their cause mattered, even if the rest of the world tried not to see.

Bernice, flushed from wine and emotion, twirled clumsily on the polished floor, her sundress swinging. "We did it," she whispered, as though afraid the moment might vanish if she spoke too loudly.

Agnes let herself laugh, soft and tired, but real. She tucked the check into her clutch and took Bernice's hands. For a few seconds, they swayed together under the quiet glitter of light, moving to a song that wasn't playing anymore but lived inside them.

Grief pressed at the edges, sharp as broken glass, but for once it didn't cut. Not in this moment. Tonight, they had built something more substantial: community, resilience, a reason to believe tomorrow might hold more than sorrow.

Agnes exhaled, her voice hushed. "Claudia would have loved this."

Bernice only nodded, blinking hard.

Outside, the neon of the casino marquee pulsed against the night sky, but in the ballroom, the air was still, the world held back, just long enough for two women to stand together in the fragile light of their victory.

9

GHOSTS OF THE PRESENT

Marsei curled into herself on the sofa, arms wrapped around her knees, hair falling forward like a curtain. The room's dim light painted her in pallor, while Michael paced the hardwood floor in restless arcs.

"It pains me to see you like this," he said at last. "Any connection to that damn family has always brought bad news for us."

Marsei's voice was muffled against her knees. "It's not them. It's the publisher."

Michael stopped mid-stride. "You have a history with them."

"They just want to postpone publishing my manuscript until Claudia's case is solved." A sharp sniffle escaped her.

"It may never be solved. Isn't that the point of your book? All those cold cases nobody cares about?"

"Maybe, until the next big case hits the state papers instead of just the reservation news. Remember that baby abduction? When they cut the child from the mother's belly up north? That made headlines everywhere."

Michael grimaced and rubbed his jaw. "Whatever." He retreated into the kitchen, his voice trailing.

Marsei remained motionless, as though the cushions had absorbed her grief.

The next day, the basement of the community center was dim and cool, its fluorescent hum softened by shadows. Bernice stepped inside with an armful of paperwork and was startled at the sight of Agnes sitting alone in the dark, her silhouette bowed forward.

"What are you doing in here, Agnes?"

Agnes lifted her head slowly. "Practicing being alone with my grief in a spot I feel safe. My office is too busy. Too many interruptions."

Bernice's voice softened. "How are you doing?"

Agnes's reply trembled. "It's difficult. Why can't I get through this? It's overwhelming."

Bernice set the papers aside and folded Agnes into her arms.

"She was your grandbaby. Don't expect so much out of yourself."

Agnes let the tears fall. "Oh, what am I doing, focusing on myself? I've got prayer circles to tend to. And other families, other survivors. Claudia was like that too, always helping someone else."

Their shoulders shook together.

"We're a sorry pair of souls," Bernice whispered through her own tears.

Agnes gave a watery laugh. "Yes. But we've got to keep trying. They've got nobody else."

"At least we have each other."

They clasped hands. From the hallway came a sudden eruption of joy as preschoolers tumbled out toward the playground. Their laughter spilled like bells into the dim basement. Both women looked at each other and giggled despite themselves, warmed by the sound of children too young to carry sorrow.

Later, Bernice's grief had hardened into fury. She paced the waiting room, stomping in small circles as she waited for Agnes.

"Chet asked for a lawyer," she spat. "So, all that's possible is being done right now."

She collapsed into a chair, face burning.

The elevator doors opened, and Agnes stepped out. Bernice leapt to her feet, words already blazing.

"They arrested Chet for the disappearance of Serena, the girl whose belongings we found in the field off 62."

At the reception desk, the young clerk threw her hands in the air.

Agnes's voice was sharp with shock. "What evidence do they have?"

Bernice's eyes brimmed, but her tone was defiant. "They say Chet confessed. He told them he had sex with her in the field, that she fought him and ran off."

Agnes stood frozen, silence widening around her.

The receptionist leaned in. "They still haven't found her body. Maybe she's still out there. Maybe her friends know something."

"He confessed?" Agnes whispered, disbelief hollowing her voice.

Bernice grabbed her hand. "Agnes, this was one idiotic mistake by a stupid boy."

Agnes corrected firmly, "Young man."

Bernice locked eyes with her. "Listen to me. Chet had his flaws, God knows I've ignored them too long. But he didn't kill Claudia. I know it in my heart."

Agnes asked carefully, "He hasn't said anything about Claudia?"

"No." Bernice's voice cracked. "I may have been wrong about his mistakes, Agnes. But he would never hurt Claudia."

Agnes straightened, resolve flickering through her grief. "Then I'd like to go down to the tribal police station. Talk to Stone. Maybe I can ask Chet myself."

Bernice wiped her eyes, fierce again. "I'm coming with you."

The glass doors of tribal police headquarters rattled as Agnes and Bernice shoved them open, their footsteps sharp and urgent on the polished tile floor. The fluorescent lights hummed overhead, too bright, too sterile, their glare magnifying the fury in Bernice's eyes and the grief etched into Agnes's face. The scent of burnt coffee drifted from the waiting area, where a few patrol officers lingered, watching the women storm toward the front desk.

"We need to see Detective Sergeant Stone. Now," Bernice snapped at the young tribal clerk seated behind the counter. Her voice trembled with rage, each word striking like a stone against glass.

The clerk, startled, rose at once. "I'll get her."

Agnes and Bernice didn't sit. They stood shoulder to shoulder, a wall of determination, until the clerk returned and gestured for them to follow. Their heels echoed down the corridor, past glass-walled offices where uniformed men and women glanced up, then quickly looked away.

Inside Stone's office, the blinds were half-drawn, leaving stripes of pale light across the desk. A large map of the reservation covered one wall, dotted with pins and notes like a patchwork of unanswered prayers. Stone sat behind her desk, steady but guarded, while Borgreve stood at the glass wall, his arms crossed as though he already expected battle.

The clerk quietly closed the door behind them, and silence pressed in.

Bernice's voice shattered it. "What the hell are you doing with my son?"

"Please, take a seat," Stone said evenly, motioning to the chairs across from her desk.

Bernice didn't move. Agnes sank slowly into one of the chairs, her hands twisting the strap of her purse.

Borgreve spoke from the wall, his voice clipped. "Chet has refused to answer further questions. He says he'll only speak to his lawyer. He also said he's too embarrassed to speak with you at this time, Mrs. O'Reilly."

"That's crap and you know it," Bernice snapped, her face flushed.

"It's the truth," Borgreve replied, tone flat.

Bernice turned on him, finger jabbing the air. "You stay out of this, just like you've stayed out of every case that's ever mattered to us. Girls go missing. They vanish. And do you give a damn? No. Never."

"Bernice, calm down," Agnes murmured, but her voice was thin and frayed.

Agnes turned to Stone, searching for answers. "Anything on Claudia's case?"

Stone folded her hands together on the desk. "We've released the scene. You can clear out her belongings from her trailer."

Agnes's throat tightened. "It's only been months." Tears welled as she fought them back. "I understand you took a lot of it already."

"That was evidence," Borgreve said, his voice matter-of-fact, as though evidence and grief were weights that balanced each other. "We won't be returning those files."

Agnes's voice cracked. "It was research. Notes for her book."

Borgreve shifted, his gaze sliding to Stone. "Stone, whose book was it?"

Stone's eyes flickered with hesitation before she answered. "Agnes, I'm sorry, but it appears Marsei somehow got hold of

Claudia's manuscript. She submitted it as her own."

The words landed like a blow. Agnes's head fell into her hands, her shoulders shaking. "No. No. Claudia had years of research. All her notes, all her work, Marsei couldn't have produced that from nothing."

"Claudia had the files. Marsei could only produce one recent draft," Borgreve pressed.

Agnes sobbed openly now. "I can't believe Marsei would do such a thing to her sister. Not my girls... not my family."

Bernice hovered beside her, torn between outrage and helplessness, her hand reaching for Agnes's back as if to shield her from the truth itself.

Later that evening, the key scraped in Claudia's trailer door. Agnes pushed it open slowly, as though stepping into sacred ground. The air inside was stale, heavy with silence, but still carried faint traces of her granddaughter like laundered cotton, dog hair, the sweetness of the candles she used to burn on quiet nights.

Bernice followed, both women balancing flattened boxes in their arms. They set them down on the counter, the sound hollow in the too-quiet room.

The trailer looked smaller than Agnes remembered. The couch where Claudia had once dozed with her dogs seemed suddenly fragile, its cushions slumped as though mourning. A stack of unpaid bills and lesson plans still lingered on the end table. The dogs' water bowls, long emptied, sat by the kitchen wall, untouched.

Agnes walked to the sink, touching the lip of a coffee mug as though it were porcelain bone. She traced her hand over the refrigerator door covered in magnets—casino coupons, old photos, a faded postcard of Lake Superior. Each small piece seemed to pulse with Claudia's absence.

Bernice opened a box and began carefully wrapping picture frames in old newspaper. One frame held Claudia's high school graduation photo, her cap tilted, her smile broad and brave. Bernice's hands trembled as she slid it into the box. "This is wrong," she whispered. "We shouldn't be the ones doing this. She should still be here."

Agnes lowered herself into a kitchen chair. The wood creaked beneath her, or maybe it was just her own weight collapsing into grief. She pressed her hands flat to the table as though bracing herself against the whole collapsing world.

"What the hell is happening," she murmured, voice breaking, "when siblings turn on each other?"

Bernice paused mid-wrap, her eyes stinging. "I'm sorry, Agnes. As much as I don't want my son to be guilty, neither do I want Marsei to have had anything to do with this." Agnes drew in a long, ragged breath, then released it in a sigh that seemed to carry decades of sorrow. "All we know is she stole the book. I shouldn't let my imagination run wild. But still..." Her words fell away.

For a long moment, the two women sat in the dim trailer light, surrounded by Claudia's belongings—objects suddenly stripped of their owner, yet saturated with memory. Each framed photo, each chipped mug, each trinket seemed to whisper her name, binding the women in their grief.

Out on Highway 62, the night stretched long and endless, prairie grass whispering in the wind as if carrying old prayers. The road shimmered faintly under the pale spill of moonlight, its asphalt fractured by years of heat and frost.

A girl walked its shoulder, shoulders hunched, hair tangled, clothes dusted with roadside grit. Serena. She hugged her arms across her chest as if that could guard her from the chill or from the weight of everything behind her. Each passing car swept her in a rush of light and wind, but none slowed.

At last, a tribal police SUV coasted to a stop, its headlights bleaching the tall weeds white. The driver's window lowered, the officer leaning into the night air.

"Serena?" His voice was careful, almost disbelieving.

She froze, then nodded. "Yes."

"Are you okay?"

Her eyes darted up and down the empty stretch of highway before she answered. "I'm fine." The words rang thin, brittle, more like a shield than truth.

"Come on in. We've been looking for you."

Serena climbed into the SUV, folding herself into the passenger seat. The warmth of the heater pushed against her skin, but she kept her arms tight around her middle.

"Why?" she asked at last.

"Your belongings were found in the field leading down to the river. We worried something had happened."

"They arrested Chet O'Reilly for assaulting you," the officer said carefully.

Serena's head snapped up. For a flicker, anger lit her eyes, anger, or maybe fear. "Let him go. Nothing happened. I don't want to press charges."

The officer glanced at her sidelong, reading the tremor in her jaw, the way her hands clenched so tightly in her lap, the knuckles whitened. He softened his tone. "You'll need to come down to the station and talk to Stone. She's running the case."

Serena turned her face toward the window, watching the prairie slide past in the headlights. The glass fogged with her breath, and in it, her reflection seemed ghostly, hollow-eyed, a girl caught between escape and disappearance.

The SUV rolled on into the night, carrying her back toward questions she didn't want to answer, toward truths she couldn't yet face.

Inside tribal police headquarters, the air was

sharp with disinfectant and the faint echo of typewriters clacking in distant offices. The hum of fluorescent lights overhead cast everything in a thin, sterile glow.

At the front desk, Chet O'Reilly stood slouched, pale and unshaven, signing a clipboard to reclaim his belongings. His hands shook just enough that the pen rattled across the paper. Beside him, a young female clerk ticked off each item returned, her voice steady, rehearsed—keys, wallet, cell phone. Each word felt like a release of weight he didn't deserve.

From the corner, one of the patrol officers leaned back in his chair, arms folded, mouth curling into a smirk. "You're lucky your mom could afford to bail your half-breed ass out."

Chet froze, his jaw tightening. Slowly, he raised his head and let a grin creep across his face, the kind that didn't reach his eyes. "Fuck you."

The clerk's shoulders stiffened, her pen scratching quicker.

The officer sat forward, his boots scraping on the linoleum. "Your truck's around back, asshole."

Chet took the envelope of his belongings, sliding it into his jacket pocket. His grin widened, teeth flashing under the harsh light. "After I fuck your sister."

The patrol officer shot to his feet, fists balled, lunging across the room, but Chet was already slipping past, quick as smoke, his laughter trailing behind him. He pushed through the double glass doors into the night, the sound of them banging shut echoing down the sterile hall.

The clerk stared at the clipboard still warm from Chet's hand. The officer stood shaking, rage quivering in his throat. Outside, the thrum of Chet's engine fired to life, a note too loud, too alive.

It carried with it the sickening weight of unfinished business.

The community center was nearly empty at that hour, its halls stripped of laughter, the walls echoing only the tick of the old clock above the reception desk. Upstairs, a single lamp glowed in Agnes's office, throwing long shadows across the clutter of files and photographs spread on her desk.

Her phone rang, sharp, urgent, cutting through the quiet. She snatched it up, her voice still raw from the day. "Hello?"

"Agnes? It's me, one of the kids you met downtown. You said to call if I saw anything." The voice was hushed, nervous, carrying the tremor of someone watching the night too closely.

Agnes sat straighter, her heart kicking. "Yes. What did you see?"

"That guy, the one who picked up Serena last month? The white dude, blonde hair. I just saw him again. He took off with another girl. Tawny."

Silence pressed into the line, heavy as

stone. Agnes forced her voice steady. "Did you get a license plate number?"

"Sorry. No. Just caught him out of the corner of my eye. Then they were gone. Fast."

Agnes closed her eyes, a wave of helplessness cresting over her. "Thank you for calling. You did the right thing."

When the call ended, the room seemed larger, emptier. Agnes sat still, the phone heavy in her hand. Beyond the office door, Bernice's laughter floated faintly from the waiting room where she and the receptionist were clinking coffee mugs, celebrating Chet's release like a reprieve, like hope.

Agnes set the phone down, her gaze falling to the picture frames beside her papers. One held Claudia at graduation, cap crooked, smile radiant. The other, older, worn around the edges, showed a little brown-haired girl with wide eyes and a solemn face.

Agnes's throat tightened, and the whisper escaped her lips before she could stop it. "Oh, Marsei. What have you done?"

The Copper Mule breathed its usual end-of-night weariness: neon signs flickered in the smudged windows, the jukebox hummed low, and a sticky film of beer clung to the floorboards. Tawny, barefoot, her sandals dangling from two fingers, spun circles in the middle of the bar with her drink lifted high like a torch. Her tank top slipped from one shoulder, her skirt swaying loose with every stagger.

The last of the patrons leaned on the bar or hunched over tables, their tired laughter dulled by drink. A waitress, hollow-eyed from a long shift, shook her head at Tawny. "Sweetheart, maybe that's enough for tonight. How about a coffee instead?"

"I'm fine," Tawny said, her voice slurred but defiant. She tipped her glass back, finding it empty, and pouted. "Besides, it's a nice night to walk."

The bartender, tall, blonde, his cap pulled low, wiped down the counter with deliberate strokes. His eyes followed Tawny in the mirror but his voice was even. "Leave her be. She'll find her way."

Minutes later, the back door shut with a hollow slam. The bar's lights dimmed. Tawny staggered into the cool night, the air heavy with the scent of spilled beer and exhaust. She slipped her sandals back on, then let them drag against the pavement as she made her way toward the bench outside.

Above her, the stars opened wide across the prairie sky. Tawny tilted her head back and laughed softly at their brilliance. "I'm a big girl," she whispered to no one. "I can take care of myself."

From the shadows of the lot, glass bottles clinked against metal. A dumpster lid groaned shut. Tawny flinched, then giggled nervously. "Guess everyone's cleaning up tonight."

A truck idled near the edge of the lot, its headlights cutting two sharp beams across the gravel. Music thumped faintly from its cab, low, pulsing, insistent.

Tawny swayed toward it, her silhouette caught in the glare. "Well, aren't you my ride home?" she called, her voice sing-song, teasing. She twirled once in front of the beams, her skirt flaring.

The door handle gleamed. She reached for it.

The passenger door opened.

Inside, the cab was shadowed, the driver's face obscured beneath the brim of his cap. He said nothing.

Tawny climbed in anyway, her laugh hollow in the dark. "What are you, my knight in shining armor? Here to sweep me off my feet?" She leaned back into the seat, eyes glassy, a hand pressed to her forehead. "As if."

The door slammed shut. The engine roared.

The Copper Mule went black behind them as the truck pulled out onto the empty highway.

The truck picked up speed, tires humming against the lonely stretch of Highway 62. Tawny slumped in the passenger seat, one hand trailing along the cracked vinyl, her other clutching the hem of her skirt.

The driver's silence pressed heavier than the music rattling the speakers. His hand hovered near the gearshift, then drifted across the seat, resting boldly on her bare thigh.

"Hey," Tawny muttered, her giggle weak, faltering. "Not so fast. You don't even know my name. I'm Tawny."

The hand squeezed harder. His fingers dug into her flesh until she winced. "Ow. You're gonna leave a bruise."

The truck swerved, lurching into the opposite lane before jerking back. Tawny's laugh died in her throat. "You're gonna get us killed!"

No answer. Only the low rumble of his breathing, the cap brim hiding his face.

She turned toward the window, stars streaking by like a smear of cold fire. "Where... where are you taking me?"

The engine growled deeper as the truck veered onto a gravel road. Dust rose behind them, ghostly in the headlights. Ahead, Claudia's trailer loomed in the darkness, the trees around it forming a wall against the highway.

Tawny's pulse hammered. "Okay, I'm just gonna walk from here, alright?" She reached for the door handle, but his arm shot across her chest and yanked her back.

Her sandals scraped the floorboard as she kicked, screamed. The driver's other hand flashed silver in the dim light, a knife, long and sharp, pressed cold against her skin.

"Don't hurt me," Tawny whimpered. "Please. I promise I won't scream. I'll do whatever you want."

He shoved the console back, opening the seat between them, and forced her down across the bench. The blade traced the line of her neck as his free hand fumbled with his pants.

Tawny's breath came in jagged bursts. Tears streaked her cheeks. She turned her face toward him, choking on the stink of sweat and smoke. His knife wavered, resting on her back now as he pulled at her skirt.

Then he slipped. The blade clattered against the seat.

In that heartbeat, Tawny bit down hard on his wrist. He roared, jerking away. She scrambled, clawing at the passenger door.

The night air hit her like a flood when she tumbled out barefoot onto the gravel. Pain shot up her legs, but fear kept her moving. She bolted toward the trailer, pounding on the door with bloody knuckles.

"Help me! Please, somebody help me!"

The porch light stayed dark. Behind her, boots crunched fast on gravel. His hand clamped over her mouth before she could scream again. He lifted her off the ground like a rag doll.

She kicked wildly, twisting, until he slammed her head against the glass of the door. It shattered, raining shards across the porch. He reached inside, unlocked the knob, and dragged her limp form across the threshold.

Tawny groaned, stirring, as he dropped her on the sofa. Her eyes fluttered open just long enough to see him on top of her, tearing fabric from her body.

She gasped, fought against him, and shoved the pillow he pressed over her face. Her muffled cries filled the room. She writhed, then kneed him hard in the groin. He bellowed, falling sideways.

Tawny stumbled up, topless, shaking, and bolted out the open door.

The gravel tore at her feet as she sprinted for the highway. The night was vast and merciless, the road empty.

Behind her, his voice tore through the dark: "Tawny! Where are you?"

She ducked into the prairie grass, thorns slicing her skin. She dropped to her belly, breath burning, ears straining for movement. His footsteps crunched closer.

The sound of rushing water pulled at her—just beyond the trees. She scrambled to her feet, running toward it, toward the river's dark, unseen current.

Branches whipped at Tawny's face as she tore through the trees, her breath ragged, heart thrumming like a war drum. The roar of the river grew louder, pulling her toward it, promising either salvation or ruin.

Behind her, his voice carried, low, taunting, close. "Tawny! You can't hide from me."

She stumbled down the embankment, feet skidding on loose stones, her hands clawing at saplings to keep from falling. The knife had left a welt along her back; blood stung where branches ripped her skin. She didn't stop.

The trees thinned, and suddenly the river was there before her, a broad, churning sweep of black water gleaming silver in the moonlight.

Tawny froze. The bank dropped steeply, jagged with rocks slicked by spray. The current foamed, fast, and merciless.

Behind her, his footsteps closed in. She could hear his breathing now, heavy, eager.

"You run like they all do," he growled.

Tawny's chest heaved. She turned, saw his silhouette break through the tree line, broad shoulders, knife flashing in his hand.

"No more running," he said.

She backed toward the edge. Pebbles slipped beneath her bare feet. The river snarled below, hungry.

He lunged.

Tawny screamed and threw herself sideways, tumbling down the embankment. Her body hit rock, then slid into the freezing current. The water swallowed her in an instant, pulling her under.

She surfaced once, gasping, arms flailing against the current's brute force. "Help!" Her cry shattered against the roar of the river.

On the bank, he watched, knife glinting, breath rising in clouds. He crouched, scanning the foaming dark.

Tawny fought, thrashing, her limbs numb, the water dragging her downstream. She caught sight of the moon above, fractured in the ripples, before the current slammed her against a half-sunken log.

Her fingers clung desperately to its slick bark. Her chest heaved, lungs burning, as she tried to haul herself up. Behind her, he paced the bank, following her shadow as the river carried her along.

"You can't hold on forever," his voice echoed across the water.

Tawny gritted her teeth, praying the current would take her far enough, fast enough, before her strength gave out.

The log tore free from its roots, spinning in the torrent. She clung to it as it lurched into the black bend of the river, swallowed by night.

10

AS DARKNESS CLOSES IN

Agnes slid the last of the files into her desk drawer. Her hand hesitated when she noticed an envelope wedged at the back, the word MARSEI written in Claudia's careful script. Agnes's breath caught. She pulled it free, the paper brittle at the corners, and opened it with trembling fingers. Inside were photographs, snapshots of places, vehicles, faces blurred by motion. She fanned them out across her desk, the fluorescent light casting pale rectangles onto the wood.

One photograph stopped her cold. Michael Abernathy, Marsei's husband, stood in the driveway, smiling stiffly, his hand resting on the polished hood of his truck. Behind him, the trailer hitched and ready, jet skis gleaming like trophies. Agnes traced her fingertip over the image, her eyes narrowing as unease grew inside her chest.

In the tribal police offices, the night was long and restless. The clock on the wall ticked past 2:30 a.m. Stone sat slouched in her chair, hair loose across her shoulders, fatigue softening the sharp edges of her face. Borgreve reclined opposite her, boots propped on the desk, a Styrofoam cup of coffee steaming in his hand. Between them, photographs lay scattered across the desktop: Hunter's truck, dark red; Chet's, a battered blue; the splintered wood of Claudia's trailer door; maps annotated with Claudia's scrawled notes.

Stone's cell phone rang, its shrill tone breaking the stillness. She squinted at the screen.

"Agnes? It's the middle of the night. You should be asleep."

On the other end, Agnes's voice wavered, tired but deliberate.

"I was going to leave you a message. I've been thinking about Marsei. Maybe she did copy Claudia's book. Claudia used to say someone tampered with her mail. Letters missing. Packages opened. I thought she was being paranoid. But what if she wasn't? What if Marsei...?"

Stone shuffled through the paperwork in front of her, barely listening. "What about the book, Agnes?"

"Marsei got a hold of it somehow. Maybe in a weak moment, she had sticky fingers at Claudia's highway mailbox. That's all I'm saying. I just needed you to know."

Stone found the photo she'd been searching for and pressed it flat with her palm. "I've got to go, Agnes."

She ended the call, her attention

sharpened. She tapped the photo on the desk with her fingernail.

"Michael Abernathy," she said. "Takes his jet skis south on vacation."

Borgreve gave a weary laugh, rubbing his face. "Vacation. Christ, I need one too."

Stone sat forward, her eyes fixed on the picture. "No. Look at the trailer hitch. Look at the tire treads. His truck is the same make, the same model as the one we've been chasing."

Borgreve's boots dropped to the floor with a thud. "Michael?"

Stone stood, pacing to the glass wall where the investigation timeline was tacked up. She jabbed at the elderly couple's statement from the night Claudia's car was found.

"His alibi was never solid. They said he was listening to UFOs on the radio. Only that night, the program wasn't UFOs, it was Bigfoot."

Borgreve frowned, shaking his head. "What the hell are you saying?"

Stone's voice dropped, threaded with conviction. "Maybe it tore him apart to watch Marsei unravel being ostracized, dismissed, cast off by her family. Maybe he saw the way she suffered and snapped. And now he's punishing women on the rez for what Marsei endured."

Borgreve stared at her, the weight of the idea sinking in. The office felt suddenly smaller, the air heavier, as though the truth had finally cracked through the walls.

Across the river, inside the Abernathy house, the night pressed against the windows. Marsei paced the office, her bare feet silent on the hardwood floor. Bookshelves lined the walls, neat and orderly, but her thoughts scattered like broken glass. She raked her hands through her blonde hair, pulled it tight, then let it fall again.

Her eyes darted to the clock—3:00 a.m.

She picked up her phone, scrolled to Michael's name, and pressed call again. The line rang into emptiness.

"Michael, where are you?" Her voice was little more than a whisper, though no one was there to hear it. "Why aren't you answering?"

The silence on the other end was vast, and it pressed in on her like the dark itself.

Borgreve's SUV barreled down the empty road, headlights carving through blackness. The highway stretched on forever, pale gravel shoulders flashing by, the prairie wind rushing across the hood like a whispering chorus. He gripped the wheel with one hand, the other pressed to his phone.

"Yeah, I need a search warrant immediately for Michael Abernathy's truck." His voice crackled through static. "Urgent. Tonight."

The call sputtered and died.

He cursed, tossed the phone down, and leaned forward. That was when he caught the faint glow of a single headlight through a stand of trees. He slowed, heart hammering. Claudia's trailer. A pale box in the night, its windows lit up like someone had come home.

He slammed the brakes, gravel spitting under his tires, and reversed into the narrow driveway. His gun was already drawn as he whispered into his phone, reconnecting with Stone.

"Stone, it's me. Something's happening at Claudia Shepherd's. There's a truck in the drive, interior lights on. Move—fast."

The engine cut. Silence pressed in heavily. He stepped out, gun up, the smell of wet earth rising from the grass. He crept to the idling truck. Empty. Doors unlocked. His pulse thudded harder.

Inside the trailer, each room gave nothing but emptiness and the echo of his boots on linoleum. Back in the living room, he froze. A tank top and bra lay tossed on the sofa, pale fabric catching the lamp light. A whisper of movement drifted from outside.

Borgreve pivoted, descended the stoop, and swept his gun across the dark yard. Nothing but the skeletal outlines of trees and the hiss of prairie wind.

Then, faint yelling. A voice carried by the river.

Stone's SUV screeched up, her door left open on the highway. The full moon hung like a blade above the tree line. She caught a glimpse of a figure stumbling through weeds toward the water.

Beyond the field, Tawny crouched in brush, her chest heaving, tears cutting streaks through the dirt on her face. Branches clawed her arms as she crawled further from the silhouette of the man. Michael's heavy footsteps stumbled somewhere close.

"Tawny!" he shouted, voice fraying. "You know I'm going to find you."

She pressed her fist to her mouth, stifling a sob. The sound of the river grew louder ahead.

Michael's breath rasped as he crashed through weeds, knife glinting in his fist. "Come back to me, honey. You've got nowhere else out here." His words trembled with something between rage and grief.

Stone sprinted through the brush, her boot catching on a root. She fell hard, palms stinging, but pushed herself up, closing in.

Michael crept toward the riverbank, knife raised, scanning the trees. His voice dropped into a low murmur, almost tender. "You don't want to go in that river, Tawny. That current will take you. Just come back. I can keep you safe."

The weeds crackled behind him. He spun.

Stone emerged, gun leveled, her breath white in the moonlight.

"Put the knife down, Michael."

"Go to hell." His shoulders rose, his eyes fever-bright.

"It doesn't have to end this way." Her voice was steady, though her pulse raced.

"You love your wife? Then prove it. Drop the knife."

Michael's throat bobbed, words tumbling raw. "She carries so much pain from this place. From you people. From your silence." He lifted his face to the sky. "Do you know what it's like to watch someone you love disintegrate into nothing? To watch her break because of what happened here?"

"Honestly?" Stone's voice dropped. "I do."

From the river came a scream. "Help! I can't swim!" Tawny's voice was high and ragged.

Stone's head turned just for a fraction. Michael lunged. The blade slashed her arm, hot blood slicking her sleeve. Her gun fell into the weeds. They collapsed together, thrashing, fists and knees and snarls tearing the night.

Michael's hands closed on her throat, choking. Stone twisted, buckled, and slammed her knee upward into his crotch. He fell sideways, fingers scrambling for the knife. Stone kicked, boot cracking across his face.

They both reached for the blade. Fingers grappled. Stone wrenched it free and slashed across his neck in one desperate arc. Michael's eyes widened, his breath rattling, his body falling back into the grass.

Stone staggered to her feet, arm dripping, vision swimming. Tawny's screams pulled her back. She tore off her jacket and dove into the freezing black river.

The current dragged, the cold burned, but she fought her way toward the flailing girl. Tawny's arms slapped the water blindly. Stone's hand caught her wrist, then her waist. With a guttural cry, she dragged her toward shore.

Borgreve appeared at the bank, his arms plunging in, hauling Tawny up. Stone clawed at the mud and finally pulled herself free. Borgreve caught her, his arm firm around her shoulder. For a breathless moment, she sagged against him, their eyes locking under the moon's hard glow.

She tapped his shoulder, wordless, and pulled away. The work wasn't finished.

The river spat them out onto the muddy bank, all three collapsing into the reeds. Tawny coughed violently, spitting river water, her whole body trembling in shudders that made her look like a child. Stone ripped off her soaked shirt sleeve and pressed it to the gash on her own arm, her chest heaving.

Borgreve dropped to his knees beside them, one hand steadying Tawny, the other sweeping his gaze across the shadows of the field. His voice was rough. "We're clear. Just breathe. You're both clear."

But the night didn't feel clear. The moon lit the prairie like a cruel floodlight, revealing every raw detail.

Michael Abernathy's body lay ten feet away, sprawled half on his side, half on his back, the weeds dark with blood where his throat had opened. His face was frozen in shock, eyes still wide, mouth parted as if he'd tried to speak one last time. The knife glinted beside his limp hand, useless now.

Stone pushed herself up, her breath ragged. She took a few slow steps toward him. Her boots squelched in the mud. For a moment, she just stared at the husband who claimed love was his excuse, at the killer who bled out for it.

She whispered, almost to herself, "You could've stopped. You could've ended this another way." Her voice broke, and she clenched her jaw until the words tasted bitter in her mouth.

Behind her, Tawny wailed into her hands, rocking forward and back. Borgreve crouched low beside the girl, trying to cover her shoulders with his jacket, but Tawny's shaking didn't ease. "He was going to kill me," she sobbed. "I thought—I thought I was already dead."

"You're not," Borgreve told her firmly. "You fought. You made it."

Stone turned back, eyes locking with Borgreve's over Tawny's bowed head. Neither spoke, but everything hung between them, the horror, the relief, the unspoken guilt of how close they'd all come.

Somewhere behind them, down the highway, the faint pulse of sirens rose, still distant but growing louder. The prairie wind carried it like a low dirge.

Stone crouched down, her wet hair

clinging to her face, and laid a hand on Tawny's arm. Her tone was quieter now, less like an officer, more like someone's sister. "We've got you. You're safe tonight."

Tawny lifted her face, her eyes swollen and red, and looked between Stone and Borgreve as if searching for proof.

Stone straightened again, glancing once more at Michael's body, then at the river still rippling under the moonlight. Darkness had claimed another, but this time, someone had lived.

The sirens came closer, flooding the night with their urgent cry, as Stone's voice carried low and steady over the wind:
"Let's bring her home."

Back at the community center the next day, Agnes sat in her office, the soft light of morning falling through lace curtains onto her desk. She held a wedding picture of Marsei in both hands, tracing the curve of her granddaughter's smile with her thumb as if the photograph could breathe again under her touch. Bernice stood beside her, arms folded gently, watching.

"Marsei, grief can take its toll on a person," Agnes whispered to the picture, her voice breaking but steadying with prayer. "My prayers are with you, granddaughter."

Bernice leaned in. "I'm so glad you've come to terms with Marsei's involvement."

Agnes placed the photo down carefully, almost ceremonially, beside a folder of community flyers. "And you've grown to look past the FBI for their misgivings and cultivate hope for future pursuits."

Bernice's face softened. "Plus, I see my son's mistakes and hold him accountable."

For a long moment, the two women sat in silence, surrounded by the faint hum of the center's refrigerator down the hall and the muffled laughter of preschoolers being dropped off outside.

In the city, Marsei lay curled in bed, the blinds drawn against the morning. She squirmed in her sheets, her breath shallow, caught in the restless turning of emotional pain. On the pillow beside her lay her wedding photo with Michael, the smiles captured forever but hollow now, the glass smudged from her fingertips. Next to it, a snapshot of Claudia's graduation rested, edges frayed, as if the picture itself bore the weight of memory and betrayal. Marsei clutched the blanket to her chest, her shoulders trembling in the dim light, caught between love and loss, sisterhood and silence.

Inside the tribal police offices, the fluorescent lights buzzed faintly. A bruised and beaten twelve-year-old Native American girl sat outside Stone's office, her feet swinging just above the floor, sneakers scuffed, knees pressed tightly together. She kept her eyes fixed on the tile until Stone came out and lowered herself onto the bench beside her.

Borgreve entered the building and paused, standing just behind them, close enough to hear but hidden from the girl's line of sight.

"What happened to you wasn't your fault," Stone said gently, her voice carrying the weight of lived truth.

The girl nodded, tears cutting quiet streaks down her face.

"Sometimes parents are really messed up and do things that end up hurting us," Stone added. Her own eyes softened, her posture bending into a kind of kinship.

"How do I forget?" the girl whispered.

Stone shook her head. "Sometimes, we can't forget. Sometimes, it makes us strong. Sometimes, it makes us who we are meant to be."

The girl wiped her eyes with the heel of her hand. "What's going to happen to me?"

"Your grandma's going to pick you up," Stone said, a small, certain smile lighting her face. "And you're going to live with her just like I lived with my grandma when I was little. Now, look at me."

Stone sat upright, shoulders squared, showing the girl not just words but proof. The girl's lips twitched into the beginning of a smile. She leaned into Stone, burying her face in the detective's shoulder, clinging with the desperate relief of someone who'd been given a lifeline.

Borgreve replaced his thin smile with a quiet clearing of his throat that startled

Stone. She looked up at him, rising to her feet, straightening, though her arm still protectively hovered near the girl.

"We tied his DNA to five women plus Claudia," Borgreve announced, his voice cutting through the hush. For a moment, their eyes locked, not just colleagues but allies hardened in fire. Their smiles were small, almost grim, but they carried the relief of ground gained in a war that never seemed to end.

The following day at the community center, the basement meeting room glowed with warmth. Agnes and Bernice moved slowly through the familiar motions: setting up a welcome sign at the door, putting out paper plates and cookies on a folding table, and arranging chairs into a wide circle. The hum of the soda machine and the smell of coffee filled the air, giving the space a lived-in comfort.

Agnes paused, standing in the middle of the room, letting her eyes roam across the walls where bright children's art hung beside flyers for food drives and vigils. "This is such a special room," she said softly. "With the birthday parties, baby showers, and support groups."

Bernice walked over, slipped her hand into Agnes's, and gave it a firm squeeze. She smiled through tears. "Where shitty endings transform into better beginnings."

The women stood together, quiet, holding

the moment between them like a fragile flame.

Outside the community center, the sun broke over the horizon, washing the prairie in soft gold. Children's laughter rang out from the playground, drifting into the still morning air, a fragile chorus against the memory of so many silenced voices. From the road nearby, Stone's SUV rolled past slowly, her window down, her tired eyes catching the sight of Agnes and Bernice through the glass doors—two women standing shoulder to shoulder, readying themselves for another day of holding the community together. The world was far from safe, but in that moment, with light touching the grass and voices rising in play, survival felt like its own kind of victory.

The End

Missing and Murdered Indigenous Women & Girls: Novella #2

1

Brimstone Butterflies

The Copper Mule's neon sign spits and flickers in the heavy dark, painting the cracked blacktop with jaundiced streaks of red and gold. The bar's back alley smells of beer-soaked cardboard and diesel fumes, the kind of place where shadows outnumber people.

Inside an FBI SUV parked across the street, two silhouettes wait.

"Just because a woman dresses provocatively doesn't mean she should be assaulted, raped, or murdered. Talk about judging a book by its frickin' cover," says Tribal Detective Sergeant Jessica Stone. Her voice cuts the silence like a blade, sharp with disdain. Taller than most, with dark hair pulled back and eyes that catch every shift in the night, Stone carries herself with the posture of someone who has learned survival isn't optional.

Across from her, FBI Special Agent Casey Borgreve stiffens. He's all broad shoulders and restless energy, his blue-green eyes catching a brief gleam from the dashboard glow. "I'm just saying the missing person photos we show might be more effective if she's dressed a bit more modestly." The words stumble out, and he knows even before he finishes that he sounds like a relic. He exhales hard. "You know what, you're right. I'm sorry. Small-town WASP upbringing."

Stone turns, her gaze sharp. "And while we're at it, just because a woman accepts a few drinks doesn't make her available to assault, rape, or murder either. And don't toss your upbringing at me like it's an excuse. I know WASPs who don't hide behind restrictive beliefs."

Borgreve smirks, trying to cover his embarrassment. "Then are they still WASPs?"

"You're just trying to agitate me now, aren't you, Casey?"

He shrugs, hand pressing against his grumbling stomach. "I'd kill for something to eat."

Stone scoffs. "We've been here thirty minutes. What kind of cop are you?"

"A hungry one."

His attention shifts to a teenage girl hauling a battered bike with a garbage bag tied to the frame. She dips into a dumpster, clattering aluminum cans into her sack. Her shoulders are squared, every movement practiced.

"Can you really make money off those?"

Borgreve wonders.

"It's worth a try versus starving," Stone answers flatly. "Some kids out here survive on a box of crackers a day when school isn't in session. Hunger doesn't care about pride."

The girl pedals away under the buzzing lamps, swatting at moths that swarm like ash. A group of drunk men spills out of a side bar, jeering. One whistles low. She flips them off without hesitation and keeps going.

"Gutsy young lady," Stone says softly. "I like her."

The SUV's cab falls quiet, both watching the churn of bodies in the street. Men stumbling, women steadying them, laughter pitched a little too sharp. It's almost normal until it isn't, until a scream slices through the noise, high and raw, from behind The Copper Mule.

Stone and Borgreve are out of the SUV in seconds, pounding across the gravel. They skid into the alley to find the dumpster diver crouched by her bike, hands trembling, eyes wide. She points at the yawning black of the dumpster.

Borgreve sweeps his flashlight inside.

The beam lands on a girl. Sixteen, maybe. Long hair matted, skin already cooling. Her eyes, gone.

Stone staggers back a step, breath ragged. "Holy shit. Her eyes have been poked out."

Borgreve's jaw tightens. "I'll get my team out here." He pivots, phone to his ear, already calling it in.

Stone turns on the gathering crowd of intoxicated onlookers, pushing them back, shielding the dumpster diver with her own body. The girl presses into her, shivering, clinging like a child to Stone's waist. Stone's hand finds the back of the girl's head and holds her there, steady, even as her own stomach twists. The alley reeks of rot and beer and death, and in that moment, Stone knows: the rez has another ghost to carry.

The Next Morning

The Spirit Pass Community Center glows pale in the gray morning light, a fortress of linoleum and hope in a place that never stops grieving. The second-floor offices smell faintly of burned coffee and disinfectant.

Agnes greets Stone with weary eyes, Bernice at her side, clutching a stack of paperwork. Between them stands Vaneeta Shah, the new Employee Assistance Program counselor. She is polished and kind, a woman in her forties who hasn't yet learned how heavy these walls can get.

"Detective Sergeant Stone, this is Vaneeta Shah," Agnes says with forced brightness. "She'll be helping with our support services. We're grateful you're in our corner, Jessica."

Stone shakes Vaneeta's hand, then lowers her gaze. "I wish this was a better day to meet. We had a body turn up last night. Behind The Copper Mule."

The receptionist covers her mouth, muffling a gasp. Bernice's knuckles whiten around her paperwork. Agnes sways, then ushers Stone into her office, closing the door with hands that tremble.

The office is lined with children's drawings, crooked on the walls. A stick figure family. A river. A dreamcatcher. Agnes sinks into her chair, blowing her nose into a tissue. "This is becoming all too familiar. Where's the FBI agent?"

"He's still at the scene with forensics."

Agnes exhales. "What can I do? Anything."

Stone opens her notebook, words scribbled in jagged shorthand. "We believe it was Arielle Flute. Her phone and ID were discarded nearby."

Agnes presses her hands together as if in prayer. "Oh, that beautiful girl."

"She was sixteen," Stone says. "Hard to confirm because—" Her voice falters. "The killer removed her eyes."

Agnes bows her head, whispering, "God help us."

Stone leans forward. "What do you know about her that I might've missed?"

Agnes tells the story: how Arielle's mother dressed her up like a doll at four for modeling gigs, makeup painting her into someone older. How her mother overdosed, leaving her with her grandparents, Helen and Isaiah. How Arielle never knew her father, a shadow from a rape at a teenage party, was swept under the rug.

When Helen and Isaiah died three years ago in a crash, Arielle was swallowed by foster care in the city. She kept running. Told anyone who'd listen that her foster parents were cruel. Then she disappeared into the hands of men with cameras.

Stone listens, pen scratching, but face impassive. "We'll have Borgreve handle the photographer. Out of my jurisdiction."

Agnes wipes her cheeks. "She hasn't been back to the rez since the funeral. Just a child trying to survive."

Stone squeezes her hand. "Thank you. That's enough for now."

They step out into the waiting room. Posters cover the walls:

MISSING AND MURDERED INDIGENOUS WOMEN—DRAG THE RIVER.

Each word feels like a weight.

A familiar voice breaks through. Verzella Chancellor, boots still muddy from her morning walk, strides in. She hugs Agnes. "You look like hell. What happened?"

Agnes clings to her. "Another girl, Verzie. Another one of our young ones."

Verzella's eyes sharpen. "More drugs? Another accident? How do we stop this?"

Stone says nothing. She just squeezes Agnes' arm and slips out as the waiting room fills with voices, grief settling into the walls like smoke.

Weeks Later

Night folds over The Copper Mule again. Stone and Borgreve sit in the SUV, watching the door. A voice cuts through the street:

"Well, shit, everyone. It's Stone and the FBI agent, watching our every move!" Hunter Daniel swaggers into the open, raising his voice so everyone can hear. "Looking for some lady killers again?"

"She was a young girl, Hunter. Have some decency," Borgreve snaps.

"Go to hell! That's where you wanted to send me. Over a dating site skank." Hunter smirks.

Stone exhales sharply. "Let's go. He just burned our cover. If it's the bartender, we're not catching him tonight."

The Next Morning

Stone's glass-walled office glows with early light. Borgreve saunters in, paper in hand.

"Forensics came back," he says, handing it over. "Six different semen donors. No match."

Stone scans the data, unsurprised. "So, we've got nothing."

"Cocaine and alcohol in her tox screen. Blunt force trauma elsewhere. Dumped in that dumpster behind The Copper Mule."

Stone shakes her head. "Small town. Same rot as the city. Drugs, gangs, rapes, murders."

"American Indian women are 2.5 times more likely to be assaulted," Stone adds.

"I know. But off-rez, nobody hears about it."

"Tribal cases don't make outside records."

Borgreve shifts. "She reminded me of that little JonBenét model."

Stone glares. "The American Indian version."

"You know what I mean."

Stone cuts him off. "We found the photographer?"

"Phillips. He lands tonight. I'll meet him at the airport."

Airport

Chauncey Phillips is thirty-something, lanky, and expensive clothes reeking of trend over taste. Borgreve corners him with airport police.

"It's good to have you back stateside. You're a hard man to find, Mr. Phillips."

"This is about Arielle? I told you, she was of no use to me."

"So, you tossed her aside."

"I made a business deal. I can't control what others did."

"Who?"

"Spence Wilder. Drake Collins."

Borgreve's jaw tightens. "The snuff film assholes."

"Simulated. Special effects. People are into that shit."

"You gave her to them."

"It was out of my hands."

"DNA test?"

"Hell no. I've helped enough. Lawyer."

Tribal Police Headquarters

Back in Stone's office, Borgreve breaks it down.

"Snuff films. Lake Street. Two assholes. That's where she went."

Stone drops into her chair. "That poor kid. Forced into modeling by her mother, sold by photographers, dumped to predators. Tossed aside like trash."

A knock interrupts. A clerk sticks her head in. "The woman being stalked by a casino guest is here again. Says it's getting bad."

Stone exhales. "Casey, this is what I mean. I can't even charge a white guy who beats one of our women at 2 a.m. on rez grounds. FBI isn't here. Locals won't show. What power do I have?"

"I get it," Borgreve says.

"No. You don't."

Their voices clash, both knowing the truth: justice depends on whose land you're standing on, and for women like Arielle, that line was always stacked against them.

That night, Stone returns to her empty rambler, its hickory floors echoing under her steps. A beautiful house, paid for with her own work, but too quiet, too hollow. She imagines children's voices filling the rooms. A family she'll never risk, not with her bloodline, not with her history.

She dials the number she knows by heart.

"Agnes?"

"Jessica. How are you tonight?"

"A little lonely. Mostly pissed at the feds. Black Thunder stalking case, and nothing's being done."

Agnes sighs. "You know how I feel about that first part. You need to get out there, date someone."

"The men I meet end up in morgues or case files."

"What about that handsome FBI agent you're stuck with?"

"Casey? He's just a friend. Took a long time to call him that."

"Maybe branch out. Try someone in the city."

"How? A dating site? No thanks."

"You meet people on the job."

"I have to stay professional."

"Is that why you won't date Borgreve?"

"He's nothing to me."

The doorbell rings. Stone frowns. "Agnes, hold on, someone's at the door."

2

Flee the Coming Dark

The doorbell drummed against the quiet of Stone's house. She pressed the phone to her chest and opened the door.

"Casey?" she said, then lifted the phone again. "Agnes? Can I call you back? Thanks." She ended the call and stepped aside.

"I'm sorry to bother you, Jessica," Borgreve said, the porch light scissoring shadows across his face. "I was feeling shitty about where we left things. I knew I wouldn't sleep—guilt would chew me up if I tried to pretend the job ends at night."

"Why?" Her voice was even, but the question hung like a hook.

"Because we're not moving fast enough on your assault and stalking cases. Can I come in?"

She waved him through to the kitchen. He perched at the island while she slid a pan of leftover lasagna into the oven, the click of gas and rush of flame filling the space between them. When she returned, she set two glasses on the counter and took the stool beside him.

"I'm feeling shitty too," Stone said. "Misdemeanor and felony assaults stacking up, sex trafficking, drugs, alcohol—"

"Especially meth," he said.

"Reservations are our killing fields. And Facebook groups are doing a better job tracking the missing and murdered than all of us in law enforcement."

She poured wine. The bottle croaked; the house settled.

"Jess, I'm deeply affected," he said, eyes down. "Please know that. My ideas about law enforcement are shattered."

"Really, Casey?"

"Hell, there's an entire population made invisible by the stats." He swallowed. "Misclassification. Systemic racism. Underreporting. And all the distrust we earned."

"Yes," Stone said.

"How can this be, and nobody does anything?"

"The tribal police can't do enough," she said. "The county doesn't show most nights."

"The state won't. And my higher-ups, half the time it feels like they don't want to." He rubbed his jaw, baffled and angry. "I don't know what to do here."

"Local departments dismiss missing women if they think she's been trafficked," Stone said. "Or if she's used before."

"Right. And we don't have the community's trust." He looked up. "I hear that. I want to earn it."

"I know reporting to the FBI is the 'priority,'" she said, bitterness soft but present, "but it's families like grandmothers who track cases for years on social media."

"That makes me sick," he said, heat in his voice. "Thousands of pages for people who vanished."

"I know you're aware," she said. "What it needs to come down to is the FBI knocking on doors before stalking turns into a white guy at a tribal woman's door in the dark."

"I hear you. Jurisdiction has always been a mess."

"And now add overworked officers," Stone said.

"Or worse, dismissive ones. Calls never returned. Reports left to rot." He tapped the counter—one, two, three—like punctuation. "Then those missing become homicides without bodies. Or bodies without names."

"And families don't want cops descending with questions they can't answer," she said.

"I see their point now," he admitted, voice low. "I really do."

"Casey, I don't mean to rail on you, but out of something like six thousand cases, only a little over a hundred made it into your database."

He let that sit. "I'm coming to terms with the scale. I'll do everything I can with what I've got. When it's a child, at least, the rules force speed, local departments have to push it up the chain."

"And even that didn't help Arielle Flute,"

she said, soft with grief. "Why poke her eyes out?"

"She saw something," he said. "They punished the seeing."

"The anger was blunt-force," Stone said. "Sixteen. What threat is a child? Her body was already a battlefield, all drug-addled, and exploited. That kid never had a chance."

He hesitated. "Can I ask something personal?"

"My mom?" Stone gave a rueful half-smile. "I'm surprised it took you this long."

"It had to be hell," he said.

"The kids at school were the worst," she said. "I feel for them now because their teens are finding the same drugs."

"And meth and fentanyl," he added.

"And meth and fentanyl," she echoed, flattening her hands on the countertop like bracing for impact. "My mom was sixteen. Wanted to break away, to play at freedom. She was beautiful. Boys soaked her in booze and took what they wanted. Shame made it easier to repeat until it swallowed her. Then the wrong man noticed. He beat and raped her, no reason needed. She fought back with a bat, then a gun someone had left lying around. She went to prison. My grandmother came to get me from that place and took me home."

"And when your mom got out?" Casey asked.

"Shame. Hounding. She slid back to the numbing with drugs, alcohol." Stone's voice thinned. "Another asshole raped and murdered her and left her in a ditch. Some kids on bikes found her."

"Did you ever feel pulled toward that path?" he asked quietly.

"Hell no," she said. "I couldn't stand the ones who judged me like they were immune to addiction. I never wanted to party. And my grandma would've tanned my hide. She saved me."

"And your grandfather?"

"Overdose, while my mom was still inside. Not much of a husband. Guilt and embarrassment carve deep."

Casey stared, stunned. "So, the teens we pick up for meth and fentanyl now, some are the kids of the same people who mocked you."

"And some still carry that air of superiority," Stone said dryly.

"Even with their kids cranked up?"

"Even with their daughter walking into the reservation barely dressed, beaten to a breath. on the same stretch of road where they found my mom." She exhaled. "That's why tonight stings. I come home to a good house with too much quiet, enough space for a small family, and I won't bring a kid into this. Not with my history. The weight of it, like being locked in a cell with her."

"Then leave," he said gently. "Find anonymity in a suburb. Have your kids. Come home to arms at that door." He pointed toward the entry, a small, pleading gesture.

She blinked it away. "Lasagna?" she asked. "I can cook."

"Yes. And I'll be the judge," he said, managing a small smile.

They ate at the island under the warm light, the conversation drifting to cop shows and lines they loved to hate. The house almost felt soft until the pounding at the door shattered it.

Stone stood, the old instincts rising. "What the hell—"

She opened it to a young woman in her twenties, beaten and listing, held up by her grandmother. Blood on the collar. Split lip. One eye is blooming purple.

"Detective Stone," the older woman said, breathless. "I didn't want everyone at the station talking. Can you help us?"

"I'll do everything I can, Clara," Stone said. "But we should call an ambulance. Head injuries hide. We can't risk it."

"No cops," Clara snapped, eyes darting past Stone into the house. She saw Borgreve, then his SUV on the street, and flinched. "Maybe we should go. I'm sorry to bother you."

"No," Stone said, firm. "If you leave, I'm calling it in. Bring her inside. Couch. Now." She glanced back at Casey. "That's Agent Borgreve. He won't hurt you."

"I'm sorry I interrupted your date," Clara muttered, easing the girl down.

"It isn't a date," Stone said. "It's a working

dinner."

"Help me," the young woman whispered. Breath sour with beer and fear. "It hurts."

"What hurts?" Stone asked.

"Everything."

"What happened? Who did this?" Casey asked.

"Her boyfriend," Clara spat. "That holier-than-thou son of a bitch."

"Name?" Casey said.

"The bartender at The Copper Mule."

"We've got him," Casey said, anger tightening his voice.

"No, he didn't," the girl blurted, trying to sit up. "Grandma, stop. You're lying."

"We need you at a hospital," Stone said. "They'll document injuries. We'll handle the rest."

"Hell no," Clara bristled. "You're not parading her like she's done something wrong. Go arrest him."

"We will try," Stone said, carefully. "But Alyssa has to press charges and name him."

"No. No," the girl said, blood threading from her mouth. "I'm not hurting him."

"After what he did to you?" Casey said, stunned. "Let me take him in. You just get examined."

"My granddaughter won't be a laughingstock," Clara said, hard. "Surely you understand, Jessica."

"Alyssa," Stone said, dropping to the girl's level, "you don't want him to do this to someone else, do you?"

"We're not here to save someone else," Clara snapped. "Nobody saved us."

Casey lifted his phone. "I need an ambulance at—"

"Casey," Stone warned, caught between care and consent.

"We came to you because we thought you'd care," Clara hissed. "Arrest him without naming my granddaughter."

"It doesn't work like that," Stone said softly. "Alyssa—let us help. The hospital will take care of you while we go after the bartender."

"Oh no, you're not," Clara said, grabbing at her. "I'm taking her home."

Casey stepped in, gentle but immovable. "She could have a head injury, internal bleeding. She could die in her sleep."

"Bitch," Clara snapped at Stone, grief and terror speaking for her, struggling against Casey's hands.

Alyssa's head dropped, eyes rolling back. She slumped across the couch and went out.

The sirens came quickly and thin through the night.

They found Matthew Morgan behind the bar, sleeves rolled, wiping the counter like it could erase things.

"What can I get you, officers?" he asked, eyes calculating.

"Your arms behind your back, Mr. Morgan," Borgreve said.

He turned the man to the bar and cuffed

him, patted him down. "You're under arrest for the beating of Alyssa Wilson."

"What the hell?" Morgan jerked. "She flipped out when I wouldn't get her more beer. Punched me while I drove. Meth makes them nuts, what they've been cooking on the rez. She jumped out at sixty. I stopped, she got up and walked off. She'll tell you the truth when she sobers up."

Stone glanced at a waitress. "Nancy, can you cover? He's coming with us."

Morgan swallowed. "Is she in the hospital?"

"How kind," Borgreve said, deadpan.

"No—I mean they'll detox her and she can clear my name."

The Next Morning

A knock on Stone's office glass. "Yes, Janine—come in," Stone called.

The clerk's face was tight. "Alyssa Wilson's somewhat sober now. She's freaking out that you arrested Matthew Morgan. She called—says let him go. She isn't pressing charges."

"Let's go," Borgreve said, standing. "Fifteen minutes?"

"If that." Stone grabbed her keys. "We'd better beat discharge. Small exurban hospital—no insurance means a quick goodbye."

Hospital

Alyssa sat half-dressed on the edge of the bed, fingers worrying around a paper bracelet. Clara stood beside her like a guard dog.

"Wait, Alyssa. Slow down," Stone said. "You're still banged up. Sit. Talk."

"No. Let him go."

"Honey, just talk to them," Clara said, gentler now, as if certainty had cracked overnight.

"Morgan says you hit him while he was driving," Borgreve said. "That you jumped from his truck at sixty. True?"

"Yes. So, he didn't do anything. Let him go."

"Where'd you get the meth?" Stone asked, steadily.

"I wasn't on meth."

"You're still coming down," Borgreve said.

"She did no such thing," Clara said quickly. "Tell them."

"Who did you cook with?" Borgreve pressed.

Alyssa slid on her shoes and shrugged off Clara's help. "I'm out. Let Matt go. I'm not pressing charges." She pushed past, Clara hustling to stay with her.

Stone watched them go, helplessness like a weight pinned under her ribs.

Back at Headquarters

"I wanted Morgan to be the guy," Borgreve admitted, a sour taste in his mouth as they sat with coffee in the late morning haze. "With the flood of misdemeanor complaints, it felt like it fit."

"Throwing fists and splashing beer isn't

the same as attempted murder," Stone said. "Too tidy if it were him."

"And we're still nowhere with Spence Wilder and Drake Collins," he said.

"They refused DNA," Stone replied.

"They were two of the last six who slept with Arielle Flute," Borgreve said, flat and certain.

Stone stared through the glass wall at the bullpen beyond. "What kind of hunger pays for simulated murder?"

"Some people really are into that shit," he said, disgust curling his lip.

"Stream a damn movie," Stone muttered. "HBO. Anything else?"

"I've seen pieces," he said. "Looks real—wounds, strangling, blood. Effects worthy of Hollywood."

Stone's gaze sharpened. "I still can't shake the eyes. Why take them?"

"Motive hides there," he said. "But what kind?"

A sharp rap at the door. Janine leaned in, breathless.

"Detective Sergeant Stone," she said, voice pitched high. "A call just came in. The tribal officer on scene wants you there immediately." She glanced at Borgreve. "He said, bring the FBI."

Stone was already on her feet, keys in hand. The coffee steamed, forgotten, as the two of them moved out of the office, down the hall, into the subsequent fracture of the day. The coming dark always had a head start. They ran anyway.

3

Fear the Drowning Deep

"What do we have, Josh?" Stone asks, stepping from gravel to the pale concrete of a new, almost-finished house on the affluent edge of the rez, not far from her own place near the golf course.

The home sits like a promise under a big sky: modern Cape Cod bones wrapped in river rock and cedar shake, provincial blue lap siding catching the late light. A barrel-vaulted porch tucks between double gables; white corbels carry the roofline; eyebrow dormers blink above. Inside, the air smells of sawdust and new paint. A master-crafted stair curls upward, splitting an open living-dining on one side from a paneled den lined with built-ins on the other.

Officer Josh leads them deeper. "Carpenter says a smell kept getting worse. Thought an animal crawled in during framing and died. He pulled some Sheetrock and found—this." He holds up a phone: a heavy-duty garbage bag cocooned in felt-like fabric, taped over and over. The outline isn't subtle. Petite, but unmistakably human.

"It's tucked in a tiny room, kids' nook, between the two bedrooms," Josh adds. "You have to crawl to it."

"Show us," Borgreve says.

They climb to the little girl's room, wallpaper half-hung, cherries and vines on a milk-white field. At the baseboard, a square opening yawns dark. Masks go on. Knees down. The crawlspace smells like a hot coin left too long on a radiator. Flies shudder and drum the plastic as Stone and Borgreve back out, gagging.

"I'll get my team and the coroner," Borgreve says, voice muffled in the mask.

In the hall, a lanky carpenter appears, tool belt slung low, eyes red from a bad night and worse morning.

"What kind of felt is that?" Stone asks.

"Underlayment, floor matting, insulation. Cheap, dense," he says. "Name's Wyatt. Wyatt Langdon. Can I grab my tools?"

"Not today," Stone says. "Crime scene now. When did you first notice the smell?"

"Yesterday. Barely there. Last night I brought another guy up—he didn't smell it. This morning it punched me. Thought raccoons, squirrel. Maybe somebody's cat. I opened the cavity, and it dropped between the studs right after I called tribal."

"Anyone out of place on site?" she asks.

He shakes his head. "The usual, flooring, painters, electricians, plumbers, a couple of us finishers."

"What were you doing in there?"

"Kid's nook," he says, thumb to the crawl. "Hideaway between the rooms. I was trimming the base and fitting a bookcase at the back."

"Everyone knows it exists?"

"Pretty much. Architects love a secret."

"Which architect?" Borgreve asks.

"Miles Crenshaw," Wyatt says. "He's dating the homeowner. She's tribal."

"How old are you, Wyatt? Where are you from?"

"Twenty-five. Bloomington. Been building since I was fifteen with my dad." He lifts a shoulder, not quite a boast.

Josh taps his phone. "License scanned. Numbers are on your cells."

"Thanks," Stone says.

"You can go, Mr. Langdon," Borgreve adds. "We'll be in touch."

The coroner works in steady, grim motions. Tape peeled. Felt sliced. Plastic parted. Heat breathes out, a sweet rot that gets into the mouth and won't leave. Inside: a decomposed young woman, petite. In the back pocket of her shorts, a driver's license. Lana Davies. Twenty-nine. Tribal. A known regular at The Copper Mule, known for men who circled her like flies do light.

"Dead about two days," the coroner says. "Blunt force to the head. Murdered elsewhere. Phone recovered and passed to your team, Agent Borgreve." A beat. "Her tongue's been cut out."

Stone closes her eyes, then opens them hard. "What the hell?"

Borgreve's gaze goes distant. "Alyssa's eyes, now Lana's tongue."

"You thinking serial?" Stone asks.

"This morning I liked Wilder and Collins for Arielle," he says. "But the dump sites don't rhyme. Dumpster versus wall. Public discard versus secret burial."

"Maybe he taped it to hide her long enough for move-in," Stone says quietly. "Kids would be the first to find her."

Borgreve exhales. "We need the architect and the homeowner."

Outside the window, laughter lifts, thin and bright as glass, kids playing Marco Polo in a bean-shaped pool two lots over. One girl keeps slipping under, milking the drama, hand in the air. Stone watches, jaw tight.

"Someday it won't be a game," she says. "Maybe not water. But drowning all the same."

At the community center, coffee steam ghosts the breakroom. Bernice leans close to Agnes. "The men fed Lana's addiction to keep her within reach. I just heard Miles was one of them."

"The architect?" Agnes frowns. "But he's seeing Kyra. The homeowner."

"He was sleeping with her to sell the design," Bernice says. "Gossip says it started as business. Ended as business too."

Agnes sighs. "Could he have had anything

to do with Arielle? The dumpster at The Copper Mule?"

Bernice shakes her head. "Different hands, I think. Different anger."

"I'll tell Jessica what I've heard," Agnes says, already reaching for her phone.

At tribal HQ, Stone ends the call. "Thanks, Agnes. It helps." She looks at Borgreve. "Clerk has Crenshaw in Interrogation."

They step into the small room. Table. Two chairs. Crenshaw is a handsome, polished, fifty approaching fast, handsomely tired too as he tries on a smile that isn't quite his.

"Mr. Crenshaw," Stone says. "Detective Sergeant Stone. Special Agent Borgreve."

"You know why you're here," Borgreve adds.

"My girlfriend, Kyra, the homeowner, she's beside herself," he says. "This happening inside her children's rooms. Wow. Have you made any progress?"

"We're making it now," Stone says.

"You were also seeing Lana Davies," Borgreve says, clean and flat.

Crenshaw blinks. "Excuse me?"

"That's the deceased," Stone says. "Found in the wall of the kid's nook you designed."

He swallows. "How—"

"Were you dating Lana?" Borgreve asks.

Crenshaw's tie tightens itself. "I wouldn't call it dating."

"What would you call it?" Stone asks.

"We had sex," he whispers. "A few times."

"How many is a few?" Borgreve leans.

Crenshaw clears his throat. "A few times a week. Lately."

"And you don't call that dating?" Stone asks.

"She knew I was with Kyra. We had an understanding. There's an age difference. I'm nearly fifty." His fingers fuss with the cap of the water bottle.

"What did you give Lana to keep her quiet?" Borgreve asks.

"A little help now and then," Crenshaw says. "Rent. Groceries. She was just a kid."

"You often have sex with 'kids'?" Stone says, eyes cold.

"That's not—I mean—don't twist—"

"When did you last see her?" Stone asks.

"A few days ago," he says. "She came to the site, asked for money. I told her I didn't have any. We planned to meet later. She never showed."

"Did she threaten to tell Kyra if you didn't pay?" Borgreve asks, table humming under his palm.

Crenshaw's temper flashes. "Who told you that?"

"Did she?" Borgreve snaps.

A beat. "Yes," he says. "But she wouldn't have. Lana talked big. She just wanted to know if I could help."

"Where were you meeting?" Stone asks.

"The Copper Mule," he says. "I waited three hours. Had a burger. Fries. She never came."

"Was that all you killed that night?" Borgreve says.

"I didn't touch her. Ask the bartender."

"Who would set you up, Miles?" Stone asks.

"No one," he says quickly. "I'm a good man who got tangled with the wrong woman."

By noon, the wind smells like rain and dirt. Out front of the community center, spring blooms flare in the daffodils, carnations, snapdragons, geraniums, petunias, and impatiens while Agnes, Bernice, Vaneeta, and Verzella plant in long, hopeful lines. Stone's SUV noses up the main road. Agnes wipes soil from her hands and meets her at the door.

"Coffee?" Agnes asks. "Inside."

They climb to the second floor. The hallway hums with low voices and printer sounds. In Agnes's office, they close the door on the world.

"I wanted to tell you more about Miles," Agnes says, pouring.

"I was hoping you would," Stone says.

"The list of women he's touched is nearly as long as our registry," Agnes says softly. "Eight years he's been here. As his plans turned to houses, he went hunting contracts and bedfellows. Four a year, give or take. Thirty-plus. He ruins marriages to land designs."

"And Kyra?" Stone asks.

"Her husband found out last year, right after the deposit. He used Kyra for her per capita checks." Agnes's face tightens. "She's been used by everyone. Only grace is her children, and that she's not the one in that wall."

"And Lana?" Stone asks.

"Like too many of our youth," Agnes says. "Started with alcohol, fell into harder. Meth took the rest. She'd been with the bartender at The Copper Mule for a while, then with Hunter Daniel after his girlfriend kicked him out. Lately, people whisper about a man in tribal housing who's cooking. No one will give me a name. They fear payback."

"Matt Morgan, Hunter Daniel," Stone says. "We start there." She sets down her cup. "Our women are hunted from every angle, inside and out. It never stops."

They pull up to a red-brick rambler that looks like a held breath. Black garbage bags are taped across windows. Broken panes are half covered with splintered pallet boards. The grass out front is beaten flat.

Stone bangs on the door. "Tribal police! Looking for Hunter Daniel."

Borgreve raps on a side window. Glass shatters out back. They sprint, rounding the corner to a scatter of men and women bolting in every direction, barefoot, half-dressed, eyes wide. No Hunter among them. The air reeks of ammonia, solvents, something metallic, and mean.

They climb through a shattered sash and immediately crawl back out, choking. Borgreve radios for hazmat. Sirens start their long approach.

They sit in the SUV with the windows cracked while suited techs bring evidence out in sealed tubs, laying it across a folding table, the sad buffet of a makeshift lab. Curious kids circle the perimeter like gnats. Officers make a line and hold it, tired but steady.

Stone and Borgreve pull on masks again and step forward among the pulled items: a pair of jeans, a torn thong, a wallet jammed half-out of a pocket. Borgreve lifts the wallet with gloved hands, flips it open, and glances at the ID.

"Hunter Daniel," he says.

He looks up at the fields, the tree line stretching toward the river, the long grass bent in a single direction like something recently run through it.

"Well," he says, dry as dust, "what are the chances anyone calls in a half-naked man sprinting through the countryside?"

The wind answers for them, hollow, endless, carrying the river's far-off rush and the quiet, relentless work of a community learning, again, to fear the drowning deep.

4

In Service to the Moon

The office lights burned low, the hour too late for most to still be working. Files lay open across the desks like discarded prayers. Stone leaned back in her chair, fatigue hidden beneath the rigid set of her shoulders, while Borgreve paced, the floor beneath his boots absorbing his frustration.

"What the hell's going on in this country?" Borgreve exploded, throwing his hands up. His voice ricocheted off the glass walls. "These numbers have to light somebody's fuse higher up the chain. Rapists, killers, they run free to do it over and over again. Heinous crimes. And they're laughing in our faces."

Stone's eyes flicked to the ceiling, then back to him, her tone low and heavy. "People think they can kill Native women because we're invisible. Invisible in the system, invisible in statistics. Invisible everywhere it matters."

Borgreve rubbed his jaw, forcing himself to steady. "How old was she?"

"Twenty-one," Stone answered. Her words

were clipped, cold. "Worked at a global engineering firm in the suburbs. Somebody dumped her in a ditch like yesterday's garbage. Boyfriend reported her missing about the same time a passerby saw the body at sunrise."

"Any ties to Morgan or Daniel?"

"Not yet. I was on my way to find out."

"To talk to the boyfriend?"

"Yes."

"I'll come." Borgreve grabbed his jacket. "My team has the ditch secured. Let's hear what the grieving husband has to say."

The Teverbaugh residence sat back in the woods, shrouded in silence. The modern farmhouse was built for privacy—shiplap walls glowing faintly under the porch lights, great walls of glass gazing into the trees, a wide lawn that kept neighbors at arm's length. From the driveway, Stone could see the silhouette of a man hunched on the screened porch, his head bowed, cigarette ember bright in the dark.

Inside, the home was immaculate. Rustic beams clashed with cold modern lines; family touches, a play nook under the stairs, and fresh flowers on the island were overshadowed by the cavernous silence.

"Mr. Teverbaugh," Stone said gently. "I'm Detective Sergeant Stone. This is Special Agent Borgreve."

He looked up, eyes red, body trembling from exhaustion or grief. "I told the officer on the phone, she's my wife. Michele. We just got married last week. Justice of the Peace in Hudson."

Stone nodded once. "I hadn't been told that. I'm sorry for your loss."

Borgreve's voice cut through like broken glass. "Why did it take until five-thirty to call it in?"

"She worked late," Teverbaugh said defensively. "Overtime at the office. Sometimes she went to dinner with one of the owners, an older man, German. Erik Möller. She stayed overnight when she had too much to drink. Nothing improper. Just company."

Borgreve's eyes narrowed. "Late sixties, right? Still possible for an old man to have... needs."

Teverbaugh shook his head violently. "It wasn't like that. Michele loved me. She just liked his stories, his garden, and the wine. We got married, didn't we?" His words collapsed into sobs, raw and wet.

"What exactly did she do at this firm?" Stone pressed.

"Mailroom. Clerical. She was planning to quit soon, go back to school."

"Mailroom staff don't usually pull all-nighters," Borgreve said flatly.

"She worked hard," Teverbaugh snapped, anger flaring through his grief.

"Do you work, Mr. Teverbaugh?" Stone asked softly.

He faltered, then whispered, "Not right

now. I'm looking."

"Will you give us your DNA sample?"

He nodded, defeated. "Anything. Whatever you need."

Back in the SUV, the night wrapped around them like wet wool. The woods pressed close, the moon caught in the black weave of branches.

"I don't buy it," Stone said, her voice quiet but sharp.

"He's too stupid to see she was slipping away," Borgreve muttered. "But that doesn't make him a killer."

"He gains nothing from her death; the prenup must've shut him out. No money, no leverage. Just a hollow house."

"Or maybe rage," Borgreve countered.

"Maybe. But rage usually leaves a mess. This body was left almost ceremonially."

The business campus the next morning was too sterile, its brick offices bland against the spring sky. Inside, fluorescent lights hummed, desks neat as dollhouses.

"Ian Galbraith," the supervisor said, extending a hand. His face was pale with worry. "Michele never misses work. Is she okay?"

"Was she seeing anyone here?" Borgreve asked bluntly.

Galbraith looked stunned. "No. Absolutely not. She was reliable. Professional."

"What about Erik Möller?"

"What? No, that's absurd. They barely spoke. He helped her carry mail once or twice. Nothing more."

Borgreve's eyes flicked to the man's desk, the empty picture frames, the calendar too clean. He filed away the absence of Michele's presence here.

"She was planning on quitting?" Stone asked.

Galbraith nodded reluctantly. "Talked about college again. Said her boyfriend, well, her husband now, wasn't ambitious. They fought a lot."

"Thank you," Stone said, though her voice was taut with suspicion.

That night, Stone sat on her porch, the moon swollen above the golf course. The silence was deep enough to choke on. She nursed a beer, the glass sweating in her hand.

Borgreve's footsteps scraped the sidewalk before she saw him. He appeared out of the dark like a shadow pulled free.

"What are you doing out here?" he asked.

"Watching the moon. Wondering what it sees that we don't. What's happening right now, in some ditch or some house, that we'll discover too late."

He sat across from her, accepting a bottle without question. For a while, they didn't speak, just listened to the hum of insects and the far-off bark of a dog.

"Hunter's slipping. Miles is lying. Teverbaugh's broken. Möller's gone to ground. And the bodies keep stacking." Borgreve finally said, voice low.

"People think we're shadows out here," Stone said. "That our women can vanish without anyone noticing. But we notice. And the moon notices too."

Borgreve lifted the bottle, his eyes on the silvered sky. "Then we work in service to it."

Stone said nothing. She didn't need to. The night had already answered.

The night stretched quietly around them, the kind of quiet that wasn't peace but weight. Out beyond the manicured lines of the golf course, the marshland breathed, frogs croaking, reeds whispering against each other, a current rolling slow and heavy beneath the moon.

Stone leaned back in her chair, her arm cradling the beer bottle against her chest. "Some nights it feels like the land is trying to tell us something, Casey. Like all the voices that have gone missing are stitched into the wind. You sit still long enough, and you can almost hear them."

Borgreve didn't answer right away. He was watching her, the blue wash of moonlight cutting across her cheekbones, catching in the dark of her eyes. Finally, he tilted his head toward the horizon. "What I hear is silence. A silence big enough to swallow every case file on my desk. And that's what terrifies me. That this country, this system, is built to keep it quiet."

The wind shifted, carrying the smell of

damp earth and something faintly metallic from the marsh. Jessica pulled her cardigan tighter, suddenly cold.

"Silence won't last," she murmured. "Not with bodies showing up in walls and ditches. Somebody's patterning this, tongue, eyes, who knows what next. The moon sees it. The land feels it. And eventually, the truth finds a way out."

Borgreve tapped his bottle against hers. "Then let's make sure it's us who find it first."

The clink was soft, lost to the night. Both of them sat in silence, listening to the crickets, the creak of wood beneath their chairs, the river carrying its unseen burdens toward darker waters.

Above, the moon rode high, pale and watchful, its face clouded yet relentless. Stone followed its arc, her chest tightening with something she couldn't name: dread, maybe, or duty. Or just the knowledge that tomorrow the phone would ring again, and another name would be added to the list.

For now, she let the silence stretch, heavy as the cases stacked in her office, heavier still with what the moon had seen and would not forget.

The night sagged heavily, full of voices that would not sleep. On her porch, Stone kept her eyes on the moon, silver, cloud-bled, eternal, and tried to quiet the gnawing inside her. Borgreve sat across from her, his face drawn in half-light, the bottle in his hand catching the faint gleam. Neither spoke for a long while.

Somewhere in the distance, a coyote called out, sharp against the marsh hush. The sound thinned into silence again, silence that pressed in on both of them like an accusation.

"Tomorrow," Jessica said, more to the moon than to Borgreve, "there'll be another call. Another body. Another family waiting for answers we may never have."

Borgreve nodded, but his jaw stayed tight. He didn't argue because there was no argument to make. Only the waiting. Only the weight.

5

Temple of the Abandoned

By morning, the moon was gone, and the casino lights burned in its place—garish, blinking, never sleeping.

"The casino brawlers are back. All officers are out on either traffic or domestic abuse calls," the tribal clerk said as she leaned into Detective Sergeant Stone's office, her voice weary with routine disaster.

Stone sat forward, rubbing the bruise still purpling her forearm from the night before. "Would you like to go to the casino with me? The hellraisers are back, and it might do us all good if they see someone who actually has the authority to arrest them."

Borgreve was already in the chair across from her, jacket draped on the armrest. He gave a half-grin, half-grimace. "Let's go make a scene."

The casino roared like a storm contained in four walls, neon buzzing, coins clinking, voices raised in drunken triumph and venom. Borgreve didn't hesitate; he surged into the barroom and slammed John Peterson and Sven Olsen against the counter in one practiced sweep.

"FBI. You're under arrest for assault."

The crowd surged with the smell of beer and sweat. Chairs scraped. The men lashed back, fists snapping toward Borgreve's jaw. Stone waded through the crush, her fist landing square on Peterson's ribs. He dropped, wheezing, while Olsen raised a chair above his head until his eyes caught the FBI letters blazing across Borgreve's back. The chair clattered to the floor. Cuffs clicked shut.

Stone steadied her breathing, scanning the faces of casino staff and tribal members alike with their anger, exhaustion, and the resignation of seeing this too many times.

"Why didn't anyone call the county sheriff?" Borgreve snapped, hauling his detainee upright.

"They do," Stone answered flatly. "Doesn't mean they'll come. More than half the time, the county leaves us hanging. Security and tribal officers can escort them out, but they can't arrest white guys, no matter how many bottles they break or women they grab."

Borgreve looked around, stunned. "This is the wild fucking west."

"Welcome to our normal," Stone muttered.

And then, out of the bathroom, stumbled a young woman, makeup streaked, eye swelling purple, lips cut. She pulled her sweater tight, head down, rushing for the door.

Stone stepped toward her. "Miss—"

But the woman flinched as if struck and bolted past.

"What the hell was that about? She needs an ambulance," Borgreve hissed.

"She won't go," Stone said, her voice low, heavy. "Her boyfriend did it to her again."

"Then let's go get him—"

"She won't press charges."

"How many times?"

Stone's throat tightened. "A few a month."

Borgreve stared after the woman disappearing into the casino haze. "What the hell is wrong with her?"

Stone didn't answer. She already knew the answer was older than either of them, woven into family histories, buried in the soil of this place.

When they returned to tribal headquarters, the world hadn't slowed. A four-year-old girl sat in the lobby, her nose bloodied, her small hands folded in her lap like she was waiting for Sunday school instead of a caseworker.

Stone crouched in front of her. "Sweetheart, is your daddy hurting you again?"

The tribal officer beside them spoke low: "This time, mommy snapped. She stabbed him. He's in the hospital. She's in lock-up. The kid's waiting for placement."

Borgreve pinched the bridge of his nose.

"History here?"

"Historical trauma," Stone said. "Grandfather molested in the orphanage. Passed it down. Kids raised in pain. Grown into abusers or victims. Binge drinking to smother the memories. And here we are."

"Christ," Borgreve muttered. "Isn't there any way to break the chain? Some relative to step in?"

"This family's lucky compared to most," Stone said softly. "When they're sober, they're hardworking. They keep their home. But sobriety doesn't always last."

Before Borgreve could respond, the clerk hurried over, pale. "Wolfie DesJarlais hanged himself last night. Agnes came by looking for you. I told her you were at the casino."

Stone closed her eyes, her chest caving as if struck. "Wolfie... He was a good kid. He saw Michael Abernathy's victim escape. He wanted college. He wanted more."

The silence afterward was suffocating.

That evening, Stone went to the community center. The Drag the River poster hung heavy on the wall, its rows of names like an unending roll call. She poured coffee, staring at it, when a bruised young mother slipped in with two children clinging to her skirt. The woman tried to turn her face away, but Stone approached, pressing her card into her hand.

"If you ever need anything, call me."

The woman bowed her head. "Thank you."

Agnes appeared in the hallway, her

expression worn thin. "Jessica, come in."

Behind her closed office door, Stone finally said it. "I heard about Wolfie. It's too damn much."

Agnes sniffled, nodding. "That boy cared for his grandmother like no other. Fifth suicide this year, Jessica. We are trying to hold back a river with our hands."

Stone looked out Agnes' window, where the casino lights pulsed like false stars. "All that money, and we can't even keep our kids alive."

Agnes reached for a tissue, her voice breaking. "It's not fair. It never ends."

The air in the office was thick with grief. Neither woman moved.

Agnes dabbed her eyes, her words trembling. "This may seem odd, Jessica, but I think you should talk to Verzella."

"Verzie?" Stone asked, her brow tightening.

"She told you she dated Miles. What she didn't tell you was how badly he hurt her and how she brought him into this community. He gets all his clients now because she opened the door for him." Agnes lowered her voice, glancing toward the hallway. "Tamryn Willow and Bethany Lufkins overheard her threatening Lana Davies to stay away from him."

Stone leaned back, her coffee untouched, cold in her hands. "You're telling me a woman in her late fifties, the landscaper everyone trusts, was tangled in this mess?"

"She's fit enough to carry forty-pound bags of soil over each shoulder. Don't underestimate her," Agnes said. "And she's working on Kyra's project. Everyone goes through Verzie."

Hours later, the call came:

"Stone, they need you at the greenhouse," the clerk announced breathlessly, leaning into her office. "Verzella just tried to hang herself from the rafters. They're rushing her to the hospital once the ambulance gets back from town."

The greenhouse loomed like a glass temple, its panes throwing fractured moonlight across rows of flowers and soil beds. Inside, chaos lingered in the damp, earthy air, pots knocked over, tools scattered. A bent rafter jutted at an unnatural angle. Verzella lay on the floor, her head wrapped, crimson bleeding through gauze. A young staffer pressed towels to the wound, shaking.

"Verzie, what the hell were you thinking?" Stone demanded, kneeling close. Borgreve stood behind her, arms folded, watching the woman fade in and out of consciousness.

"She was arguing," a worker said, voice high and panicked. "With that architect—Miles. He shoved her. She threw rakes at him."

Another chimed in. "She yelled something about a tramp. Asked if he screwed her the same night he screwed Verzie."

"And then?" Stone pressed.

"She sent us out and told us to feed her cats if anything happened. We thought she was joking, but..." The teenager's voice cracked. "Then we heard the crash."

Stone closed her eyes briefly. "Give me the keys. I'll check on her house."

Verzella's home was no ordinary dwelling, it was a curated gallery. A dramatic curved staircase swept upward, lit by a chandelier that dripped glass like frozen tears. Her paintings, which were bold, abstract, eight feet across, hung on walls of Spanish tile and polished stucco.

But beneath the surface polish, there was a fracture. Two wineglasses sat broken on the mahogany bar, their stems snapped, shards gleaming faintly in the recessed light. Cats darted nervously from counter to floating shelves. Upstairs, men's clothing lay strewn in trails across the hall, shirts twisted, trousers marked with what looked like dried blood.

Stone's hand went instinctively to her gun. Borgreve stepped into the master bath, whistling low. "Christ. This place is bigger than my whole apartment."

Stone ignored him, eyes fixed on the soaking tub. Crimson streaks dried along its porcelain lip. She pressed her fingers to the frame of the window above it. The backyard landscaping was immaculate with curved hedges and perfectly laid stone paths. The kind of perfection only Verzie could shape.

"There's a box here," Borgreve said, pulling out photographs. A beach scene with Miles and Verzie together, smiling, a couple. Intimate. Happy. At least on the surface.

"Jesus," Stone muttered. "She wasn't lying. She loved him."

But the blood told a different story.

At the hospital later that night, Verzella lay pale against white sheets, throat raw, head wrapped. Her eyes flickered open as Stone approached with Borgreve looming just behind.

"Verzie, why did you do this to yourself?" Stone's voice was gentle, but hard beneath the gentleness. "Was it for Miles?"

Verzella's cracked lips curled bitterly. "What the hell are you talking about?" Her voice rasped like dry reeds.

"We went to your house," Stone said. "We saw the blood. The broken glasses."

"You had no right," Verzie snapped weakly, trying to sit up before collapsing back, gasping.

"Did you and Miles fight?" Borgreve asked.

Her laugh was hollow, edged with pain. "He'll tell you anyway. That bastard. Sleeps with anyone who hands him work."

"And Lana Davies?" Borgreve pushed.

Verzella's eyes darkened. "That little tramp. I told her to stay away from him. He was poison. But she wouldn't listen."

"Did you kill her?" Borgreve demanded.

Verzella's breath caught. She coughed, the

nurse rushing to hold a cup to her lips. "Kill her? No. She wasn't worth the waste of time."

The nurse raised a hand, firm. "Enough. Her throat needs rest."

Stone leaned in one last time. "Then tell me, Verzie, what was worth your time?"

But Verzie closed her eyes, retreating into silence, and the machines around her hummed on, steady as a heartbeat.

Back at headquarters, the air between Stone and Borgreve was thick with unease.

"Agnes was right. Verzie's tied up in this, but murder?" Borgreve rubbed the back of his neck. "I don't buy it."

"Neither do I," Stone admitted. "But the blood in that house doesn't lie."

Borgreve turned to the glass wall, marker squeaking as he listed names:

Matt Morgan. Hunter Daniel. Wilder &
Collins. Miles. Verzella—question mark.

Stone watched him, arms folded tight. "The question is—who's next?"

"Stone," a young officer poked his head into her office, hesitant. "You wanted updates on Matt Morgan? He's gone north on a fishing trip. His brother's filling in at the bar."

Stone nodded slowly, then glanced at Borgreve. "Let's pay the brother a visit. And ask around."

The bar was dim, its neon beer signs buzzing

faintly, the air thick with fryer grease and old cigarettes that clung to the walls like tar. Dominic Morgan, stockier than his brother, with the same hard eyes, watched them from behind the counter, polishing a glass that didn't need polishing.

Pam, a weary waitress with dark hair pulled back, slid plates across tables, moving fast but not hurried, like someone who knew survival meant efficiency.

Stone waited until she came by their booth with menus. "Thanks, Pam. Mind if I ask you a few questions?"

Pam's shoulders stiffened. "I'd rather not. I need this job."

"It's not about Matt," Stone reassured. "Unless you've got something to share about him."

Pam hesitated, then leaned closer. "No. Then who's it about?"

"Verzella Chancellor," Stone said. "She come in often?"

Pam's eyes widened. "Verzie? Hell, yeah. A few nights a week. She's got a new friend too, some counselor lady from the community center, Indian but not Native. Vish... Vaneeta? Something like that. They're thick as thieves."

Borgreve scribbled it down, eyes narrowing. "And Miles Crenshaw?"

Pam gave a dry laugh. "Miles is here with anything in a skirt. That man gets around."

The bartender's whistle cut across the room. "Pam! Right now!"

She rolled her eyes. "They're not even asking about your brother, you jackass." She turned back to Stone. "The night you found the girl in the dumpster, Miles and Verzie were both here. They fought. She splashed beer in his face. I thought he'd strangle her, but he just stood there, soaked, grinning like he could take whatever she threw at him."

"And Hunter Daniel?" Borgreve pressed.

Pam snorted. "Him too. He and Matt were fighting over his bar tab, as usual."

Borgreve slid two photographs across the table. "Ever see these two?"

Pam studied the faces of Spence Wilder and Drake Collins. A slow smile curled. "The jackpot winners. They tipped me a hundred bucks. Whole place saw it."

Stone and Borgreve exchanged a glance. Everyone, *everyone*, had been there that night.

Pam straightened, balancing their orders on her tray. "It was a full house. Loud, rowdy, but happy until you found her in that dumpster. She was a pretty girl. Who does that—throwing someone away like trash?"

Her voice softened for the first time, almost reverent, before the bartender barked her back to the counter.

Stone leaned back in the booth, jaw tight. "So, everybody was here. Miles. Verzie. Hunter. Matt. Even Wilder and Collins."

Borgreve drummed his fingers on the table. "Which means nothing, or everything. Dumpster girl didn't end up there by accident. Someone dragged her out the back while the whole damn town was drinking."

Stone's eyes swept the barroom, the cracked linoleum, the faces half-lit by neon, the jukebox spilling a low, mournful country tune. "The question isn't who was here," she said, voice low, "it's who slipped out long enough to kill her."

Stone and Borgreve left cash on the table, untouched burgers cooling under the low hum of neon. As they pushed through the bar's heavy door, the stale warmth gave way to the sharp bite of night air.

Outside, the parking lot lay cracked and uneven, lit by a single buzzing light that cast long, broken shadows across oil stains and cigarette butts. The Copper Mule's sign flickered red against the dark rez road, its glow bleeding into the black horizon like a wound refusing to close.

Borgreve shoved his hands deep into his jacket pockets. "Everyone's alibi collapses into the same night, the same place. Too many faces, too much booze, not enough truth."

Stone scanned the darkness beyond the glow, her jaw tight. "One of them slipped out while the music kept playing and the drinks kept pouring. Someone used the chaos as cover. And no one's talking."

They stood there a moment longer, listening to the faint pulse of jukebox bass leaking from the bar, before heading toward their separate SUVs. The night swallowed them quick, the road ahead stretching wide and empty, as if the reservation itself held its breath, waiting for the next body to surface.

6

The Memory of Someone
Else's Dream

Stone leaned back in her chair, one boot braced against the desk leg, the other crossed over Borgreve's in a silent tug-of-war. Her voice was flat, but her eyes were sharp. "I just saw Spencer Wilder and Drake Collins eating steak at the casino."

Borgreve didn't move at first. He let his head fall against the ceiling's hum of fluorescent light, the kind of sound that drilled into the bones. "Full moon tonight. Everyone's out, fresh out of hospitals, out of hiding, back on the streets. Hot nights shake loose all the ghosts."

"Verzella's probably back on her feet," Stone muttered. "Maybe we should swing by her house."

"She was scheduled to show up at the greenhouse today." Borgreve pushed his chair upright. "Let's start there. Easier to find out if she's back to work."

They'd barely reached the SUV when Stone's radio crackled, Pam's voice jittering through static: *"Detective Stone? It's Pam from The Mule. Big disturbance, Verzella and Matt. Bad one."*

"Copy," Stone snapped. "We're en route."

Borgreve jerked the SUV into a hard U-turn, gravel spraying across the ditch. The tires groaned against the road.

Then Stone stiffened, her hand snapping to the dash. "Stop. Back up. Jesus—back up."

She pointed up a weed-choked service road, the kind that barely existed anymore, leading toward a rotting farmhouse. The wind shifted, bending tall grass just enough to reveal the pale shape hidden in the ditch.

Borgreve slammed the brakes and threw the wheel, headlights cutting across the body sprawled in the grass. Naked. Motionless.

For a breath, neither of them moved. Then Stone hissed, "She's breathing. Barely."

Borgreve was already out of the SUV, kneeling in the dirt, his flashlight strobing over ruined flesh. "Call an ambulance."

At St. Luke's, the reek of disinfectant couldn't mask the violence carved into the girl's skin. The charge nurse shook her head as she relayed details. "Severe head trauma. Extensive bruising. She's late teens. No ID."

Stone pressed her palms against her thighs, grounding herself. Borgreve's jaw ticked. "She's in a coma. That could take hours." He looked toward the doors. "We hit The Mule now. See what Verzie and Matt were tearing into."

Stone nodded once. "That house... no one's lived there in decades. Whoever left her there knew it was dead ground. She wasn't supposed to be found."

The Copper Mule's parking lot was a haze of neon and cigarette smoke. Pam stood just outside, arms looped around Verzella, who twisted like she was ready to bite through the leash.

"They nearly came to blows," Pam said breathlessly. "Customers scattered. Sheriff showed up, shrugged, left. Typical."

Verzella's face was raw, streaked with sweat and manure. "He's a dumb motherfucker," she spat.

"Where'd you come from before this?" Borgreve asked.

"The greenhouse. Can't you smell it on me?" She barked a bitter laugh.

Pam's eyes darted back toward the bar. "Matt told Miles he should 'fuck them younger, less batty.' That's when Verzie snapped. Miles was here too, drinking like nothing touched him."

Stone's shoulders tightened. "So, everyone's paths cross here again."

Inside, Matt's voice roared from behind the bar. "Pam! Get your ass back in here."

Borgreve stepped in close, voice cold. "Matt, where were you before clocking in?"

Matt sneered, towel in hand. "Home. You want me to punch a timecard for you now?"

Stone's radio crackled again, sharp as a

gunshot: *"That victim at St. Luke's just slipped into a coma."*

Verzella's fury faltered, her eyes wide. "Oh my God. I'll pray for her."

Later, parked outside the hardware store, the SUV idled while the neon from The Mule bled into the dark rez road behind them. The silence inside was heavier than the hum of the engine.

Stone rubbed her eyes with the back of her hand, jaw trembling.

Borgreve looked over. "That girl, she reminded you."

Stone's voice broke. "The ditch. My mother. Same placement, same helplessness. I thought I was past it."

"You're not broken, Jess. You're human."

Then movement in the lot. Hunter Daniel sauntered out, a cocky smirk plastered on his face.

"Who turned up dead now?" he called.

"No one," Borgreve said evenly. "Where were you before this?"

Hunter only shrugged, sliding into his truck. "Driving. Do I need an alibi?" His laugh echoed off the brick as he gunned the engine and disappeared into the trees.

Stone stared after the taillights until they vanished, her hands clenched so tight her knuckles whitened. "Feels like I'm living someone else's nightmare," she whispered.

Stone stared after Hunter's taillights until they bled into the dark trees. Borgreve let the silence hold a moment, then checked his phone.

"Missing person report just hit HQ. Eighteen-year-old. Amber Lauzier. Parents waited two days before calling it in."

Stone let out a low curse. "The good ones always take too long. By then..." She let the thought die. "What's her story?"

"Two-parent household. Both casino execs. Clean reputation. Too clean, maybe."

"Amber's name came up before," Stone muttered. "Pretty, model-type. Perfect bait for the likes of Wilder, Collins, Matt Morgan, Hunter. Hell, even Miles."

Borgreve turned the SUV toward the north subdivision where the reservation blurred into affluence. "Let's see how the other half lives."

The Lauzier home rose out of the manicured cul-de-sac like a showroom. Wide stone pillars held up a front porch dressed in hanging baskets, each bloom engineered to impress. Beyond the glass walls, Stone could already see enormous abstract paintings glowing in warm light. The place was part penthouse, part museum.

"Doesn't look like anyone goes missing here," Borgreve murmured as they mounted the travertine steps.

Randy Lauzier opened the door before they knocked, his face flushed, phone still in his hand. "Jessica—thank God. And the FBI, too." He shook Borgreve's hand hard. "We'll have her back soon, right?"

Sara Lauzier appeared behind him, composed in a beige sweater, voice brittle. "Come in, please. We've been beside ourselves."

Inside, the house smelled of citrus cleaner and money. The open floor plan sprawled with glass and stone; a chandelier glittered above a dining table set for ten, though no meal had touched it.

"She's never run away before," Sara said quickly, as if rehearsed. "The angriest she's ever been is slamming a door."

"Any boyfriends?" Stone asked.

"Absolutely not," Sara snapped. "Amber's been focused on school. She started community college classes this summer. Maybe her friends want to pretend she's dating someone, but that's just gossip."

"Her friends say older man. Flowers. Jewelry," Borgreve countered.

Sara's eyes went hard. "Teenagers lie to one-up each other. My daughter wouldn't lie with her body."

Randy tried to soothe her with a hand at her elbow. "You can look through her room, if you want. We don't hide anything."

Amber's bedroom was too neat, too curated. White walls, grey bedding, a laptop perched on a floating nightstand. But the closet whispered a different story: lingerie folded between sweaters, jewelry scattered in tangled chains, none of it in boxes.

Stone lifted a drawer, eyes narrowing. "She was dressing for someone."

Borgreve hauled the mattress off its frame and pulled out a baggie of weed. Sara gasped, one hand to her mouth.

"That's impossible," Randy muttered, voice cracking.

Stone didn't answer. She sifted through the jewelry, the provocative lace. "Parents are always the last to know," she murmured.

On the desk, Borgreve flipped open Amber's laptop. "Password?"

"Thor," Randy said, hollow. "Her puppy's name. We checked it ourselves. Nothing there."

"Then you won't mind if I take it to our lab," Borgreve replied. He slid it into an evidence bag.

Behind them, Sara whispered, "She wouldn't. She's not like that."

Stone turned and met her eyes, not unkindly. "She's like any girl. Looking for someone to tell her she's more than she thinks she is."

Randy's phone buzzed. He stepped into the hall and returned pale. "Is it true? An unidentified girl was brought into St. Luke's today. Beaten? Left for dead?"

Stone stiffened. Borgreve gave the smallest nod.

"We need to see her," Randy pressed.

Sara's scream ripped through the sterile air of the house when they reached the ICU.

Amber's body was bandaged, swollen, hair shaved away from the wound.

Sara collapsed against the rail. "It's her. Oh, God, it's her. The toenails, she picked that color two days ago. Wild purple. A mother knows."

Stone swallowed the lump in her throat. "Then listen to me. If this is Amber, we keep it quiet. Whoever left her there may try again."

"Who did this?" Randy demanded, eyes locked on Stone. "You, of all people, should know."

Stone had no answer, only the echo of the girl's shallow breathing and the weight of her own memories pressing like stones in her chest.

The night air outside St. Luke's was heavy with humidity, the kind that clung to skin and hair, pressing grief deeper into the body. Stone and Borgreve stood just beyond the sliding glass doors, the fluorescent hum behind them giving way to the drone of cicadas and the low rumble of distant semis on the highway.

Stone lit a cigarette she didn't really want, more for something to occupy her trembling hands. "It's always the same scream," she muttered, watching the smoke curl upward. "Doesn't matter if it's a mother, a sister, a friend, it's always the same sound when the body on the table is someone they love."

Borgreve leaned against the brick wall, jacket unbuttoned, tie loose, his face ghosted by the parking lot lamps. "Sara recognized the toenails, Jess. That's all we've got. No ID, no testimony. Just paint on her feet and a mother's grief."

"She'll carry it like a stone around her neck." Stone flicked ash into the darkness. "And if Amber survives, she'll carry her own. Different weight, same drowning."

Borgreve let the silence stretch, then said, "You saw her body. Someone didn't just want her gone; they wanted her destroyed. Head trauma like that, it's rage. And it's personal."

"Or it's practice," Stone countered, her voice low. "A killer refining the message. First Arielle's eyes, then Lana's tongue, now Amber's skull. Piece by piece, they're trying to strip these girls of something essential."

The full moon climbed higher above the tree line, pale and indifferent. Stone followed its arc, the glow reflecting in her damp eyes. "You ever feel like the moon sees more than we do, Casey? Like it watches every scream, every body dumped, every secret buried in these ditches?"

"Yeah," Borgreve said, pushing off the wall. "But it doesn't do a damn thing to stop it. That's on us."

Stone crushed the cigarette under her heel, the ember snuffing into nothing. "Then we'd better be ready. Whoever's out there— they're not finished. Not by a long shot."

They walked toward the SUV, their shadows stretching long and distorted across the asphalt, swallowed by the night as the hospital's glow fell behind them.

7

More Solemn
than a Fading Star

"It's shitty that the third leading cause of death for American Indian women is murder," Stone said, her voice flat, the words echoing against the glass wall of her office where she'd scrawled names and case fragments in looping marker.

"And I'd bet the stats don't even scratch the surface," Borgreve added. His reflection in the glass looked as exhausted as hers.

A knock on the frame broke the silence. A tribal officer leaned into the doorway. "Erik Möller's here. Want him in the interrogation room?"

"Yes. Thank you." Stone glanced at Borgreve, then whispered as they watched the older man shuffle past the glass. "He looks older than I expected."

Inside the sterile room, Möller folded his hands neatly on the table. His European composure was almost theatrical, a contrast to the violence circling the case.

"Mr. Möller," Stone began, "I'm Detective

Sergeant Stone. This is FBI Special Agent Borgreve. Thank you for meeting with us."

"Absolutely. I'll do anything to help find Michele's killer," he said, his accent faint but distinct.

Borgreve leaned forward. "How much did you know about Michele's marriage?"

"Quite a bit. She confided in me often. Sometimes it felt as though I was her therapist, but I didn't mind. We ate together, steak, burgers, Chinese. She drank wine, sometimes beer. She would talk, I would listen." His voice softened, reverent. "She was a good friend. That's all we were."

"Nothing romantic?" Borgreve pressed.

"We danced. Jazz clubs, big band nights. She humored me. Perhaps I was her companion, perhaps she was mine. But no, there was nothing beyond that."

"Did she truly love Teverbaugh?" Borgreve asked. "She married him the weekend before her death."

"She married him for health insurance. Michele was practical. But I told her, wait. Marry for love, not for convenience." Möller's gaze hardened. "The truth is, she had someone else. A carpenter. Wyatt. Wyatt Langdon."

Borgreve stilled. "Wyatt Langdon?"

"Yes. They were together often. I was in Germany much of the time, but I knew."

Stone's tone sharpened. "Did you have anything to do with Michele's death?"

"No." Möller's reply was immediate,

steady.

"How late was she with you that night?"

"Until seven. I made her steak. One glass of wine, nothing more. She left to meet a friend. I don't know who."

"Do names like Alyssa, Amber, or Lana ring a bell?" Stone asked.

Möller's brow furrowed, then smoothed. "Amber. Yes. That's who she mentioned."

"You're certain?"

"Yes. Certain."

"And you're willing to give us a DNA swab?" Borgreve asked.

"Of course."

"Then that's all for now." Stone stood. "We'll be in touch."

Wyatt Langdon entered next—broad-shouldered, younger, carrying the casual arrogance of someone used to impressing people with his hands.

"Wyatt," Stone gestured to the chair. "Thank you for coming in."

He sat, guarded but not rattled. "I was dating Michele. I suppose that's why I'm here."

"We'll get there. First, the body you found in the wall—Lana Davies. Did you know her?" Borgreve asked, pacing behind him.

"I knew her from The Copper Mule. Bought her drinks a couple of times. That's it. No romance. She was older, meth had worn her down."

"Did you know it was her when you tore

that wall open?" Stone asked.

"No. And if I had, I'd have told you."

"Back to Michele," Borgreve pressed. "How long were you seeing her?"

"Three months. I wanted more. She married that asshole for insurance, but it wasn't going to last. He wanted kids, she wanted college. They were opposites."

"Did you and Michele fight?" Stone asked.

"Yeah. I pushed for more, she pushed me away. But I'm not a killer. If it's bad, you walk away, you don't bash someone's skull in."

"Were you with her the night she died?" Borgreve's eyes narrowed.

"Yes. We danced. We had sex in my truck. Then she went back in for a last drink. I went home. I had work."

"People saw you together?"

"Yeah. The waitress said we looked cute. The bartender—Matt—was hitting on her."

Stone leaned in. "Matt Morgan?"

Wyatt nodded. "That's him."

They dismissed him after agreeing to the DNA swab, but as he left, Wyatt paused in the hallway. Stone and Borgreve caught it, the slight hesitation when the clerk mentioned Amber Lauzier was waking from her coma. A flicker of recognition he tried too late to mask.

At the hospital, Stone and Borgreve stood outside Amber's room while her parents hovered protectively at her bedside.

"She has zero short-term memory of what

happened," Borgreve muttered, reading from the agent's notes.

Inside, Amber turned her bruised face toward the window, refusing to look at them. "Didn't my dad tell you? I don't remember anything."

"Amber, I'm Detective Stone. Can you tell me who your boyfriend is?"

"He didn't do this." Her voice cracked, tears streaming. "He loves me. You'll just try to arrest him."

"The man who did this might come back," Borgreve said, voice tight. "You could help us stop him before he hurts someone else."

Amber shook her head violently. "Nobody stopped him from hurting me. Why would I help now?"

Sara Lauzier cut in, her tone sharp. "That's enough. My daughter needs rest."

The nurse stepped forward, firm. "They're right. This has gone far enough. Leave now, or I'll have security escort you out."

Outside in the corridor, Borgreve muttered, "Did she just threaten to throw my FBI ass out on the curb with a teenage rent-a-cop?"

"Don't take it personally," Stone said, though her face was bleak.

"Not sure I can take it at all." His voice darkened. "Nobody wants to get involved. Meanwhile, a possible serial killer is walking free."

"Native women are invisible," Stone said, pressing her back against the wall. "Invisible partners. Invisible victims. Nobody cares if we vanish."

"Why?"

"Because they say we dress wrong, we drink too much, we act the wrong way. That's the excuse. That's always the excuse."

Borgreve slammed his fist lightly against the cinderblock wall. "And the family doesn't even want to help."

"Would you? If you thought the FBI was just here to dig up every other dirty secret you had? Trust doesn't come easy out here."

He growled low in his throat, pacing the hallway. "Jess, I care. I really fucking care. I want to catch this bastard."

"I know."

"But no one will believe that. And it's eating me alive."

Stone looked at him, her eyes shadowed but steady. "Welcome to the rez, Casey."

The hospital's fluorescent lights buzzed like gnats overhead as Borgreve ground his jaw, still pacing the hallway. Stone hadn't moved from the wall, her eyes following the scuffed tiles as though they might whisper the truth if she stared long enough.

Then she straightened, her voice low. "Did you see him pause? When the clerk mentioned Amber coming out of the coma?"

Borgreve stopped. "Wyatt."

"Yeah. He froze. Just for a second. But he heard us."

Borgreve's mouth pulled into a tight line. "He's our carpenter who claims he just found

Lana Davies in the wall. The boyfriend Michele was sneaking around with. The guy who says he wanted more, but she 'distanced' herself. That pause tells me he's scared of what Amber might say."

Stone peeled herself from the wall, a new edge in her voice. "Let's move. If he's rattled, he'll do something stupid."

They pushed through the sliding hospital doors into the night. The summer air was heavy, smelling of wet asphalt and faint smoke from distant backyard fires. Their SUV sat under the jaundiced glow of a parking lot light.

"Where do you think he'll run?" Borgreve asked as they climbed inside.

"Not far," Stone said, buckling her belt with a snap. "Men like Wyatt—they think they can still control the story. He won't leave. He'll circle close to whatever secret he's guarding."

Borgreve started the engine. The headlights cut across the dark lot like blades. "Then let's circle, too."

They rolled out slowly, shadows bleeding across the cracked pavement, hospital windows glowing in their rearview like watchful eyes. Ahead, the rez road stretched black and endless, broken only by the occasional neon flicker from gas stations and bars.

Stone leaned forward, scanning each passing car. "If Wyatt's spooked, he might head back to The Copper Mule to drown it out. Or back to that worksite. Or..." She trailed off, her thoughts already knotting into darker places.

"Or he might want to make sure Amber Lauzier doesn't wake up after all," Borgreve finished.

Stone turned to him, her face pale in the dashboard light. "Then we can't let him out of our sight."

The SUV surged forward into the night, chasing taillights that might belong to Wyatt or to someone else entirely.

They caught him easy enough. Wyatt's dusty half-ton truck nosed out of the hospital lot not long after them, headlights blinding in the rearview for a moment before he swung east. Borgreve cut in behind, easing the SUV back a hundred yards, just far enough to keep the carpenter's taillights in sight.

The road unspooled into darkness. Out here, the night swallowed sound and shape, leaving only the crunch of tires on gravel and the restless sweep of the moon through thin clouds.

Stone leaned forward, elbows braced on the dash, eyes narrowed. "He's not heading for town."

"Nope," Borgreve muttered. "He's staying on the rez roads. These lanes are like veins, and you only run them when you don't want to be seen."

Wyatt's brake lights flared suddenly, glowing red through a patch of trees. He slowed at a fork, lingered like he couldn't decide, then swung left toward a narrower road that stitched between low hills and floodplains.

"Where does that lead?" Borgreve asked.

"Back ways to the housing tracts. Old work sites. And the river," Stone said, her voice thinning.

The SUV hummed low, steady. Borgreve killed his headlights for a stretch, letting the moon do the work. They trailed through tall grass waving silver in the night wind, past sagging barns and shuttered trailers that leaned like drunks in the dark.

Wyatt's truck swerved once, right tires dipping into the ditch before correcting. His window was down, one arm visible in the blur of light, fingers tapping, nervous.

Stone whispered, more to herself than to Borgreve, "He's not just driving. He's circling something. Like he's checking the perimeter."

Borgreve flexed his hands on the wheel. "If he stops at that river, I swear..."

Up ahead, the gravel turned to dirt. The truck's taillights bounced with the ruts, deeper into the trees, toward the low shimmer of water catching the moon.

"Jess," Borgreve said, low and taut.

"I see it." She had her hand on her holster already. "Stay close, but not too close. If he's going to bury something, or someone..."

They followed, silence thick but for the thrum of engines and the high, lonely cry of an owl echoing across the riverbend.

The road narrowed to little more than a track, weeds licking their bumpers. Wyatt's truck slowed, brake lights glowing again, then clicked off.

Darkness swallowed them whole.

Stone's voice was barely a breath: "This is it."

The truck rolled to a crawl, gravel crunching more softly as it slid into a clearing by the water. The engine clicked off, and the sudden silence felt unnatural like the world itself had stopped breathing.

Stone and Borgreve cut their own headlights, letting the SUV sink into shadow beneath the trees. Through the windshield, they watched Wyatt climb out of his truck. His shoulders looked broader in the pale light, lumbering, as if the weight of something unseen dragged against him.

He stood for a long moment, hands on his hips, staring at the black ribbon of river. The moon shimmered across the current, broken silver shifting in the ripples. Then, slow and deliberate, he circled to the bed of his truck.

"Binoculars," Borgreve slowly whispered, reaching under the seat.

Stone raised them, the lenses catching Wyatt's silhouette as he pulled something out—long, wrapped in a canvas tarp. Heavy. He staggered under its weight, half-dragging it toward the bank.

"Jesus," Borgreve muttered. "Tell me that's not..."

Stone swallowed hard. "We need to see

what he does before we move."

Wyatt paused at the edge of the clearing. The wind off the river lifted his hair, tangled it, and set the tarp flapping in ragged little breaths. He crouched, fumbling at the knots, his face tightening in the moonlight.

Stone and Borgreve leaned forward in tandem, hearts pounding the beat of the night.

Wyatt froze. His head turned, not toward them, but toward the far bank, as if he'd heard something move across the water. For a long, brittle second, he simply stood there, holding the dark like a man listening for ghosts.

Then, with a grunt, he pushed the bundle closer to the river's edge.

Stone whispered, voice like ground glass: "Casey... if he dumps it, we've got him."

8

The Mystery
Behind the Chime

Two weeks later, the air in Stone's office was heavy with the stale scent of burnt coffee and the scratch of markers squeaking across the glass wall. Files fanned out on her desk like the wreckage of lives: photographs, autopsy notes, timelines. Borgreve sat opposite her, flipping through his phone with the posture of a man waiting for a storm.

The storm came.

"Borgreve," he answered, voice clipped. A pause. His eyes widened. "Okay, go ahead." Another pause. His chair scraped the floor as he shot upright. "No shit." He slammed his palm on the desk, then raised one hand like a victorious signal flare. "I got it. Thanks."

Stone's pen froze above her notes. "What?"

"Wyatt Langdon's semen was inside Amber Lauzier." His voice carried the edge of triumph, almost savage.

Stone leaned back, arms crossed, a shadow falling over her face. "We both saw him freeze when he heard she'd woken up. He knew then. He's going to try to finish her off. She doesn't realize the danger she's in."

"Has she been released yet?" Borgreve demanded.

"Today. This morning."

Chairs toppled behind them as they bolted. The corridor blurred, doors and clerks passing like smears of color. They were out into the damp daylight in seconds, slamming into Borgreve's SUV, tires spitting gravel.

Stone was already on her shoulder mic, calling ahead. Her face turned pale as she clicked off. "She's out. Already on her way home."

Borgreve spun the wheel in a violent U-turn, the SUV fishtailing across a line of casino-bound traffic. Horns blared. Rain pelted the windshield in fat drops, smeared by wipers working too slowly for the storm. He floored it, weaving through cars, headlights flashing off wet asphalt.

The Lauzier Home

The Lauziers' house glowed like a glass jewel against the slate sky, modern lines, polished surfaces, too much light for the kind of conversation Stone and Borgreve had come to have. The rain chain beside the neighbor's porch clinked in the wind, a fragile chime that sounded like time running out.

"Mr. and Mrs. Lauzier," Stone said, voice taut, "we need to speak to your daughter."

"She's napping," Sara replied from the doorway, arms folded, eyes bloodshot. "Please don't disturb her."

"Randy, Sara," Stone pressed, "this is important. We have lab results from Amber's rape kit. It wasn't forced, which means it was probably her boyfriend. We need to talk to her now."

Randy stiffened. "Who is it?"

"Wyatt Langdon."

"The carpenter?" His face went crimson.

"You know him?" Borgreve asked.

"He did work for us months ago. You mean that son of a bitch was in my house screwing around with my daughter?" Randy's fury cracked the polished calm of their home.

"Please," Stone urged. "This could help us catch whoever nearly killed her."

Reluctantly, they let the detectives in. The glass walls of the great room revealed Amber before they even reached her, leaning against the sectional, staring blankly into the storm-streaked windows. She didn't move to greet them. Didn't blink. Just stood as if she were somewhere else entirely.

The Interrogation of Amber

"Amber," Randy said gently, "Detective Sergeant Stone and Special Agent Borgreve need to ask you some questions."

Amber turned her head at last. Her eyes were swollen, her expression flat. "It's not him," she said. Tears streaked her face, but her voice was almost monotone. "Wyatt would never do this. He loves me."

Stone crouched low, her tone softer. "Amber, the hospital's rape kit shows you had sex with Wyatt the night of the attack."

Amber shook her head violently. "Then I must've been with him before. And afterward, someone else hurt me. But it wasn't Wyatt. He's stopped answering my calls because of you. You've scared him away. You're ruining everything!" She pounded her fists into the cushions, sobbing.

Borgreve leaned forward. "So, you don't know where he is now?"

"No," Amber snapped, wiping her face.

"Where did you meet him?" Stone asked quietly.

"He was working for my dad. On the house."

Randy cursed under his breath, pacing the gleaming floor. "That bastard. In my house."

"For what, Dad?" Amber's voice cracked. "I'm an adult."

"You weren't when this started," Randy shouted back.

The room fractured, Amber collapsing into her mother's arms, Sara crying, Randy pacing like a caged animal, Stone kneeling with photographs in her hands.

"Amber," Stone said, pushing the pictures gently toward her, "do you recognize any of these men?"

Amber's finger hovered over each one: Miles Crenshaw. Arielle Flute's boyfriends. Hunter Daniel.

"Are these all your suspects?" Randy roared. "Why hasn't someone been arrested?"

Stone's jaw clenched. "We're working on it."

The Interrogation of Wyatt

Hours later, Wyatt sat in the hard metal chair of the tribal interrogation room, his face pale under the humming light.

"You want to guess why you're here?" Borgreve asked, pacing.

"Amber told you we were dating."

"No," Borgreve said, voice low and cutting. "The rape kit told us. Your semen was inside her. Same week, she was beaten nearly to death."

Wyatt dropped his eyes to his hands, fidgeting. "Because I'd just told you about Michele. I didn't want you thinking—"

"Thinking what?" Borgreve barked.

"That I had anything to do with them being hurt."

"You expect us to believe it's a coincidence? That two women you were sleeping with ended up beaten, one of them murdered, the other barely alive?" Stone's voice cracked like ice.

Wyatt winced. "I loved Michele. Amber was just company when Michele couldn't be there. I know it was wrong. I just wanted attention."

"You're about to get all the attention you need," Borgreve growled.

Agnes

Stone went to the community center for air she couldn't find. Agnes greeted her warmly, but the warmth was strained.

"I heard you locked up the carpenter," Agnes said. "The Lauziers are telling everyone he manipulated their daughter."

"We can't hold him long. No proof beyond consensual sex."

Agnes's eyes darkened. "And yet he says he got 'caught up with the wrong women'? That's poison, Jessica. That's exactly what men, here and out there, tell themselves so they can keep destroying us. At every age, we're raped, beaten, abandoned. Nobody cares. Not the FBI, not the courts, not the state. I'm surprised your partner is still here at all."

Stone's fists curled at her sides. "I wanted to wring his neck when he said it."

Agnes leaned closer, her voice sharp as broken glass. "We need a wall against that kind of thinking. A wall that doesn't crack."

Kyra's House

The call came in as Stone was leaving the center: a domestic disturbance at Kyra's home, the house where Lana Davies had been sealed into the wall.

Rain slicked the roads as she pulled up, the glow of ambulance lights splashing against siding. Outside, Kyra sat on the gurney, face bruised, mascara streaked, screaming through the fog of alcohol.

Inside, Miles Crenshaw stood bleeding, EMTs wrapping a deep gash on his arm. Furniture was overturned, glass crunched underfoot.

"What happened?" Stone demanded.

"Nothing," Miles muttered. "Accident."

"Kyra says different."

"She won't talk. She says she hurt herself." Borgreve appeared from the kitchen, jaw tight.

"That's not the call dispatch got. She screamed, you were going to kill her," Stone shot back.

Miles's voice cracked. "She went crazy. Threw a chair, a toaster. I threw them back. She came at me with a knife."

"And the fight was about Lana Davies?" Borgreve pressed.

Miles looked away. "It was just sex. It meant nothing."

That was when Kyra stormed through the doorway, baseball bat in her hands, her scream raw. "You motherfucker!"

Borgreve caught her, wrestling the bat away as she thrashed. Her voice was ragged, spilling years of rage. "You're too old for them! All you do is screw young girls to get work! You don't give a damn about me or my kids. Everything's been a lie!"

Stone cuffed her, walking her out into the wet night as Kyra kicked and screamed.

Back inside, Borgreve looked Miles dead in the eye. "And you're under arrest for domestic battery. Hospital first, then jail."

Rain battered the windows. The rain chain outside clinked like a metronome to the chaos, a steady reminder that the storm wasn't ending anytime soon.

9

Night Has a Thousand Eyes

Agnes, Bernice, and Vaneeta arranged bottled water and snacks along the reception tables inside the community center, their movements practiced, solemn. They were the hostesses of Drag the River weekend, guiding volunteers who scattered across mud, brush, and current, combing for signs of the nine missing tribal women.

"Due to the rains, the river's high, land's soft," Bernice told a cluster of young searchers, voices hushed under the low roll of thunder. "Mark anything you find, clothing, jewelry, bags. We'll follow the trail."

From the waters, a canoe team paddled back against the current, their jackets soaked, faces grim. "Nothing floats long out there," their leader reported. "If it's not snagged at the bottom, it's already miles downstream."

Then radios cracked. *"I've got a purse and a garbage bag—clothes trailing north."* Another voice chimed in: *"Cell phone near a washed-out fire pit."* A third: *"Engraved watch by the roadside."* Orange flags snapped in the wind, planted in tall prairie dropseed and bluestem, the field now a makeshift graveyard of markers.

Agnes's hands trembled as she lifted her phone. "Jessica, you'd better come."

At the River

Stone and Borgreve arrived in tandem, SUVs splashing mud as they cut into the brush. Stone hugged Agnes briefly before following Borgreve toward the flags, the scent of wet earth rising thick.

"What do you make of it?" she asked, crouching near the scattered purse.

"Could be a hitchhiker," Borgreve said, squinting, "or somebody dumping a victim's trail." His jaw hardened. "Annabelle McLaughlan. Number four."

They moved deeper, rain hissing through leaves, until Borgreve lifted a small, mud-caked watch. "Congratulations, Dana. Love Mom." He turned it over. "Dana Rancour. Number seven."

"Just because they drank or partied doesn't mean they deserved to vanish," Stone muttered.

"I didn't say they did," Borgreve snapped, then softened, gesturing at the cans scattered in weeds. "I'm saying whoever left them wanted us to think that's all these girls were."

At the riverbank, Stone plucked up a soaked pink phone plastered with stickers. Her sigh was long. "Tiffin. Number nine."

Borgreve cursed low. "That's three in one

sweep."

"They're seen," Stone said bitterly. "People just don't care. These girls are invisible."

The Truck Stop

Later that afternoon, Stone and Borgreve steered into the glaring lights of the truck plaza by the interstate. Diesel fumes, fried food, neon hum. It was the kind of place where too many stories ended.

They spotted her first, thin legs, short skirt, hair whipped by the wind, climbing down from a cab. The man beside her looked fifty, beard flecked with gray. When Borgreve waved them over, the girl bolted into the tall weeds, gone before anyone could move.

"Who was she?" Borgreve flashed his badge.

"Just a hitcher," the trucker said quickly, raising his palms. "I'm not that kind of guy."

"Of course not," Borgreve drawled, unimpressed.

Stone stepped closer, photograph in hand. "Have you seen this girl? Annabelle McLaughlan."

The man squinted. "Yeah. Last week. Wanted Denver, but I was headed south. Pretty thing. Exotic. She knew what she wanted, trust me."

"She's a missing tribal member," Stone said sharply. "Not a conquest."

The man shifted. "I can give you names. Truckers she might've gone with. Some guys get pushy when a girl backs off, but—"

"It's their fault," Stone cut in, eyes blazing. "Don't you dare put this on her."

The trucker ducked his head, scribbling names onto Stone's pad. Other truckers passing by slowed, eyeing him with suspicion, realizing he'd cooperated. Borgreve raised his voice on purpose: "Thanks for all the help, sir. Your testimony about your fellow truckers is going to be *very* useful."

The man flinched as heads turned his way, and he slunk back toward his rig.

"You kind of painted a target on him," Stone murmured.

"He's an asshole," Borgreve replied.

"I won't argue that."

Borgreve tucked the notepad into his jacket. "I'll run these names through long-haul registries. See if anyone's logged Denver. Maybe she made it that far."

"And I'll check in with Annabelle's family. See who she knows out there."

They exchanged a weary glance, rain streaking the windshield when they climbed back into the SUV. The neon glow of the truck stop bled into the night road, swallowed whole as they drove back toward the rez.

Annabelle's Family

The rain followed them back onto the rez, a steady percussion on the SUV roof. By the time Stone and Borgreve turned down the gravel drive, the house ahead glowed warm through sheets of water—too bright, too normal for the kind of conversation waiting inside.

Annabelle's parents, Miriam and Thomas McLaughlan, ushered them in with stiff politeness. The foyer smelled faintly of sage and lemon cleaner. Photographs lined the wall, school portraits, family reunions, Annabelle as a child with a gap-toothed grin. No photos from the last two years.

"We've already talked to officers," Miriam said quickly, wringing her hands. "We've put her picture out everywhere."

"We're not here to ask you to relive everything," Stone said softly. "But we do need details. Anything recent, calls, friends, someone new."

"She was restless," Thomas admitted, his voice gravelly. "Talking about Denver. Said she had people there. But when we pressed, she wouldn't say who."

"Did she leave with anyone?" Borgreve asked.

"She said she'd find a ride. Just threw it out there like we weren't supposed to worry." Miriam's eyes shimmered with anger under her grief. "She wore that skirt, the one she knew I hated. Like she wanted someone to see her."

"Clothing doesn't invite what happened to her," Stone said sharply, meeting Miriam's gaze. "Don't let anyone make you believe that."

Silence thickened. A clock ticked loudly in the next room.

"Did she have money?" Borgreve asked.

"Only what she took from her dresser. Twenty dollars, maybe thirty," Thomas replied. "She wasn't prepared for a trip like that. She was just a girl." His hands trembled on the armrest of his chair. "Still just a girl."

Stone studied the mantle. Annabelle's face stared back in a graduation photo, cap tilted, her eyes bright with possibilities now clouded by silence.

"We found some of her things near the river," Stone finally said. "We're still piecing together the timeline. If she reached Denver, we'll track her. If she didn't, we'll find where the trail ends."

Miriam crumpled into tears, pressing a tissue to her face. Thomas turned away, jaw clenched so hard the veins stood out.

Stone left a card on the kitchen counter. "If she calls, texts, anything, even a whisper of her name, let us know immediately."

They stepped back into the rain, the house light glowing like a false beacon behind them.

Outside, the SUV hummed to life, windshield wipers beating back the storm.

"Family's already halfway erased her," Borgreve muttered. "Blaming skirts, blaming attitude."

"That's how it starts," Stone said, staring into the downpour. "And that's how the killer counts on it ending."

Denver Leads

By the time they were back at tribal HQ, Borgreve's phone was alive with updates. His FBI team had pulled the truck stop names into manifests, mile markers, weigh station logs, and delivery records.

"Two of them made it west. One all the way into Utah, the other stopped in Denver." Borgreve scrawled lines across Stone's glass office wall, linking trucker names to dates. "Guess which one hasn't checked in since last week?"

Stone leaned against her desk, arms crossed. "If Annabelle made it to Denver, she might still be alive."

"Or she never got out of this county." Borgreve rubbed his eyes, frustration leaking through. "Either way, I've got Denver PD circulating her picture tonight. Truckers, diners, motels, and the Greyhound terminal. If she surfaced there, somebody saw her."

"And if she didn't?" Stone asked.

"Then she's still here. Which means your killer isn't just a drifter, Jess. He's close. He knows the back roads, the blind spots."

Stone stared past him, out the rain-smeared window toward the casino lights burning against the night sky. "And he knows nobody will raise hell when another Native girl disappears."

The Rez Whispers

Later that evening, Stone slipped into the community center. The Drag the River volunteers had gone home, leaving only

Agnes and Bernice stacking chairs. The smell of wet earth clung to their clothes.

"You found something?" Agnes asked immediately, hope flickering in her tired eyes.

"We found things," Stone said. "Clues, but no bodies. And families who'd rather swallow their grief than face what's happening."

Bernice crossed her arms, voice hard. "Because grief doesn't bring them back. It just opens you up for gossip. People would rather whisper about skirts and bottles than admit a predator is hunting us."

Stone didn't argue. The posters on the wall, MMIWG flyers, missing faces in red, spoke louder than words.

A door slammed somewhere in the building. For a second, all three women froze. The wind howled down the hallway, rattling a loose vent cover like a chime.

"Every sound feels like him," Agnes whispered.

Two Roads

Back in the SUV, Borgreve was waiting. His laptop glowed with a map pinned with trucker routes stretching west.

"My team's convinced Annabelle was picked up. If that's true, we're looking interstate. Could be Denver, could be beyond."

Stone buckled in, jaw tight. "And if it wasn't a trucker?"

"Then it's someone right under our noses."

They drove in silence, the reservation road slick with rain. On one side lay Denver—distance, uncertainty, hope. On the other lay the rez—familiarity, silence, fear.

"Two roads," Borgreve said finally. "We'll have to chase both."

Stone kept her eyes on the blacktop unraveling ahead. "And pray one of them leads us to the truth before another girl goes missing."

Denver: Shadows in the Mile High

By the next afternoon, Borgreve was in a rented sedan, weaving through Denver traffic, the mountains like bruises on the horizon. He'd already shaken hands with two local detectives, but their skepticism followed him like cigarette smoke.

"Runaway hitchhiker," one muttered. "They always are. Give it a week and she'll turn up broke, begging a bus ticket home."

Borgreve bit down his irritation. "She's not a runaway. She's a target."

At the Greyhound terminal, he walked the concourse with Annabelle's photo in hand. The air reeked of diesel and sweat. A janitor nodded and said he'd seen a girl like her two nights back, climbing into a rig idling by the curb.

"She wasn't alone," the janitor added. "Guy had her by the elbow, steering her like he owned her."

Borgreve's jaw tightened. He jotted the truck's description, white cab, company logo half-scraped away, and sent it off to his team. Then he sat in his car, staring at the terminal's neon clock as the night pushed in. Somewhere between Denver and the rez, Annabelle was either alive or gone.

Stone: Circling Wolves

Back home, Stone walked the dusty lots behind The Copper Mule, where cigarette butts and broken glass glittered in the mud. Pam, the waitress, met her by the back door with arms folded tight.

"Everyone's saying it's Wyatt. That he's the one hurting these girls," Pam said. "But I don't buy it."

"Why not?" Stone asked.

"Because he's not smart enough. This—" Pam gestured to the dumpsters, the shadows, the silence "—this is a game. Someone's staging things. Wyatt's a dumbass, sure, but he doesn't think like that."

Stone filed it away. Pam wasn't the first to hint that the killer was calculating, deliberate, and rehearsed.

Later that night, Stone parked outside Verzella's greenhouse. Lights still burned inside. She watched through fogged glass as Verzie moved alone among the hanging baskets, talking to herself, or maybe to ghosts.

"Everyone's unraveling," Stone whispered into the dark. "And whoever's doing this... he's watching it happen."

Convergence

At midnight, Borgreve called from Denver, his voice tight. "Jess, I've got a witness placing Annabelle with a trucker two nights ago. White rig. Logo half-scraped. It's solid."

"And here," Stone said, watching Verzella's silhouette move under the lamps, "everyone's still circling the same wolves—Wyatt, Miles, Matt, Hunter. Pam says Wyatt doesn't have the brains for it. Maybe she's right."

Borgreve exhaled. "Then we're chasing two killers. One who rides the interstates, and one who hides in plain sight."

Stone closed her eyes, listening to the greenhouse chime rattle against the glass in the wind. "Or one man who knows how to play both sides of the line."

Rez Roads and Highways

By the time Borgreve drove back from Denver, dawn was just beginning to gray out the interstate, the silhouettes of rigs like silent guardians against the skyline. His phone buzzed twice with updates, one from his team about Annabelle, the other from Stone, short and tight: *Meet me by the river pull-off. We need to talk.*

The pull-off was empty except for Stone's SUV and the churn of the water below. She leaned against the hood, hair loose from its tie, eyes hollow from another sleepless night.

"They found Tiffin safe," she said before

he could ask. "But she's refusing to talk. Too scared. Too ashamed. The cycle continues."

Borgreve set his coffee on the hood beside her. "And Annabelle was last seen in a white cab, logo scraped. Heading west. She's probably gone, Jess. Or she's waiting for us in some truck-stop motel, another name on the list."

Stone rubbed her temples, staring at the river as if it might confess something. "So, we've got two lanes of hell—one running through the rez, the other stretching out on the highway. And maybe..." she trailed off.

"Maybe they overlap," Borgreve finished. "A contractor who moves between job sites. A trucker who drifts in for a casino run. A bartender who knows when girls are alone. One man, or two? Doesn't matter. The bodies keep piling up."

The river hissed against its banks, swollen from rain, dragging branches and scraps of debris downstream.

Stone whispered, "Night has a thousand eyes, Casey. But out here, no one's looking. No one sees us until we're gone."

For a moment, the two of them just stood together, watching the water swallow the evidence of storms past. The cases were no longer scattered pieces; they were bleeding into one another, threads pulled taut between the rez backroads and the endless highways beyond.

And somewhere, out there in the shifting dark, the predator was watching too.

10

Melody of the Stars

Stone and Borgreve pulled up outside Annabelle McLaughlin's parents' home, tires crunching the gravel of a broad circular drive lined with birch and oak. Wyatt Langdon was balanced on a ladder above the detached garage, a trim gun in hand, while Verzella, brisk and purposeful, directed landscapers across the pavers toward a wildflower garden. Two Weimaraners streaked past in pursuit of a rabbit, their sleek bodies glinting in the late sun.

The McLaughlin residence loomed over them, a French chateau cut from pale stucco and crowned with steep rooflines. A fountain sprayed in the courtyard, guarded by a stone lion that bared teeth at visitors. Through ten-foot steel-and-glass double doors, Stone and Borgreve were admitted by the maid service into a foyer that rose three stories, light striking the granite floors and curling wrought-iron staircase like fire over water.

"Hello? Anybody home? The maid service let us in," Stone called, her voice echoing through marble archways and the designer kitchen beyond. The house breathed wealth, every surface polished to a gleam, the walls studded with inlay mosaics and crystal chandeliers.

Shane and Dani McLaughlin appeared at the base of the staircase, their faces drawn but polite.

"I have FBI Special Agent Casey Borgreve here with me," Stone said. "We'd like to ask some questions about Annabelle."

"Absolutely," Shane replied, voice gruff. "The more eyes on this, the better."

Dani led them upstairs into Annabelle's room, French-inspired and ethereal, creams and pale pastels washed with sunlight. A dainty chandelier glittered over the vintage bed, while selfies and snapshots covered a fabric pinboard. Borgreve crouched, checking beneath the mattress and desk, while Stone studied the photos.

Several showed Annabelle in party scenes with familiar faces—Amber, Wyatt, and even Michele.

"She worked at the greenhouse?" Stone asked, pointing to a photo.

"Yes," Dani said. "Miles set her up with the job."

Stone and Borgreve shared a look. Too many names were circling back to the same nexus.

Outside, Verzella was brisk and vague, *a wonderful girl, antsy to travel.* Wyatt, intercepted before he could leave, was blunt.

Belle liked to flirt. Belle wanted out. Belle was bored. He claimed they last drank beer at the river only two days ago.

Stone's phone rang and it was Tiffin's mother. The city alibi had collapsed. A new lead.

By nightfall, Stone and Borgreve were back in the SUV, eating casino takeout at Stone's cluttered desk. Files stacked high, phones buzzing with fragments of new sightings, they were interrupted by the intercom: *possible abduction near the natural food store.*

They raced into the night.

Amber Lauzier stumbled toward them, pale and shaking. "It was him again," she sobbed. "Michele's old boyfriend. Alyssa's, too."

Moments later, the chase was on— shadows tearing across powwow grounds under construction, through fields of spruce and oak, past startled teens on lovers' lane. The suspect vanished, reappeared, vanished again. Each time Stone and Borgreve closed the distance, he slipped away, a phantom in the dark.

At the mini-storage facility, their break came. A garage door rattled, a lock clattered to the ground. Inside, duct tape-bound Tiffin, trembling on a makeshift bed. Above them, Hunter Daniel stood on the roof, gun drawn. His shot went wide, shattering beer bottles, and then he fled, a ghost slipping off steel and into the trees.

The hunt drove them across the rez—casino lots, liquor store back alleys, woods crawling with patrols. Finally, Stone cornered him near the dumpsters, gun raised.

Hunter sprang like a feral animal. They fought dirty with kicks, fists, and blood in the mouth. Hunter laughed, spit mixing with crimson, as he confessed:

"She screamed, so I cut her tongue. Lana was garbage. Michele stiffed me on money, so I made her pay. Arielle saw my buyer. Amber? Just a laugh, just another ditch bitch like your momma."

Stone clawed for her weapon, blood stinging her eyes.

"And you," Hunter whispered, pressing her down. "You're nothing more than a bastard child."

The shot rang out. Stone's bullet caught him full. His smile broke, body jerking backward under the county highway's lone streetlight. They both fell, Hunter bleeding into the dirt, Stone collapsing with him, the night alive with sirens and the thrum of distant bass from parked cars at lovers' lane.

She woke to the hum of machines, IV tugging at her arm, Borgreve slouched in a chair nearby.

"He's been here the whole time," the nurse said softly.

"A week," Borgreve admitted, moving to her bedside. "You got him, Jess. Hunter's done."

Stone closed her eyes, a tear slipping free. "But Annabelle?"

"We did what we could," Borgreve whispered. "We'll keep fighting for the rest."

Released against medical advice, Stone returned to duty pale but steady, Borgreve shadowing her. At the community center, the elevator doors opened to a chorus of voices: *surprise.*

Agnes beamed, clasping Stone's hands. "Who knows how many women and girls you saved?"

Stone shook her head. "We couldn't save Annabelle."

Agnes squeezed tighter. "But we don't give up. We live to fight another day."

Stone gazed out the office window at the casino lights, the hotel, and the childcare center glowing against the dark. "Are we just raising girls to become women who'll be victimized again and again? How do we make ourselves visible?"

"We keep working," Agnes said. "We never stop. We never let them vanish into the night."

Below, in the memorial garden, Borgreve looked up at her. Stone lifted her chin, the weight of grief and survival heavy, but steady.

The melody of the stars hung above them, faint but unbroken, a promise against the darkness.

At dawn, the rez was hushed except for the

laughter of children chasing each other across the cracked basketball court behind the community center. Their voices rose like bright sparks against the pall of night, carrying over the memorial garden where names were etched in stone. Stone sat in her SUV at the edge of the lot, hands folded on the wheel, watching as the sun broke through a veil of cloud, soft gold spilling across the asphalt. For a moment, the air smelled of wet earth and sweetgrass, and she let herself believe that one day the girls here would run free without fear—that the night, with all its thousand eyes, might finally blink closed.

The End

The Lasting Echo of Lost Souls: Novella #3

1

Late October Dreaming

The day wore a borrowed summer, thin blue sky, light sharp as glass, while the maples burned down the roadsides in spilled wine and honey. Red-twig dogwood flashed its veins, smoketree smoldered from blue-green to embered orange, and every trail in the exurbs filled with leaf peepers and lenses and the other kind of watcher too, the sort who came to the edges of things with their pockets full of trouble.

A timber stair stepped through boulders into the pumpkin rows where Detective Sergeant Jessica Stone, Agnes GreyEagle, Vaneeta Shah, and Bernice O'Reilly shepherded twenty preschoolers down the hill like bright leaves in a gust. Jackets shed by midmorning hung from volunteer arms like molted skins the parents would definitely ask about later. The barn smelled of hay and tempera paint; tiny hands jabbed brushstrokes into orange domes, making lopsided faces that grinned like saints and goblins.

Jessica, tall, athletic, with paint on her knuckles, laughed when a kid stamped a fingerprint mustache across her pumpkin. Agnes watched from a beat-up stool, palm warming Jessica's shoulder. It pleased the old woman to see the detective's face unarmored for once.

"You need a couple of your own, Jess," Agnes said, half-teasing, wholly sincere.

"No prospects," Jessica answered, rinsing a brush. "Unless you count the grumpy guy in the unmarked SUV."

"FBI Special Agent Casey Borgreve?" Agnes arched a grandmotherly brow. "He's single."

"He's married to the job," Jessica said, but the corner of her mouth twitched.

Sun poured through the open barn doors. Beyond, cottony seed drifted like ash. A dark SUV rolled in behind the school bus; Agnes sighed. "That's him. Never a good omen."

Jessica handed off three paint-sticky kids. "Two minutes," she told Agnes, then stepped into the light, flagged Casey, and tugged him back toward his vehicle.

"What's up?"

"Sorry to cut your field trip," he said, voice low. "Body in a drainage pond. A few miles out. Early morning dump, witnesses saw a garbage can tip. Thin wallet in a side pocket: Malia Glenbow."

Jessica's jaw set. "Malia, we were in school together. She was younger. Brilliant." The word snagged. "What happened?"

"Prelim tox shows GHB. Blood alcohol point three two." He glanced at a screen, winced. "Coroner says likely blunt force trauma before submersion and full autopsy pending."

"She barely drank," Jessica said. "Her grandma lives with them. Dry house. That level, that's not a choice."

They stood a heartbeat in the warm October light, the barn behind them loud with kid laughter, and then Jessica nodded once. "Take me to HQ. I'll call in. Agnes!"

Agnes was already there, pressing a Tupperware of pumpkin cookies into Jessica's hands like a talisman and lunch in one. "Go," she said. "Be safe. I'll take the corn maze, too."

On the drive back, the maples flickered past like a slow-rolled fire. Casey drove in silence until the low brown building of tribal HQ rose from prairie grass. Inside, the air smelled of coffee and dry-erase ink. Jessica set the cookies down untouched.

"Family?" Casey asked.

"Family," she said.

They nearly clipped a bicyclist at the boulevard, braked hard, then turned between river-rock retaining walls toward the Glenbows' circular drive. Two St. Bernards came like a tide, tails thudding. The log home sat deep and wide, all glass and timber and warmth, hand-peeled pine posts, skylights stitched into trussed ceilings, pine wainscoting catching the sun. Jessica felt the familiar wrongness of bringing bad news into a beautiful room.

Grandma Glenbow opened the door with soft hands and sharper eyes. "Come in," she said, already reading the answer in Jessica's face. "Sara and Darby went to the natural foods store. They'll be right back. Water?"

"Yes, thank you," Jessica said to buy seconds. The front doors opened with the rustle of paper sacks. Sara and Darby froze at the two badges in their living room, and groceries slid to the children who appeared as if conjured.

"Dear God," Sara said, sitting before anyone asked. "Is it a car—"

"Honey," Darby murmured, steadying her with a palm between her shoulders. "Let them tell us."

Jessica glanced once at the window wall, the pines beyond it spearing the sky. "I'm so sorry," she said. "Malia died last night."

The room folded in. Sound became breathing. Casey took the part that required edges. "There are signs of foul play. We're waiting on the medical examiner."

"Who?" Grandma asked. "Why?"

"We don't know yet," Jessica said. "We'll tell you as soon as we do."

They moved through the house on soft feet. Wide-plank oak under the spiral stair. A loft sitting area where Malia's laptop waited like a quiet animal. Down past a two-sided stone fireplace into a bright kitchen that smelled faintly of cedar and citrus. A phone charging by a ceramic mixing bowl; Casey bagged it. "People live on their phones," Jessica said gently to Darby. "Why was hers here?"

"It kept dying," he said thickly. "She ordered a new one. The old one was useless half the time."

Malia's suite wore silver and turquoise like a prayer. The bedframe had a curve like a smile; the soaker tub in the bath looked like it could float. Jessica touched nothing she didn't have to. Casey did his usual magic: under the mattress, behind framed beadwork, beneath the lamp's felt pad, nothing.

"Grandma didn't take the main-floor master?" he said to say anything, to hang onto the normal.

"She has the in-law suite downstairs," Darby said. "Fountain. Garden door. She sleeps to water."

"May we take the devices?" Casey asked. "We'll return them."

Darby nodded, blinking. "Her password's usually AspenAngel. Her dog. Christmas pup."

"Thank you," Jessica said. It felt small.

Back at HQ, the digital forensic tech tapped keys with the calm of a surgeon. Jessica and Casey peered over shoulders, eyes grainy from coffee. A calendar entry: J, 8:00 p.m., the night before she died.

"Don't spike your hopes," Jessica said. "She's got two close friends—Josie and Jewel. Both Js."

"Phone intel coming in," the tech said. "Texts, GPS, voicemail, browser history."

"Which tower for browsing?" Jessica asked, pointing at a dating site tab.

"Nearest the Glenbows'," Casey said, scrolling through bland profiles and too-white smiles.

Jessica's desk phone rattled. She listened, asked two questions, hung up. "Josie and Jewel are home. Trailer park off the north road."

"I'll drive," Casey said, shrugging into his jacket.

"Princess," Jessica deadpanned.

"I bruise easily," he said, and they were out the door.

The trailers sat under a sky that had gone pewter by afternoon. Some yards were tidy, with asters by the steps and wind spinners clacking. Others were stacked with broken refrigerators and three-legged sofas. A pair of ravens picked at an overflowing dumpster.

"Why the split?" Casey asked softly.

"Some folks are from other tribes, work the casino, save what they can. Some burned their per capita and haven't found bottom yet," Jessica said. "Josie and Jewel live with their grandma. All three work, catering for her, poker club for them."

Jewel answered before the second knock: twenty-seven, pretty, athlete's posture, eyes like storm water. "Jess. Come in, but excuse the towels." Every mirror wore a dishcloth shroud. Casey stared a second too long. "Storm coming," Jewel explained. "Grandma covers them."

The home smelled like yeast and butter. "She baked this morning. Take some," Jewel ordered, already nesting golden dinner rolls into a plastic pan. "Josie's in the shower."

"We're here about Malia," Jessica said.

"I was supposed to meet her two nights ago. She ditched." Jewel's mouth measured worry and affection in equal parts. "She did that sometimes."

"Are you the 'J' on her calendar?" Casey asked.

"She didn't calendar us," Jewel said with a small laugh. "That was the problem."

Josie burst out with a towel around her head with the same face, a slightly softer set. "What are we... oh. Malia's calendar. She never writes us. And if you're about to ask, no—she didn't drink. Like, at all."

"Men?" Jessica asked.

"She thought about online," Josie said, rolling her eyes, "then spooked herself with serial killer podcasts. But there were two guys at school who crushed on her big time. Justin and—"

"Colby," Jewel finished. "Justin lives in the valley. Runs cross-country with her. He's a blackjack dealer till he finishes at the U in public affairs. Colby's in her class, lives in Dinkytown."

"Thank you," Jessica said, meaning it. "Save me a roll."

"Bring the pan back," Jewel said, not meaning it.

The casino floor poured a thousand small noises into the air with chips kissing felt, muted cheers, the rinse of a sax over the sound system. At a blackjack table, a lanky young man with a receding hairline dealt mechanically, eyes skittering. Casey flashed the badge just long enough. "Justin Jankowicz? We need a room."

The supervisor slid into the dealer slot. Justin led them to a glassed room off the floor, hands already wiping sweat at his jeans before guilting them into stillness at his sides. "What is this?"

"When did you last see Malia Glenbow?" Casey asked.

"Three nights ago," Justin said. "Trail run near the river. Seven, maybe."

"Where'd you split?" Jessica asked.

"Fast-food by the track," he said, voice quickening. "She used the bathroom. I ran home. She's close? She was fine. You're scaring me. Where is she?"

"Would you consent to a cheek swab?" Casey asked.

"Sure, yes, just tell me—"

"Malia is dead," Jessica said evenly. "She was found in a drainage pond."

Justin's face emptied. "So not a car accident," he said, as if he'd rehearsed a safer version. "We weren't dating. I wanted to. She wasn't into it. School first."

A supervisor poked her head in. "We okay?" she asked, eyes the size of chips.

"We're done," Casey said, already standing. "Justin, swing by tribal HQ as soon as you can."

Justin nodded and didn't move for a long time after they left. Outside, the light had shifted again with that late October trick where day pretends to hold but night's already climbing the trees. Jessica paused at the doors, breathed in cigarette smoke and cold metal and the faint, clean edge of coming rain.

"J could be Justin," Casey said.

"Or Jewel," Jessica said. "Or Josie. Or someone who never gets written down."

They walked into the parking lot. Leaves scudded in circles, little cyclones of color spinning and dying against the curb. Somewhere on the rez, a chime stirred in the first wind of the storm.

2

Finely Embroidered Heartbreak

By the time the school bus sighs back into the community center lot, the sky has traded its morning lacquer for a pewter sheen, the kind that presses sound flat. Jessica hands out last hugs and high-fives, little fists clutching paper sacks half-full of apples like trophies. Agnes stands in the doorway with her cardigan sleeves pushed to her elbows, the benevolent queen of this small kingdom, and Jessica folds her into a quick, rib-squeezing embrace.

"Corn maze," Agnes reminds her, smiling into the wind. "I'm holding you to it."

"Scout's honor," Jess says, backing away toward her tribal SUV.

She's barely in the seat when the radio flares: shots fired outside the Copper Mule. One fatal. Units en route.

"Stone, can you meet me there?" Casey's voice, clipped, too steady.

"I'm on my way." She swings out, skims the edge of the casino's brick-and-glass sprawl, and hits the main road. The cottonwoods along the ditch toss their last coins of yellow at her windshield. Dispatch comes back with a name, and the inside of her chest goes empty.

Shay Proulx.

The Copper Mule's neon horse-kick is still blinking when she pulls up. Blue strobes bounce off plate glass and the pharmacy's brick across the way; a crushed Styrofoam cup corkscrews down the gutter toward the sewer grate.

"Casey," she calls, sliding from the seat. There's a smell here she never gets used to, cold air, hot metal, the copper film of blood. A small, neat body lies near the curb, hair splayed like spilled thread. Someone's put a towel over the torso, but the head wound is a black red flower she can't look at for long.

"Did anyone see who—" Her voice fractures on the question.

"Jess," Casey says, reading the break. "You knew her?"

"Shay's ours," Jessica says, and the words scald, tribal member, seamstress, teacher of careful arts. The Copper Mule's waitress came to her classes for baby blankets and powwow regalia; she turned cotton into ceremony with a steady backstitch. "Her shop's by the natural foods. Kids came to her Halloween class for felt pumpkins." She bites down hard on the rest.

The county sheriff strolls up, hat in hand, boots wet with alley water. "Detective Stone—she one of yours?"

"Shay Proulx is a pillar," Jess says evenly. "The last person I'd expect to pull a bullet."

Casey points across the two-lane at the pharmacy's camera clusters. "Deputy—pull everything you can. Street, sidewalk, front door. Push it to my secure unit. Now."

"Roger," the deputy says, already trotting.

The air hums with onlookers murmuring themselves braver; someone laughs too loud, the wrong sound in the wrong place, and it dies quickly. Jess feels her throat close. She backs to the SUV, palms braced on the door, sips from her water bottle until the street stops pulsing.

"What's up, Jessica?" Casey asks softly, leaning on the frame.

"These are my girls," she says. "First, Malia. Now, Shay." She tips her head toward the body. "Could've been me. Any of us."

Pam, the Copper Mule's waitress, pads over in non-slip shoes and heartbreak mascara. "I told the deputy," she blurts. "She and her boyfriend were arguing. They took it outside. I swear—if I thought he'd—" She presses knuckles to her mouth. "I would've done something."

"It's not on you," Jess tells her gently. "Name?"

"Dawson LaVigne. I think? That's what it said on his card." Pam wipes at her cheek. "White guy. Short, stocky. All bark until it wasn't. You know the type."

Jessica does. "Thanks, Pam. Go back in. We'll find you."

By late afternoon, the sky has sunk closer still, pressing a dulled light through the glass walls of Jessica's office. She and Casey watch the small monitor as Dawson LaVigne is led into tribal lockup by a tribal patrolman and an FBI agent. His mouth moves in a steady stream; the audio crackles on as the door closes.

"Stone—you asked if he said anything," the patrolman says, head around her door with Casey's agent double. "When we pulled him at the casino hotel, he said—and I quote—'stupid bitch didn't know her place.'"

The thin file in Jess's hands bends under her grip. She sets it down very carefully. Casey thanks the officers; the door snicks shut.

"Asshole," Jess breathes. "As if an educated Indian woman is a provocation."

"I know," Casey says. "We'll get this one. Then we keep going."

"Until when?" she asks, but she already knows the shape of his answer.

"One at a time," he says anyway. "Let's get back to Malia."

Dinkytown smells like espresso and rain. The coffee shop is narrow, with a brick wall, a chalkboard menu, and strings of warm bulbs, and the barista, Colby, is behind the counter, a gangly twenty-something with bottle-blonde hair and eyes still rimmed in salt.

"Colby Perrier?" Casey flashes his badge low, voice pitched not to carry over the milk steamer. "We'll wait over there."

Colby nods, finishes a pour, waves the supervisor over, then slides into the corner booth opposite them, a damp napkin twisting between his long fingers.

"We're sorry to reach out like this," Casey begins. "We're trying to build a picture of Malia's last days."

"I haven't stopped crying since you called," Colby says, eyes going glassy again. "She was—she was kind. Focused. Maybe too focused for me," he admits with a tiny, crooked smile. "I wanted more. She had goals."

"Anyone in her circle with the initial J?" Jessica asks.

"Jeremy," Colby says instantly. "Professor Beaujolais, Strategic Management. Everyone loves him. And Justin, her study partner, is a blackjack dealer at the rez casino. Oh—and me. Colby, not helpful." He flinches at the joke. "I'm sorry."

"Jeremy's last name?" Casey asks.

"Beaujolais," Colby repeats. "He's from Louisiana. Teaches like a TED Talk. Horses, kids, the whole Instagram family thing."

"Your alibi for Thursday night?" Jessica asks, gentle but firm.

"Here until midnight." He points to the woman steaming milk. "Kennedy can vouch. Walked home after, and my roommate, Donovan, saw me come in at twelve-fifteen. Stayed in."

"You've been helpful," Casey says, and

means it.

Outside, rain freckles the sidewalk. They walk past a rack of bikes strung with wet leaves and slide into the SUV. The highway west takes them around the darkening basins of Lake Minnetonka and Wayzata's tidy million-dollar porches, Orono's seamed stone walls, Mound's marinas gone skeletal with the season, Minnetrista's horse fences slick with mist.

"Last J on the list," Jessica says, staring at the GPS arrow inching through lakes and marsh.

"Married with kids," Casey says. "Tact. Thoroughness."

"You missed the turn," she says mildly.

He reverses into a gravel lane and the scene assembles like a wealthy man's dream: a fence rimming a handful of horses—two Mustangs, a paint-spattered Appaloosa, sleek Arabians, quarter horses with patient eyes. A barn hand in a rain shell swings a gate. The house lifts behind it all. It's a modern mountain style in the Midwest, heavy timbers and steel, pitched roofs and glass, trusswork like a skeleton laid bare. A covered deck elbows along two sides, offering sightlines into rooms lit with the kind of warmth you buy.

Jeremy Beaujolais meets them in well-worn boots, a plaid shirt that knows a dryer, a wedding ring bright, that soft-easy professor energy Jessica recognizes a mile off. His wife, a perfect knockout, with kind eyes, shepherds two children back inside at his wave.

"Call me Jeremy," he says, extending a hand.

"Jeremy," Casey says. "Tell us about Malia."

"Bright," Jeremy says without reaching for adjectives. "Ambitious, but not hollow with it. Wanted to build a community development agency, you know, housing, pathways to ownership. She cared about the unglamorous parts."

"Her personal life?" Casey asks, watching for a flinch.

"Her peers adored her," Jeremy says. "She kept them on task by refusing to flirt." He grins, self-effacing. "I overheard, now and then. Professor hears more than he's told."

"Any personal interest on your part?" Casey keeps his tone cool like river stone.

Jeremy's laugh is small, not offended. "No. My wife would shoot me, and anyway, I didn't believe she was dating. She asked for a mentor visit once and tore the idea up because it felt too personal."

"Last time you saw her?" Jessica asks.

"She was meant to meet me Friday, after class," he says. "She didn't show, which was unlike her. She wanted my take on an internship application."

"DNA swab?" Casey asks.

"Of course," Jeremy says, holding out his cheek like a schoolboy for a shot.

Back at HQ, a CSI tech rolls his chair over, pushing hair off his forehead. "Fast-food footage across from the track is clean," he says. "But the manager remembered an Indigenous woman, Thursday, ponytail, bright turquoise tee, and running pants, who waited while they cleaned the restroom. Didn't buy anything. He clocked her for that. Said he watched her cross to the inn by the racetrack, stand under the pergola."

"The inn footage?" Casey asks.

"Exterior camera's dead," the tech says, grimace apologetic. "Lobby cam's garbage. I can try to clean it."

"Do," Jessica says. "Grab the employee's info too."

When Casey turns back to Malia's browser logs like route maps, council meeting minutes, an online fabric store she'd favorited, Jessica stands, stretches out the ache, and heads for someplace she can breathe.

The community center breathes like a heart with a lobby full of movement and murmurs, kids' art tacked up in spirals, the smell of frybread sneaking down the stairwell. Jessica pours coffee, nods at Vaneeta's patient posture, at Bernice's sensible shoes and teddy-bear calm, then tap-taps into Agnes's office.

"Corn maze?" Agnes asks, smile loaded.

"Put me down," Jess says. "And no updates I can share beyond 'working.'"

Agnes's mouth softens. "She was a good one," she says simply, and they let that sit a beat, the way you sit with someone's name in your mouth.

"New faces on the rez?" Jess asks, defaulting to inventory.

"A few white boys chasing our girls," Agnes says, dry. "Nothing flagrant yet. But I'm decorating for the preschool Halloween party and the domestic abuse room. Want in?"

Jess's yes is immediate. They ride the elevator down to the basement, where the preschool lives with its paint-smudged tables, cubbies labeled in shaky handwriting. Agnes opens a box: streamers in harvest colors, balloons, a hand-pump, paper pumpkins with toothy smiles, witches with underbites.

"I want kids," Jess says to a sagging bit of crepe she's coaxing to the ceiling. "I don't know that it's in the cards."

"You have time," Agnes says. "And that handsome FBI man looks at you like you're the only leaf left on the tree."

"Nonsense," Jess says, but her ears go warm. She tapes up a goofy spider and lets the silence breathe. Agnes breaks it with a tilt of her head.

"You know that old barn near the abandoned house where Amber was found last year?" she asks. "We've got a client who's seen a transient girl living there. Dumpster-dives behind the dining hall. Calls herself CJ. Named after a movie star, poor thing,

Chardonnay Jolie. From out west somewhere. Family history of mental illness; our client says hallucinations run in the lineage." Agnes's eyes flicker with that nurse's blend of worry and competence. "She's been telling people there's a clown trying to rape her."

Jess looks up sharply. "A clown."

"I know," Agnes says. "But we've both seen worse truths start with ridiculous words." She takes Jessica's hand. "Will you check on her? Before winter closes its teeth?"

"Today," Jess says. "I'll also run her name. And if you can get her in here, we'll push insurance paperwork, housing waiting lists, whatever it takes."

Agnes squeezes back. "You're family, Jessica," she says softly. "Don't forget."

Rain needles sideways as Jess turns onto the county road. Prairie grass has gone to blond and rattles in the wind. Dispatch logs her destination; she kills the siren long before the broken driveway, and the place unspools out of the weather like a bad memory: the house a flayed ribcage of board-and-batten and busted jalousie glass, the barn a scabbed relic with one hinge weeping rust. The red paint is long gone; what's left is the gray of bones.

She checks her flashlight, her Taser, layers of habit clicking into place. The grasses slap her knees, slick with rain; boulders hide in the thatch like old teeth. Bottles green and brown glint at the bases of reed canary, barnyard grass, and wild rye. Something scuttles. She keeps going, careful of the marsh she knows is here somewhere, seasonally, with regret.

By the barn door, the wind shifts. Tacos, she thinks, surprised. The door's missing a hinge; a barrel props it from the inside. She pushes, and it answers with a scream, so much for stealth.

Inside, there's the thin light of a farm museum: rusting cultivators and tires, soda bottles in milky stacks. Stairs cling to one wall, each step a petition, each reply a louder squeak. At the top, the loft is arranged with the kind of care that breaks you: hay and prairie grass mounded under cardboard boxes; a scatter of clothes in three sizes; fast-food clamshells; a pair of mismatched sneakers drying nose to nose. Two pails catch rain tapping through the roof. On a flattened carton, a small meal gone cold.

She edges to a narrow awning window and works it up. The house fifty feet away shows a slice of interior where the stairs inside have collapsed; you can see the spine of the place like a fish left to bleach. Something moves in that cavity, shadow, animal, person. Jess blinks into the rain. The weather vane atop the cupola squeals, a chicken-voiced alarm.

A flicker at her feet makes her jerk back. Mouse, almost certainly. Enough for today. She takes the stairs sideways, weight near the wall where what strength remains still lives, breathes steadily, eyes on the barrel at the threshold, then the gray open.

"Chardonnay Jolie," Casey repeats, fingers drumming keys back at HQ. "CJ." His brow lifts. "Old socials. A missing-person flyer from—hell—four years ago. A cousin posting prayers, then nothing."

"It's a haunted place," Jess says, rubbing damp from her sleeves. "Even in daylight. Mice, spiders, that weathervane shrieking like it's alive."

"And the person in the house?" Casey asks, too lightly.

"The girl," Jess says. "Or my brain is trying to put a body to worry." She balls up a printout and wings it at him when he smirks. "Don't say clown."

"I wasn't going to say clown," he lies. Then, more seriously: "I'll ask patrol to swing by. Pairs only."

"Good," Jess says. "Before snow hits. Let's not lose another one to the edges."

3

Love's Darkest Road

The sky had gone the color of hammered pewter when the clerk cracked Jessica's door. "Stone, we have a video call from a girl who says the men next door are threatening to rape her. I patched it through. Name's Kaia."

Casey was already half out of his chair. He slid in front of Jess's monitor and hit accept. A young Native woman filled the screen with cheeks slick with tears, a braid ragged over one shoulder, eyes jumping toward a door splintering under fists.

"We're in the guest cottage," she rushed. "Small lakeside of a four-acre property—southeast of the casino. We rented the little one. The big house up the hill is a separate place where those guys are—" The feed hitched, then came back under the drum of boots and coarse laughter. Someone banged on the glass; the pane shivered in the frame.

"We've got your address," Casey said, voice flat and steady. "Units are en route. Stay on the line if you can. We're coming."

Jess was moving before the call clicked off

with her belt, jacket, and keys. The corridor outside their offices smelled of copier toner and rain, the kind of weather that sits in the bones. By the time their convoy of two tribal patrol SUVs and Casey's Bureau truck slewed down a maple-lined gravel lane toward a strip of wind-wrinkled water, the cottage lights flickered like a plea in the lake's reflection.

It was too late for the worst of it. Patrol had kicked the next-door drunks back across the grass and pinned them on the main house's porch rails; one of them still pounded his chest and slobbered threats until an FBI agent leaned in and made the air go quiet. Inside, Kaia lay curled on the edge of a narrow bed, knees to chest, a thin blanket bunched around her. On the other side: her fiancé, pale and slack-mouthed with booze, one hand still on an empty bottle like a child clutching a toy.

Jess crouched to make herself level with Kaia's eyes. The cottage smelled like pine cleaner and lake damp, a cheap candle guttering on the kitchenette ledge.

"Kaia, I'm Jess," she said softly. "From tribal police. I'm so sorry. You're safe now."

The girl swallowed. "We came from South Dakota. It was supposed to be—" Her breath hitched. "They broke the glass and just opened it."

"We'll need to get you to the hospital," Jess said, keeping her voice an anchor. "There's a kit they do; it collects evidence. It helps us put them away."

"The officers pulled them off me," Kaia whispered, shaking. "You saw. Why do I have to—"

"Because a prosecutor needs more than what we witnessed," Jess said, hating the shape of the answer and saying it anyway. "You won't be alone. I'll call ahead. The ambulance is outside."

Kaia's gaze slid to the man snoring beside her. "Will Ryan be okay?" Her voice was small, bewildered.

"He'll be fine," Jess lied to the moment, not the future. "Let's get you taken care of."

Behind them in the doorway, Casey murmured to the CSI tech to photograph the glass, the latch, the scuffs on the painted floorboards where a struggle had kicked up dust. Outside, the lake smacked its little shore like a hand too tired to make a fist.

Morning brought a clean, cruel fact: while a deputy sat watch in a cruiser at the end of that pretty lane, Ryan had woken, heard, and left. He shoved his things in a duffel and told the deputy to tell Kaia he couldn't do it, couldn't unsee what he hadn't seen, couldn't be a fiancé to a woman who three men had raped while he slept.

"That ass," Jess said flatly in the doorway of dispatch. "How's she getting home?"

"The hospital released her," the clerk said, cheeks pinched with anger. "She's sitting on a bench in a too-big hoodie asking for a ride."

"I'll get her," Jess said, already dialing Agnes. "We'll get her all the way home."

She drove Kaia through a mist of leaf-littered roads, past the community's fall banners hanging limp in the damp, NATIVE WOMEN ARE SACRED, past the hotel tower shouldering out of cattails, past the little playground's red slide bright with rain. Inside the community center, warmth and the smell of coffee wrapped around them like a cloak. Vaneeta brought soft-voiced steadiness and a Styrofoam cup with a lid. Agnes materialized as if willed into being, her hand small and fierce in Kaia's.

"We'll drive you back ourselves," Agnes promised. "No buses. No waiting."

"You'll be okay," Jess said, and meant you're not alone. She hugged the girl, felt the tremor in her bones, and tasted rage like pennies. "Our driver's a tribal admin officer. She won't leave your side."

"Thank you." Kaia's eyes glossed, not with relief but with the shock of being held up by strangers when family split and ran.

At the stairs near the reception desk, Jess paused with Agnes. The foyer's tile gleamed; kids' shoes squeaked by in tiny herds.

"He didn't deserve her," Agnes said under her breath. "What is a thirty-six-year-old doing with a twenty-one-year-old if not borrowing shine?"

Jess nodded, jaw tight. "She thinks she's tarnished. He told her that without using words."

"Then we'll replace every mirror in her life with women like us," Agnes said, steel in satin. "Onward, Jessica."

Days later, dressed for warmth and weather, not ceremony, Jess and Casey stood at the arboretum's Japanese garden and watched a wedding unfold like a lantern. The maple leaves were lacquer red, the stones black with rain. Bridesmaids in autumnal satin lifted their hems to pick their way over stepping-stones. The groom waited under a white trellis that framed the waterfall like a painted scroll; the bride came down the terraced slope on her father's arm, veil snagging once in a low branch, and the two of them laughing through it. The officiant's words were carried off by a breeze and returned in pieces: love, patience, home.

They said nothing as they walked afterward through a cathedral of weeping willows, the breath in the leaves a soft applause. The sculpture garden held its metal and marble creatures in the wet light, antlers of steel dripping. In the tea room, heat sighed from a wood-burning fireplace, and the glass doors looked out on a slick stone terrace and beyond it a lawn dotted with pumpkins and puddles. Agnes had saved two seats, as promised; she patted Jess's hand and Casey's shoulder and slid away to let them sit with a difficult grace in a soft place.

By midweek, the rain had rinsed the sky to

China gray. Jess and Casey sat shoulder to shoulder in her office with the glass walls catching the dull daylight while they were scrubbing through camera footage from the gas station near the racetrack inn. The frames clicked by: a kid in a hoodie, a minivan, a man with a Lotto ticket who looked at his shoes like they might answer back.

"Oh, shoot," Jess said, checking her watch. "Corn maze bus. Agnes will kill me."

Casey glanced up, mouth lifting. "You're good with kids," he said. "Good for you to be with joy instead of just this." He gestured at the screen, at the stack of files banded in red elastic.

"Thanks," she said, meeting his eyes in the gleam of the monitor. It was a warm look, brief as a match.

The clerk broke the moment. "Agnes says the bus is loading."

"Tell her I'm coming," Jess said, already halfway up. In the community center lot, Agnes fitted a lime-green vest over Jess's jacket and looped a child leash into her hand like she was issuing a badge. Two new girl, identical, shy, sharp-eyed, clutched each other's sleeves until Jess dropped to their height, introduced herself, and made them laugh. The wind had a bite under the sunshine; the school bus was a yellow casket of sound. At the corn maze, wristbands snapped, hayride breath huffed from the tractor in white gusts, and Jess gathered her brood like a shepherd, ponytail flinging sun when she looked back to count heads.

While Jess was a bright dot in a field of corn, Casey sat with the CSI tech in the hum and tick of HQ and ran Malia's laptop through one more sieve.

"How was the wedding?" the tech asked casually, tapping keys.

"Nice," Casey said, eyes on a progress bar. "The clerk looked happy. Jess looked—" He stopped himself. "It was good to be somewhere; the worst thing was wet shoes."

"How was it being with Jess away from work?"

Casey smiled without looking. "She's a friend."

"Uh-huh."

A patrolman stuck his head in. "Is Jessica back? She said she wanted to ride along to that barn with the reported transient."

"She's still lost in corn with a pack of four-year-olds," Casey said, standing. "I'll go."

Maintenance had laid a safe path through the grasses, mowed a swath, broken glass swept to the ditches, and the house taped with bright warning lines like a crime scene on pause. The barn still hunched like a tired animal. The patrolmen waited hands-on-hips as Casey came up the lane.

They checked the house first: empty, rotten stairs, more suggestion than wood, jalousie slats like missing teeth. "We'd need a ladder for the second floor," Casey said.

"Save it for the day, with more bodies and better insurance."

In the barn, oil and old hay made an ache in the nose. They moved slowly, the way men move when the floor could turn traitor. Mice stitched the shadows. Up the narrow stairs, the loft was laid out like a careful lie: a bed of hay and grass under flattened boxes, a nest of clothing in three sizes, water bottles lined up along a beam. Near the far window, a neat ashtray of cigarette butts made its own small landscape, brown filters like seeds, a spoon blackened at one edge.

"Receipts," Casey said softly, lifting one between gloved fingers. "County Assistance Program voucher. Thrift store down the highway."

The shorter patrolman nodded. "They outfit folks with clothing and basics. CAP office does food vouchers, too."

"The butts," Casey said, peering toward the window. "Only here. Not near the bed."

"Maybe she didn't want ashes by where she sleeps," the taller officer offered.

"Maybe someone else stands here and watches her sleep," Casey said, voice gone hard and narrow. He looked out through the warps of old glass and traced the line of trees that ran from the casino's conference wing down and out like an umbilical made of shade. "We'll keep an eye on it. Two-officer checks. No heroes."

That night, wind prowled Jessica's eaves and

made the maple bang a branch against the gutter like a knocking hand. Dinner was a bubbling comfort, featuring pasta shells stuffed with cheese, hot Italian sausage that had gone ruddy in marinara, and the inexpensive wine tasted like cherries and a hint of smoke. They ate at her little kitchen table, then migrated to the living room where the fireplace threw a friendly orange and their case files lay in a messy geography between them.

"You were right to get Kaia out," Casey said. "The longer she sat there, the more that man's absence would burrow into her."

"She'll hear it in every silence for a while," Jess said. "I keep hearing it for her."

They worked in companionable quiet until Jess rubbed her arms, eyeing the window. "Hard freeze tonight. I'm thinking about CJ in that barn."

Casey hesitated. "You're going to hate what I'm about to say."

"Try me."

"Does the casino ever hire clowns? For birthdays?" He held up a hand as she laughed once, incredulously. "Listen. I know we joked. But up in that loft, Jess, there's a second presence. Butts by the far window, not the bed. A view line straight from the event wing through the trees to the barn. If someone wanted to go unseen, he could. And if she were actually assaulted and told it, the only way anyone would listen—"

"By calling him a clown." Jess blew out a

breath, the shape of resistance turning to thought. "Agnes said CJ's family has a mental illness. Hallucinations. The community believes what's easy to believe."

"So, ask Agnes about clowns," he said gently. "And we keep both things in our hands, what's likely, and what's dangerous if we dismiss it."

"Done," she said. "And the gas station video? You said the CSI pulled something."

"Only thing that stuck was a cyclist in a red tee," Casey said. "Caught from behind, quick. Bulldog graphic."

Jess straightened. "Brown bulldog? Red background?"

Casey's eyes lit. "Where'd you see him?"

She closed hers, chasing the memory like a skittish thing. "I've seen that shirt. Exactly that shirt. Gas pumps? Grocery? Somewhere on the rez property. It pinged, but I didn't know why." She set her glass aside. "I need sleep, not wine."

Casey dug out the print. He turned it toward her with its red tee, blocky bulldog, the posture of someone pedaling away fast. She pressed her lips together, nodding, frustrated. "Tomorrow," she said. "It'll come."

Morning shook off night like a dog out of water. Jess took the stairs two at a time at the community center and nearly collided with Agnes, who steadied both their coffees with the reflexes of a saint.

"Do you know where one can rent a

clown?" Jess asked, deadpan.

Agnes blinked, then laughed softly. "Jessica, are you asking me about a clown?"

"I know how it sounds," Jess said, and laid it out: CJ, the barn, the cigarette butts, the tree line, the way danger dresses itself as a joke long enough for everyone to look away.

Agnes's face sobered. "I have not met the girl," she said, "and I did tell you what our client heard about her family. But you're right, we make sport of gossip in this town. It's not the same thing as truth." She tilted her head toward the preschool murmur on the other side of the wall. "Yes. Clowns exist. Daycare has had them. The preschool here once in a blue moon. Birthdays. I remember a teen who hired one after that horror remake, you know, the red balloon business."

The memory slid into place like a key. Red balloon. Sewer grates strung with them by kids who wanted to scare each other silly. "Can you find out where they rented?"

"Of course," Agnes said, already reaching for a sticky note. "I'll call the daycare first, then that boy's mother. I'll text you before lunch."

They took their coffee to the memorial garden anyway, though fallen leaves matted the stones and the wind nosed cold fingers under their collars. The playground beyond was a bright tangle of color, blue slides, red monkey bars, and a little boy in a green coat hung upside down from a bar, hair making a punctuation mark in the air.

"We turn over every rock," Agnes said, eyes on the boy, on the future. "And if the rock is heavy, we call each other to lift it."

4

Let the Angels Fall

Wind came knifing down the corridor of Nicollet like it had a score to settle with gusts that lifted grit from the curb and set the tarp walls of the encampment shuddering. Shonna White moved through it with her chin tucked into a scarf the color of winter berries, a backpack slung high, latex snap of gloves each time she reached for the next handful. Her voice was soft and sure, a steadying metronome amid the endless shuffle of tired feet and bad bargains.

"Hey, dear—these are for you." A palm-to-palm transfer: condoms, a wallet card with the women's crisis line, her own name in block black ink. "Take care of yourself, okay?"

She bent to the next girl, tiny, bleached hair lifting like thistle in the wind. "Sweetie, take these. Be safe. Call if you need help." Behind them, a space heater chattered in a tent doorway; a woman laughed too loudly, then stopped.

Shonna paused at the corner to fish deeper

in her pack. A city bus sighed at the curb. Somewhere, a bottle broke. She stepped off the curb on the walk sign, lifted her face into the cold, and the sound came hard off the facades, a metallic pop that made the pigeons fling skyward as one. The cardboard box of packets jumped from her hands. Cards and condoms pinwheeled into the wind, bright and helpless. Shonna folded at the knees and then all the way down, a red varnish pooling under her cheek on the slick November asphalt as a white sedan fishtailed and roared away.

Women on the stroll flinched and backed, an instinct born of survival. Passers-by ducked behind cars and called 911 from behind glass and steel. The pharmacy camera at the corner watched without blinking; its pixels later would give up a plate, the mean tilt of a jaw, a history. Half a mile away at a neighborhood market, that same driver had played bully in a fluorescent aisle, barking at a Native mom and her lanky teen son. Clerks remembered. So did news anchors, for a few hours.

The break room TV at tribal HQ showed all of it on a loop, the banner shouting DEVELOPING, the chyrons marching bad facts across the bottom. Jess watched without sitting. Casey came in late, a little gray at the edges, hair askew, poured coffee like penance, and took up a place beside her. Someone stood to offer a chair; he shook his head and stood anyway, hands braced on the laminate counter.

Jess's phone buzzed. "Hey, Agnes, Shonna White, really?" Her voice dropped as she paced into the hall. "Her grandma—was anyone with her when they, okay. Call me if she needs me."

"What is it, Stone?" voices called from the doorway.

She came back and said it flat: "The Indian woman shot in Minneapolis was Shonna White."

A hush drew down like a curtain. The clerk at reception, eyes glossy, said, "I went to school with her. Shonna was—God, she was so smart. She was going to be a doctor."

"We've pushed the APB to surrounding counties," a patrol sergeant added. "Cameras pulled a plate. They think the driver might head out this way to the casino."

Dispatch crackled as if on cue: a white sedan just parked in the main lot under the bright casino banners.

Chairs scraped. Doors banged. Officers poured down the corridor like a weather front.

Security had boxed the sedan in by the time Casey and Jess swung wide into the lot. Floodlights bleached the asphalt. For a heartbeat, the main doors breathed out a crowd, and the man was just there, coming down the stairs fast, big shoulders in a grubby jacket, chin out, eyes mean with beer. Jess's voice on the radio, "I see him coming out, main steps," and then she was moving, and everyone else was, too.

"Police! Stop!" The word tore into the cold. He didn't. He turned instead, a crude pivot, gun up, and fired once with a greasy spark that made the air itself cower. Jess dropped behind a concrete planter, stone biting her palms. Casey kept coming, then caught the whip of a bullet past his ear and stopped just long enough to make the math. He fired, controlled, and the man's knee went slack. The gun clattered. Hands went up.

"Chris Gohlke," someone breathed. A name to put teeth in the anger.

"You're under arrest," Casey said, voice low enough to make the words heavier. He Mirandized while hauling the bleeding bull of a man to the SUV, away from phones and the hungry circle of onlookers. Officers formed a wall. The ambulance washed blue and red across the casino façade.

Gohlke couldn't help himself. He spilled poison whenever a Native face came near. "Indian women play coy," he jeered, laughter bubbling like something rotten. "Alluring me until they fleece me. I'd take out more if—"

Nobody bit. Not the patrol, not the paramedics. The words dissolved on cold air and pavement.

But Jess took them like a blow to the ribs. She carried them, silent, all the way back to headquarters, up the steps, through the glass doors, and into the tidy fluorescent.

Casey stepped into her path at her office door. "I need a hug," he said simply.

"Back off, Casey."

"I mean it, Jess."

She stood there a second longer than she felt safe, then stepped into him. He wrapped his arms around her without squeezing, like victory, more like ballast. "He's an asshole," he said into her hair, soft. "He doesn't get a room in your head."

She let go first, wiping at her eye as if it were dust and not grief. Casey paused to speak a word to the clerk who'd known Shonna, gentled his voice, then came in to find Jess staring at the glossy print of a man on a bicycle in a red bulldog tee, caught from behind, neck cords taut, anonymity smug.

"If only we had his face," Casey said, knowing it added nothing and saying it to keep the air moving. "We could run FR and pull him from every social feed he ever—"

"I know." Her eyes didn't leave the page.

"What if we post it at the community center with a small reward? Even twenty-five."

He tilted his head. "Would anyone move for that?"

"Hunger is a motivator," she said. "Single moms. Elders on fixed incomes. It buys diapers. It buys soup. We'd get calls."

"Then we do it."

The community center breathed steam and coffee and the lemony disinfectant of the clinic. Jess stood waiting on the elevator, watching tiny kids trail their mothers like ducklings, each with a new hat or a new cough. Inside the lift, she tilted her head back and pressed the heel of her palm between her brows, one small tear sliding down without permission.

"Oh, Jessica." Bernice came around a corner like a comforting aunt, and behind her stood Agnes, eyes full. Vaneeta lifted the stack of flyers from Jess's hands before Jess even asked. "I'll hang them everywhere," Vaneeta said. "Every corkboard, both restrooms, the clinic desk."

"Coffee," Agnes announced, the commander of a kinder army. "Sit."

Jess set the Styrofoam on Agnes's desk and sank into the familiar armchair. Outside the window, the playground kite tails snapped in the wind; a row of memorial stones caught the light like old bones.

"How's Shonna's grandma?" she asked.

"Devastated," Agnes said quietly. "She heard about his mouth. Words travel faster than grief."

Jess stared into her cup. "There are so many who look at Native women as something to handle, or erase."

"They are intimidated," Agnes said, chin lifting. "By girls who are bright and ambitious and unafraid. It's always been so." She tapped the flyers. "Tell me."

"We have a person of interest in Malia's case," Jess said. "The only shot we have is his back on a gas station cam. Bicyclist. Red shirt. I've seen him, Agnes. I just can't place where."

Agnes didn't answer right away. She watched Jess instead. "Part of my quiet is Shonna," she admitted. "The other part is you. You're carrying too much alone, Jessica. That anger, earned as it is, keeps you braced all day, and bracing is exhausting."

"I'm not crazy."

"Therapy isn't a verdict," Agnes said gently. "It's a tool. After Claudia died, I went off-rez because I needed to say things without worrying how it would ripple." She opened a drawer, sifted like she knew exactly where the thing lived, and handed over a simple cream card. "Megan. Across the river. Warm. Unafraid of hard truths."

Jess held it, thumbed the embossed number. "I don't want to talk to Bernice about the community. It'd put her in a bind."

"Then don't," Agnes said, smiling. "Let an outsider love you a little."

By the time Jess came back down the highway, she had an appointment on her calendar and Casey waiting by the door, two to-go coffees, and a plan. They hit the gas station first; the manager squinted at the print and said the shirt rang a bell, promised to ask his night clerks, and pointed them to the corkboard by the Lotto display.

At the racetrack inn, a clerk with a neat part and a bored expression took two copies, one for the lobby, one for the breakroom. "Is this the drainage pond lady?" he asked. Jess nodded once and watched him tape their hope to cheap oak veneer.

At The Copper Mule, Pam met them mid-aisle with menus and a look. "What are we hunting today?"

"A man in a bulldog tee," Jess said.

Pam's nose wrinkled. "Oh, that shirt. He's been here, sure. Twice? Three times tops. Not exactly Mr. Personality. Gave off 'still lives with his mother' vibes. Sat at the bar, stared at the TV like it owed him money."

"Anything else?" Casey asked.

"Thirty-something, maybe. Cobalt eyes," Pam said, surprising herself. "One of the ladies mentioned them."

"Show Matt?" Jess asked. "See if he remembers."

Pam carried a flyer to the bar. Matt glanced, snorted, and pitched his voice too big. "Guess I should be grateful I'm not a suspect this time."

"Matt," Jess said evenly.

He shrugged. "Yeah. Saw him. Quiet. Watered his whiskey for an hour. Light tipper. Hot eyes, if you're into that kind of deadness."

"Thank you," Casey said through his teeth as Pam walked away.

"What is that saying?" he muttered when Matt was out of earshot. "Honey, flies."

"Matt's never been accused of honey," Jess said, pushing the menu back. "I need a breakfast platter and orange juice."

"Burger," Casey told Pam, "And water."

Jess fiddled with the corner of a flyer. "Do you think I need counseling?"

"For your anger?" he asked, not unkindly.

"That's a yes."

"I think you carry a lot," he said. "And I think you'd breathe easier if you had a place to put some of it down. That doesn't make you weak. It makes you smart."

"Agnes thinks so, too."

"See someone off-rez," he said. "Clean edges. No echoes."

"Would you ever go?"

"If I were bleeding on the people around me," he said. "Or if it made the job blur."

"Okay," she said, half to herself. "Okay."

The counseling center lived in a pair of glass-and-stone buildings across from a mall where the parking lot sprouted ornamental pears. Wild turkeys ambled like small armored cars along the nature trail behind the offices. Inside, the lobby smelled of bergamot and rain. An enormous chandelier made of glass leaves hung like frost.

Megan's office had lighting that understood how to hold a nervous person without overhead glare, just lamps, a rug soft enough to anchor thoughts, and a settee by a window with a thin view of water.

"You have a beautiful space," Jess said, sitting where the chair let her see the lake.

"In summer, you can hear loons," Megan said, and then let the quiet invite whatever came. "What brings you in, Jessica?"

"I'm angry," Jess said. "People see it. I can't carry it as far as I have to go."

Megan nodded. "Anger is often the bodyguard for sorrow."

Jess told the abbreviated version about Malia and Shay, and Shonna under the cold city light; men with opinions about disappearing Native women; the dirtier truth, the one she said without flinching now: I'm the product of a rape. My mother went to prison for killing him. When she got out she was found in a ditch. They call me 'prison baby' when they want to cut me down.

"It eats at me all day," she said. "I don't show it. But it eats."

"Cognitive behavioral therapy," Megan said, not like a prescription, more like a tool held out for inspection. "We learn to catch the thought behind the feeling, examine it for accuracy, and then decide if we want to keep it. Over time, that gap between trigger and reaction gets a little wider. Enough to breathe."

"Thoughts to actions to moods," Jess said. "And when someone says something cutting in the middle of an arrest?"

"You do your job," Megan said. "Later, sometimes ten minutes later, sometimes at red lights, you replay it, name the thought, name the feeling it birthed, and then choose a counterthought on purpose. It's work. But it's a way out of carrying poison that isn't yours."

Jess let out a breath she didn't know she'd held. "So, am I cured?"

Megan smiled. "We practice. We add relaxation tools. Coping strategies. We build resilience like muscle. Let's start biweekly and see how it lands."

Jess stood at the window afterward and watched a V of geese drop into the lake like a black seam being sewn shut. On the walk back to her car, wild turkeys looked up from pecking and, unimpressed, went back to their business. She put the business card in her wallet behind her badge, a talisman beside an oath, and drove back into the work.

5

Dreaming Through the Noise

The call bled through the intercom with the flatness of bad news. "Detective Sergeant Stone? Debi Lawson is being reported missing. Do you want the family here, or should we send someone out to take the report?"

Jess's hand froze above the mess of files on her desk, then she flicked a look at Casey and stood. "Tell them I'm coming to them."

"Who's Debi?" he asked, already reaching for his jacket.

"My best friend in high school." Jess's voice softened, then tightened. "Dartmouth, then Berkeley for Ethnic Studies. She did NGO work like refugee shelters, church basements, police station lobbies and then moved back last summer on fire to change the world. I... we lost touch. I was proud and—honestly?—jealous." She took a breath. "Her parents are pillars. Mom's an attorney, and Dad runs loans at the tribal credit union. Two younger sisters nearby, both married, are tight-knit. If they called us, it's bad."

"Keys," Casey said gently, palm out. "I'll drive."

The Lawson house sat at the last bend of a ridge road where the oaks fell away and the horizon came in as a long thought. The place seemed to inhale light: a timbered mountain of a home with a glassy prow and a roofline like a gull's wing. Stone columns shouldered the entry; the wraparound deck caught the whole sky.

Inside, the great room rose two stories under a ribcage of beams, the kind of space that made conversation hush. Motorized shades whispered up at Karsyn's touch, giving the valley back to the room. Walnut floors ran like a river from the stone hearth to a long bank of windows; soft Persian rugs pooled here and there. Light found marble, found buffed oak, found the old inlay of an antique buffet built into a wall that looked like it had always been there.

Karsyn met them halfway, eyes rimmed and steady with effort. "Jessica—thank God. If you're here, I know someone's going to take this seriously. Debi did not run off."

Wallace came from the kitchen with a hand out, jaw set in that way men get when they've decided not to break. "Agent Borgreve, good to have you. We appreciate both of you."

"We've kept the drapes closed," Karsyn said, as if answering a question they hadn't asked. "People slow down on the road. We've got our girls and their little ones staying here for now." She swallowed. "I can't lose another child."

"Any unusual cars? Hang-up calls? Anyone hanging around?" Casey asked.

"Nothing," Wallace said. "Just idiots saying she finally met a man and took a long weekend." His mouth twisted. "Ask Jessica—that's not our Debi."

Karsyn nodded. "Friday night, she ran into town for Chinese. Chloe offered to ride along; Debi teased that she'd only slow her down. Keys, phone, a wave, and that's the last we saw of her. The gossip says she was sneaking to meet someone. They're wrong."

"Can we see her room?" Casey asked.

"Of course. The house cleaners don't touch personal things."

They took a broad staircase that made you want to run your hand along the rail. The lower level was its own small resort with two master suites, a pocket-sized spa with a massage table and warm stone, an art studio with a kiln whose metal mouth looked like an embered cave, a library with a ladder on tracks, a card room and billiards under amber lamps, a home theater with seats like small starships. The air had that cinnamon-cedar undertone of careful wealth.

Debi's suite sat farthest from the stairs. The door opened on white stucco and whitewashed planks, a spill of cobalt that felt like sea and sky had been bottled for winter. Arches winked and repeated; a wrought-iron canopy bed held the room like a line of poetry. A credenza wore a flat screen and a scatter of travel trinkets like teacups painted with Greek keys, indigo throws, and a bowl of sea glass. The bath gleamed: a slipper tub with one swanlike end higher than the other, nickel fixtures, stacks of towels tied with twine. French doors opened onto a private nook with quarry tile and citrus in pots, the little patio stepping down to an infinity edge that spilled the country right into the pool.

"She called it modern Mediterranean style," Karsyn said, drifting a hand over a pillow. "Half her life's in here. Blankets and baubles from everywhere. She loved Greece and said the patterns felt like home."

Jess put a palm on Karsyn's shoulder while Casey worked the room the way he always did: under the mattress, behind frames, fingertips checking the undersides of nightstands, a cautious pass along the baseboards. He lifted the laptop from the desk, turned it, and bagged it. In the bath, he opened the medicine cabinet and found nothing but sunscreen and a cracked-open bar of Marseille soap.

Back upstairs, the family had gathered as if the house itself had called them. Chloe, ten years younger, hair in a dark braid, stood with her arms locked across her chest; Emma, five years closer to Debi, hugged a mug with both hands. Wallace watched them from the hearth; Karsyn kept a hand on a counter stool as if the room might tilt.

"Debi dating anyone?" Casey asked. "Crushes? Messages?"

Chloe shook her head immediately. "Nobody here. She's always... going. Grad apps, planning trips. Men here feel small to her, if that makes sense."

Jess softened the edge. "Anyone paying her attention she didn't want?"

"Not that she told us," Emma said. "She wasn't cagey. Just busy."

Casey handed over cards with both their cell numbers. "We'll take the laptop for a bit. If anything—anything—comes up, call."

Chloe came back from the kitchen with the laptop charger and a slip of notebook paper. "Her phone's been glitchy. She had a new one on order; it was supposed to arrive on Saturday. The password for the laptop might be 'nautilus' or 'Aegean' as she was on a theme."

They were back in the SUV, gravel spitting, when the river called them. Dispatch: a canoeist had hit something big near the sandbar where the valley narrowed and the water ran slow as glass. Jess felt that little drop in her stomach that comes when you already know, and you keep going anyway.

The dirt road gave way to a little pullout where an athletic young man in hydrophobic layers paced with his hands in his hair. His canoe bumped lazily against the mud; a patrol unit idled, lightbar asleep. The air smelled like wet leaves and the metallic chill of November water.

"Agent Borgreve. Detective Stone," Casey said. "You're…?"

"Colton Reed. Linden Hills," he said too fast. He swallowed. "I come out for the quiet."

"Start to finish," Casey said. "Where'd you put in?"

"Trailhead lot. Forty-five minutes downriver."

"And then?"

"I skimmed something near that berm," he pointed, "reached down, caught a cord. When I pulled, it surfaced. Wrapped tight in a blue sheet, both ends duct-taped, concrete block on it." He swallowed again. "I cut the cord at the block, tied it to the canoe, brought it here. I thought maybe—" He stopped.

"Thank you," Casey said. "We'll need your information. Are you willing to provide DNA for elimination?"

Colton's eyes flicked from Casey to Jess and back, as if gauging judgment. "Of course."

The coroner's van came in low gear, crunching gravel. The coroner and her assistant moved with practiced quiet, no drama, just respect. She gloved up, bootied, clicked her thermometer, and worked like this was her liturgy. "Body's likely been down two days at least," she murmured. "I'll know better at the table." The gurney straps whispered.

Casey turned toward the river, eyes scanning the way debris snagged against fallen branches and drifted free. Jess watched a hawk work its slow geometry above the cottonwoods and felt something in her chest unstring.

Back at HQ, the day became small squares: file directories, cached maps, emails with subject lines that meant everything and nothing. The CSI unit cloned Debi's drive; Casey worked with one screen on texts and another on bank logins. Everything about Debi's life on paper echoed what the house had already told them: ordered, determined, relentlessly forward.

Late, the coroner's report buzzed Casey's phone. He read it once, then again out loud, the list clinical until it wasn't. "ID confirmed by driver's license and dentals. Postmortem interval consistent with 48–72 hours. BAC point-three-two. Primary cause: acute alcohol poisoning. Postmortem blunt-force trauma to the head and face. Body wrapped and placed in the river."

Jess slid her palms into her hair, fingers resting at her scalp until it hurt enough to be a different feeling. A single tear slipped, and she let it. "I'll tell them."

"You'll tell them with me," Casey said, already on his feet.

The following morning, the counseling office felt like it had remembered Jess overnight and saved her a chair. Megan met her in the doorway with a slight nod, and Jess felt herself exhale for the first time since the riverbank.

"I can't do CBT in the moment," Jess said as soon as the door clicked behind them. "I can't 'reframe' while I'm standing over duct tape."

"It isn't for the duct tape," Megan said, tone like warm water. "It's homework. Field medic on scene, surgeon in the OR. Tell me about your night."

Jess stared out at the scrape of the lake through the window. "We found a friend. My friend. She was drowned in liquor before someone rearranged her face. Wrapped like garbage. Sunk like a problem to solve later."

"And the thought that came with that?"

"That Native women are trash to be discarded." Jess heard her voice and almost didn't recognize it. "It's not fact, but it's how it lives in me."

"That's interpretation," Megan said. "Not lie, not truth, but an interpretation built on a lifetime of evidence you didn't ask for. We'll look at thought, feeling, body, and behavior. What did you do after?"

"I drank a bottle of wine and slept like a rock thrown in a river."

"Okay," Megan said, no judgment in it. "Boots and bootstraps can coexist with softness. Today we plan alternatives. Social ones. Bowling. A class. A walk with someone who makes you laugh."

"I have a treadmill."

"We're looking for people," Megan

pointed out. "Not machines."

"I don't want to be seen," Jess said, softer. "In public spaces I feel... read. Judged."

"Can you read minds?" Megan asked lightly.

Jess almost smiled. "Feels like it."

"Then you're omnipotent," Megan said, eyebrows up. "Or maybe folks have their own jobs, kids, bills, toothaches, and are barely noticing you. We hold both possibilities and choose the one that hurts less and is no less plausible."

Jess nodded, slowly. "I was trying not to think that it could have been me."

"That's a true fear," Megan said. "And it didn't happen to you. Both are true. Who in your life proves your generalization false?"

"Casey," she said immediately. "Others, too. But him, most."

"Good," Megan said. "Notice your body with the thought. Stomach, head, breath?"

"Tight. Sick. Weak."

"Now we start catching the thought, naming the feeling, breathing three slow counts, and offering yourself a counterthought on purpose. We do it in the car, at red lights, in parking lots, after the scene is cold." She smiled. "This is practice. We don't white-knuckle alone—we make it a partnership."

Jess sat with that, turned it around. "Okay."

"Okay," Megan echoed. "Go to work. And after work, do one small social thing on purpose."

River Road undid itself in gray ribbons and fallow fields. Hobby farms slept in the hush between harvest and snow. Bare cottonwoods showed their architecture; maples and ash stood like shadow plays against a pale sky. Jess drove it slowly on purpose, letting the valley keep her company, and found herself turning into the dirt track almost without deciding. The old barn hunched against the wind like a sinister secret. The house beside it sagged into itself.

She moved through the grasses with her flashlight and the patience that comes when your clothes are already wet and your socks are already cold. The barn door gave with its old complaint. Inside, the smell of oil and dust, old hay, and rodent. Upstairs, the loft had the same lived-in ache with layered wrappers, bottles, the messy nest of a bed. The food was fresh in the way trash is fresh like last night's grease, this morning's onion. No CJ. No anyone. She left a note tucked under a water bottle: *CJ, come to the Community Center. Ask for Agnes. Safe people. —J.S.* Then she backed out, checked the house from a distance, and went to work.

Casey met her at the door like a guilted brother. "Called you a dozen times," he said. "Almost drove by. Figured you were hiding from the job, which meant hiding from me."

"I was," Jess said. "I drank the wine like an idiot and slept. Saw Megan this morning. I'm working on it."

"Good," he said, the word like a porch light.

That night, his taillights trailed her home like a promise. They ate on the floor in front of her fire, knees knocking the coffee table, laptop screens reflecting in their glasses. They made notes; they scrolled, they filled silence with the slight noise of companionship. When the bottle went empty, Jess laughed once, rueful. "This is exactly what Megan said not to do. But she did say be social."

"She's right," Casey said. "I'm glad you're not alone in this. And I'm glad you're letting someone outside of me carry part of it."

Jess tipped her head back against the couch. "I'm just going to close my eyes—" she said, and then she was asleep, her breath evening out, the fire painting the room with its small, moving gold.

Casey turned the gas down until it purred. He shook a throw and covered her shoulders, another across her feet. He washed their plates, set the glasses in the sink, and turned off the lights with his elbow. He locked the door behind him and stepped into the deep cold.

The road out past the casino ran black and empty. The barn rose ahead like a darker dark with a single square of dull light in its loft window. He slowed, checked the mirror, turned down the dirt track, and rolled to a stop with his headlights off, the engine ticking as the cold took it.

He took a flashlight and his taser, not because he thought he'd need them but because habit is a kind of prayer. The barn door gave, and he moved the way you do when a staircase has already told you once it's thinking about failing. On the main floor, his light balled over implements and spilled oil, mice darting away at its edge. Upstairs, the lantern threw a campfire halo against the roof ribs. The air wore three smells: cigarette, beer, and cheap burger. The pile of butts in the far corner had a red glow barely there, a whiff of heat he could almost believe he imagined until it smarted the nose. On the bed, a carton with a half-eaten burger slumped under wax paper. The blankets, layer on layer of thrift, rose like a small hill.

Casey crossed to the window and leaned out enough to catch a slice of the hill beyond the barn. Two figures—human as language—ran down the slope under the spill of light from the county road, shadows lengthening like frightened things. Farther off, the casino's uplights painted the low clouds like an artificial dawn. Somewhere, an owl called the world back to itself.

He stood a long minute, thinking about cold, and girls, and the way a place can keep secrets just by being inconvenient. He took a small evidence envelope from his pocket and pinched a half-dozen butts into it with the kind of delicacy that looks like care and is also procedure. Then he clicked off the lantern, let the loft go to darkness, and felt the chill lay its hand across his neck as he found the stairs.

Outside, his breath made ghosts. He looked once more at the barn's black square of window, then at the road back to town, and thought of Jess asleep under a throw, of Megan's card in her wallet, of the way the noise of this job fills every room. He started the SUV and let the heater thrum, the dirt road opening ahead in the beams like a ribbon unfurling, the reservation beyond, dreaming through the noise.

6

Sympathy for the Damned

Morning came thin and pewter, a frost line etched along the curb where the sun hadn't reached. When Stone and Borgreve swung through the sliding glass doors of tribal police HQ, the lobby smelled of burned coffee and lemon cleaner, and the humming fluorescents made everyone look a shade too pale. Janine lifted a hand from behind her computer—her eyes flicked past them toward the far wall.

The young woman there was all edges and tremor: early twenties, runner's calves in scuffed trainers, a casino-logo hoodie tugged over a tank top, hair in a hurried knot with wisps stuck to tear-damp cheeks. The alcohol came off her like a ghost of last night, sweet, sour, a stale bite.

Jess crouched so they were level. "I'm Detective Sergeant Stone. This is FBI Special Agent Borgreve. What's your name? How old are you?"

"Ashlynn Bissette." The voice tried for steady and failed. "From out by Glacier in

Montana. I'm twenty-three. I waitress in the poker club." She sniffed hard, like that might keep her from coming apart.

"Can we help you today?" Jess asked, softly.

Ashlynn folded forward, elbows to knees, the sob taking her in one long shudder. Jess guided her up, palm to elbow, cool skin, gooseflesh, and steered her down the hall. In Stone's glass-walled office, the light was kinder, filtered by the dry-erase notes scrawled over everything, a city of names and arrows and times. Jess shut the door; the world muted to HVAC and the faint tick of her wall clock.

Ashlynn clutched her phone like a talisman, then thrust it out. "I went for a run and... I don't remember. I woke up in the brush by the river. I hurt everywhere. I felt like—" She swallowed. "I felt like I'd had sex. I checked my phone and there's a video."

Jess slipped a glove on, tapped play, watched without blinking. When it ended, she passed the phone, glove, and all to Casey. His jaw hardened as he watched. On the glass wall behind Jess, the reflection of the video stuttered: fractured light, a figure too close, the disorienting rainbow of some cheap prismatic filter that turned horror into something unreal.

"I didn't know what was happening," Ashlynn whispered. "I can't remember a thing. I swear."

"Have you showered?" Casey asked.

"No. I thought—like in the movies—you're

not supposed to till they do the test."

"That's exactly right," Jess said, heat in her throat. "We'd like you to go to the hospital for a rape kit. It'll take a while, but it's important."

"And the clothes from last night?" Casey asked.

"I kept them. On my bed. I just put this on and came here."

Jess nodded. "We'll have Janine take you to the hospital and then back to collect your clothes. Is that okay?"

Ashlynn's eyes searched both their faces, desperate. "You believe me, right?"

"We're going to do everything we can," Casey said, and for once his voice didn't carry any steel, just a promise.

They worked gently through the timeline. Jess laid a laminated map on the desk; the plastic was cool under Ashlynn's fingernail as she traced.

"Out the door at four," Ashlynn said, closing her eyes to find it. "I saw an older couple with one of those tiny Pomeranian cloud-dogs around four-thirty. Then a young couple with a stroller. I ran the valley trails till full dark. It got so cold that my fingers hurt through my sleeves. I turned back. A white or silver sedan kept rolling past slowly. He stopped. Brown hair? I can't. His face was chubby. Not fat, just full. Late twenties? And his eyes—I'll never forget—but I can't remember the color when I try." She pressed the heels of her hands into her eye sockets. "I woke up on gravel. I threw up on this rock the size of a basketball. Here." Her finger tapped the map by a familiar bend where river searches always started.

Jess slid out to the squad room, touched Janine's shoulder, and enlisted a backup clerk to cover the phones. When she brought Janine in, Ashlynn's breath steadied at the sight of a woman with gentle hands and practical boots. "We'll be with you the whole way," Janine said, and Ashlynn nodded like it hurt.

After the door closed on them, silence pressed in. Jess exhaled. "Is he our guy?"

"The video's junked up with that prism effect." Casey scrubbed back and forth, eyes narrowing. "He's hiding something red in his hand. The edge looks wet. He's draped a black sweatshirt over it."

"Knife?" Jess asked.

"Could be." He set the phone down like it might bite. "She reads credibly. Running is part of her life. The GHB window's tight— we're pushing the twelve hours. Blood draw might save it."

By the time Ashlynn returned, paler and wrapped in a hospital blanket like armor, the CSI tech waited with evidence bags. A sketch artist arrived with charcoal and newsprint, and they settled in the conference room under the humming light. The pencil moved with a heavy brow, receding hairline, boyish cheeks on a grown man, and those eyes, deliberate as pins. Cobalt. Ashlynn's breath hitched when the artist finally shaded them the right depth.

Casey sent the finished sketch to his team in one tapped message. Thirty seconds later, it was on a path to every newsroom within a hundred miles.

They drove Ashlynn home, where the trailers clustered near the racetrack, plastic Halloween ghosts still twisting from porch rails in the wind. Her door was flimsy; the linoleum inside had those crescent scuffs of chair legs. A plant in a coffee can leaned toward a small window. Jess bagged Ashlynn's running gear while Casey canvassed the neighbors, holding up the sketch. Nobody had seen the chubby boy-man with the bright eyes. People shrugged, squinted, and closed curtains.

They took the gravel road to Debi's place with the heater turned high and the air smelling faintly of antifreeze. Karsyn and Wallace were already in the front yard, coats pulled tight, as if waiting outside might bring better news faster.

"Any word?" Karsyn's voice had that crack in it like thin ice.

"Not yet," Jess said. "We'd like to show you something."

Inside, the house felt colder than before, as if grief had lowered the thermostat. Casey unfolded the sketch on the coffee table; the paper looked too rough for this room. Karsyn's hand flew to her mouth; her eyes went wide and then glassed over.

"He was on his bike by our mailbox," she

said, voice gone hoarse. "At the trail. He said he was looking for his buddy Jack."

"Jack who?" Casey asked, then caught Jess's look, softened it. "If you remember."

"Laframboise," Karsyn sobbed. "Jack Laframboise. Oh, God. Debi would have... she would have stopped. She always—she would have told him his eyes were striking. She would have introduced herself." The thought broke her; Wallace's arm was around her before she finished.

"We'll have extra patrols through your road," Jess said. "We won't let him circle back on you."

Chloe shook her head. "I haven't seen him." Emma frowned. "Maybe... the bowling alley? In the arcade? I'm not sure. Those eyes..."

"Thank you," Casey said, folding the sketch. "We'll be at the funeral tomorrow."

Jess glanced at him, surprised. He met it with a small shrug: *for you.*

They were rolling down the boulevard when memory landed in Jess's chest like a dropped stone. "Stop—here." She pointed. "Last time we were here, you nearly clipped a cyclist. Red shirt. Bulldog on the back. That was him."

They didn't have a face then. Now they did.

At the Glenbows' place, the St. Bernards thundered up as if joy hadn't learned grief, tongues out, tails batting the air. Sara and Darby opened the heavy doors to Jess's knock with eyes ringed, shoulders squared for bad news that didn't get better. They studied the sketch in the light that poured through those high windows, shook their heads, unhappy to be of no help. "Thank you for telling us first," Darby said. "Not hearing it from the TV."

Back in the SUV, Casey's phone buzzed twice with lab notifications. He read, jaw set. "GHB traces in Ashlynn's blood. BAC point-two-six this long after. They found semen."

"He's poisoning and filming," Jess said, voice flat. "Our guy."

"We'll stack charges like cordwood," Casey said. "He won't see daylight for a long time." He glanced at the clock. "Paperwork now, or...?"

"The bowling alley," Jess said. "Arcade. See if those cobalt eyes haunt the skee-ball lanes."

The bowling center along the southern stretch of the rez always smelled like shoe spray and fryer oil, like Saturday afternoons in a town that couldn't quite decide if it was a city. Kids shrieked; pins crashed like small avalanches; the arcade thrummed with pixelated gunfire and the tinny martial music of machines. They paid for two lanes, taped a flyer to the counter, another to the soda machine, a third near the prize counter. Staff nodded solemnly and took more to the breakroom.

Men who looked too old for air hockey stood around pretending not to watch children. When Jess and Casey laced up rental shoes and started tossing strikes like they'd been born to it, the loiterers evaporated into the parking lot one by one.

"Where'd you learn that?" Jess asked after his fourth clean frame.

"Unrequited love," he said, grinning. "She worked here. I had to get good enough to impress her."

"Did it work?"

"Not even a little."

They watched the arcade entrances between frames. A cluster of kids in matching camp T-shirts swarmed the ticket blaster; an exhausted parent rubbed her temples with her knuckles. Somewhere, a prize bell dinged. No cobalt eyes. No red bulldog shirt.

"Let's ask Jack about his 'buddy,'" Jess said.

Jack Laframboise's house was all magazine spreads and antlers. The covered porch made a cathedral of the front door; inside, timber beams crossed and recrossed like a high mountain trail. Modern ironwork stair rails cut clean lines through all that wood. A wall of windows poured the afternoon over stone columns. The wild game mounts looked down like old kings.

The maid let them in to the hush of money. Downstairs, the family room stretched in a long, low glamour—double see-through fireplaces, an eighty-inch screen, a glossy bar that could seat a small team. Through glass, the subterranean sport court held Jack in a sweat-dark tee, breathing hard as he took jumpers under a ceiling with more air than most houses.

Destiny breezed in from the screened porch with autumn air in her hair. "Jessica? How'd you get in?"

"The maid," Casey said apologetically.

Destiny's smile flattened a degree. "What can we do for you?"

"We need a word with Jack," Jess said. "It's about the murders."

Jack came in with a towel looped around his neck, impatience already on his mouth. "I'm not a suspect."

"Good news then," Casey said, tone neutral. He passed the sketch.

Jack glanced and snorted. "Yeah, I've seen him the little chunk who haunts the arcade. Likes to hang around teenage boys. Bit of a creep."

"Girls?" Jess asked.

"Mostly boys," Jack said, flipping the towel end to end. "Doubt the guy could get a date if he tried. Awkward. Peculiar."

"Can you contact him?"

Before Jack could answer, a voice from upstairs called, "Jack, your trainer's here!"

Jack tossed the towel on a barstool and waved a vague hand. "No idea how to reach him." Then he peeled off toward the corridor, the trainer, a younger man built like a plank, falling in step with him.

Destiny kept her smile on. "Anything else?"

"Post the flyer," Casey said. "Call if he shows."

They took the long way out, letting the

house parade past with its custom cabinets in a kitchen the size of a chapel, Cambria stone gleaming, a breakfast nook tucked into a banquette beneath arched windows. Two children had colonized the cushions with crayons and crackers. Through French doors to a study, a maid dusted a walnut desk with reverence.

"Thank you," Casey told her, reflexively polite to workers. She startled, then smiled back, surprised to be seen.

Twilight lifted as they drove. Jess lifted a hand toward the dark smudge on the horizon, where the familiar ruin of house and barn was. "Can we check on CJ?"

They split the property with an old cop's choreography with Jess at the front of the barn, Casey slipping around the back where the grass grew waist-high and seedheads rattled. Inside, the smell of cold wood and mice. Jess tapped with a stick at the corners of the loft before advancing; the floor creaked like something deciding. The air had that knife-edge of November. Her breath plumed in the dim.

"Lost and Found," she read off a beat-up liquor box filled with scarves and dollar-store gloves, a baseball cap with a logo from three states away, sunglasses with one arm mended in tape. "She lifted this from somewhere. Bar? Diner?"

"Or someone dumped a bin out of pity," Casey said, toeing a pile of pilled sweaters. "She's building a nest."

"Warm is generous." Jess rubbed her forearms through her jacket. "How long on those cigarette butts you grabbed last week?"

"Couple of weeks out," Casey said. "Backlog at the lab."

"Agnes hear anything?" Jess asked as they clattered down.

"Ask her," he said. "She's your antenna to this place."

She was already thinking the same. At the Community Center, the second-floor hallway smelled like paper and lavender hand cream. In Agnes's office, lamps turned the corners warm. A mug waited on the desk like Agnes had known the minute Jess would walk in.

"It's hard, what you're doing," Agnes said as soon as the door clicked. "Harder than people say."

"I started seeing someone," Jess said, cradling the cup. "A therapist off-rez. It helps. It's work."

Agnes's whole face lit. "I'm proud of you." She eased back in her chair. "CJ?"

"Any word?"

"She's made friends," Agnes said, mouth a worried line. "Some of ours bring food and clothes. They're good-hearted. But she keeps talking about a clown. I think she needs warmth and medicine and a locked door she can choose to open."

"Names?"

"Charity and Savannah Harris have been

kind to her. They're at the natural foods store most days." Agnes hesitated. "They may clam up if they think you're taking CJ."

"I'll go gently," Jess promised. "Ask sideways. Talk lettuce and apples first."

"Any luck on your bicyclist?"

Jess set the sketch on Agnes's desk. The cobalt eyes felt electric in this gentle room. "We sent this to the news an hour ago. He's getting boxed in."

Outside, late wind skated dry leaves along the walk. Through the south windows, the casino's uplights cut the dusk, bright and indifferent, while the rez settled toward night with porch lamps flicking on, kitchen windows gold as loaves fresh from the oven, and, somewhere out beyond the last streetlight, a cold barn holding its breath.

7

Paper Cuts Still Bleed

By the time Stone and Borgreve gave up on the natural foods store, the Harris twins were polite and unhelpful, the produce misting system hissing like a snake, the afternoon had thinned into a gray that made the parking lot feel colder than the air deserved. Back at HQ the lobby's heater rattled like an old bus. Janine looked up from her monitor, then tipped her chin toward the waiting room.

A small girl sat alone on the vinyl bench, legs swinging, ponytail askew, a pink backpack hugged to her chest. Her sneakers didn't reach the floor; the rubber toes knocked a small rhythm against the bench's metal leg. Behind the reception glass, Janine's voice was low and urgent.

"Her mother just came in, barely conscious. Passers-by picked them up off the shoulder out by County 6. They were afraid whoever hurt her was trailing them, so they brought them straight here. Mom is on the breakroom couch till the ambulance can get here. Looks like cardiac, maybe stroke, hit her right as she came in."

Jess knelt so the girl didn't have to look up so far. "Hey. I'm Jessica, and this is Casey. What's your name?"

"Shelby." The teeth she flashed were small and new, the smile a brave thing that didn't reach her eyes.

"How old are you, Shelby?"

"Five. I'm in kindergarten." Pride glowed for a second, then faltered as a moan carried down the hall from the breakroom.

"That's my mom," she whispered. "Can you help her?"

"We're going to check on her right now," Jess said. "We'll be right back."

Janine slid a printout across the counter as they passed—Beaudoin, Marni; prior calls, prior bruises, and the paper rasped like a bad omen.

The breakroom smelled of burnt coffee and lemon cleaner and fear. On the couch, a woman lay turned to one side, hair stuck to her forehead, a purple bloom of a bruise rising on her cheekbone. Her breath came ragged; her mouth drooped on one side. Jess said her name, not loud, just firm enough to cut through the fog.

"Marni Beaudoin. You're back. Did he do this to you again?" Jess kept her voice even. "Will you press charges this time? Your daughter shouldn't have to see this."

Marni blinked slowly, like the words were far away in the room. "Shelby's strong," she mumbled. "She'll get over it."

A rustle in the doorway. Shelby had edged close; crayons and a sheet of copier paper pressed to her chest like armor. Jess went to her and crouched again.

"Your mom says you're strong," Jess said gently.

"That doesn't mean it doesn't hurt," the girl said, voice small but clear, and tears slid without the drama of a sob. Jess wrapped her arms around the bony little shoulders and felt how tightly they were wound.

"Do you have family nearby, Shelby?"

"My grandma and my auntie live next door. In the big trailer," she sniffed.

"Good. I'll have someone get them, okay? Janine up front is going to sit with you. She's really nice."

"What's going to happen to my mom?"

"An ambulance is coming. They'll take her to the hospital and fix what's wrong." Jess brushed a tear with her thumb. "We're not going anywhere till your grandma gets here."

"Are you going to arrest Presley?" Shelby's eyes were dark and steady, the way kids learn to be when grownups won't.

"We'll see," Jess said, because anything else would be a lie. She walked Shelby back to the front desk. Janine leaned out with a smile that was all warmth and motioned the girl around the counter to a chair with markers and a coloring book.

Back in Jess's office, the glass walls turned reflections into paler ghosts, two tired cops, a mess of case notes, the white hum of winter coming. Casey leaned against the glass and scanned his phone, the blue light sliding across his face.

"What are you thinking, Jess?"

"That I'm supposed to be thinking differently," she said, and managed half a smile that wasn't for him. "Replacing 'the world sees Native women as punching bags' with 'bullies are a loud minority, and a lot of good men exist.'"

"Good," he said, not patronizing, just relieved. "I've got tip line notes. A few possibles. A lot of pranks. And a lot of people who needed to talk to someone, anyone."

"Same read here," Jess said, tapping her keyboard. "Let's triage. I'll print the credible community names. We can divide the rest and phone-bank."

They made three calls before the next lead wore their names, and then they were past the river, climbing into a neighborhood of big porches and poured concrete driveways. Frost hadn't touched the south-facing deck; the sun turned the boards to honey. On the back porch, a couple who looked like they'd walked out of an L.L.Bean catalogue waved them around: Charlie in an oatmeal sweater and jeans, Daisy in duck boots, a little Yorkie vibrating against her ankles.

"It's almost pretty enough to forget the calendar," Charlie said as he led them down the spiral stairs to the lower patio. "Daisy, sit please." Then to Stone and Casey: "I'm sorry. She fusses with the dog when she's nervous."

"Mrs. Durand," Jess said, flipping open her notebook. "Tell us about the sighting?"

Daisy smoothed a flyaway hair behind her ear. "I was headed to the car wash after a call with our daughter in San Francisco. You know that stretch? He shot out in front of me on a bicycle. I had to swerve—I mean, really swerve. He tipped over, and I thought, God, I've killed some young man. I got out, and he stood up. He had the prettiest dark blue eyes." She flushed, embarrassed to say it. "He looked harmless. Pudgy face, kind of doughy. I apologized. He apologized more. Then he pedaled off toward the fitness center, maybe the bowling alley."

"She told me as soon as she got in," Charlie said, nodding. "Last Thursday. Four-ish."

"You don't think?" Daisy's hand hovered at her throat. "You don't think he's the one hurting those girls?"

"That's helpful," Casey said, not committing, not comforting with lies. "Knowing his haunts is half a net."

They were halfway to the SUV when Jess's phone buzzed, and the dispatcher patched through Ashlynn's call.

"Detective Stone?" Ashlynn's voice was breathless, thready. "He just drove by my trailer. Silver car. I know it's him. He's going to finish it. I need you. Please."

"We're coming," Jess said. "Fifteen minutes. Don't answer the door. Don't move toward the windows. Hide if you can."

She clicked off and keyed Janine to

dispatch two patrol units directly. Casey threw the lights and siren; traffic threw up its hands. The main drag was a river of brake lights: hotel staff clocking in, office workers clocking out, buses lumbering in from the Cities with backs full of croupiers and line cooks. Horns answered the siren; cars parted like tired schools of fish. The slot tower flashed over the pines, red and white and indifferent.

"Stone—Ashlynn again," dispatch said, and patched her through.

"Where are you?" Ashlynn gasped. "A patrol car's out front, but they're just sitting. Nobody's looking!"

"Let the officer in," Jess said. "He'll stay with you. We're fighting traffic."

"How long?"

"Five minutes," Jess said, and Casey shot her a look she didn't like. She held it. "Stay right with the officer."

When they finally bumped into the trailer court, dust kicked up and caught the low sun. A patrolman met them at the door, hat pushed back, hand on his radio. Ashlynn stood behind him, eyes red, jaw set.

"Thank you," she said, gripping Jess's forearm. "Did they catch him?"

"Not yet," Jess said. "We're going to circle the corridors now. You stay inside with the officer. Locks on."

"Call me," Ashlynn said, like that might be the same as safety. "Either way. Please."

They made a slow sweep of the crossover

road, past the racetrack and down into pure commerce: big-box rectangles and light poles and a sky netted with bird wires. They eased through the parking lots like fishermen dragging a net, membership club, orange-apron home store, the neon tangle of the craft outlet, the pet place, a handful of drive-thrus where cold fries always smelled better than they tasted. Nothing. At the convenience store, they stepped into air that smelled like hot dogs and motor oil and coffee gone dark, and the clerk shook her head at the sketch.

Back at the trailer, the apology felt like cardboard in Jess's mouth. "We didn't find him."

"You sure you saw him?" Casey asked, and the room went colder.

Ashlynn bristled; tears came fast with anger behind them. "I made your sketch," she said. "I remember his eyes in my sleep."

"I believe you," Jess said quickly, shooting Casey a look like a shove.

"I can't run anymore," Ashlynn said. "I can't even check the mail."

Jess felt the decision bloom before the caution could stop it. "I'll run with you tonight. After work. I'm not your pace, but I'll be company. If he's watching, maybe he shows."

"Stone?" Casey warned, because that was his job.

"I'll be fine," Jess said. "We can't ask her to walk into the world alone."

"I'll set a stakeout along the valley," he said after a beat. "Eyes on the parks. Radios up."

"Oh, thank you," Ashlynn said, relief washing her voice thin. "I feel better, just knowing."

They drove back to HQ without the radio on. It made the engine sound too loud, and the silence started to itch. In Jess's office, Casey stood in the doorway and kept his voice low.

"Jess."

"How could you ask her that?" she said, not looking up. "Like she made it up?"

"Fear narrows vision," he said. "It's not about her character. It's about a brain on overload."

"She knows what she saw," Jess said flatly. "She knows what he did to her."

"Then where's our corroboration?" he asked and lifted a hand before she could jump him. "It's my job to ask both questions."

"I'm going home to change," she said, shoving her chair back.

"I'll get eyes in the lots," he said. "Don't go dark on your radio."

In the truck, she pounded the steering wheel once, hard, because anger needed somewhere to go that wasn't a human. "You're not an asshole," she told the windshield, a breath later. "You're trying to keep me breathing. But doubting her out loud? Come on, Casey."

At home, she moved quickly, putting on running pants, a light jacket, a radio clipped at her hip, and hair in a ponytail, which she yanked a shade too tight. In the mirror, she caught her own jaw set like her mother's used to, and loosened it with a stretch.

Ashlynn opened the door on three locks and a chain. "I added those," she said, cheeks flushing. "Hardware store. I couldn't sleep otherwise."

"You did well," Jess said and pulled her into a short, firm hug. "Let's move."

On the shoulder of the access road, they stretched while the last light slipped between birch trunks, turning the white bark into ribbons. The casino rose behind them, the glass catching the sky like a lake turned on its side. Across the ditch, red pine stitched the horizon; undergrowth pressed in damp and green. Jess keyed her radio.

"Casey, we're starting."

"Copy," came from the speaker. "Stay on the shoulder till you hit the trailhead. Team is posted at the lots."

They ran. The first mile was breath and pavement, and the rhythm of footfalls syncing. The air had that leaf-mold sweetness that only shows up when the ground goes soft under the first frost. Traffic thinned; the racetrack slid by, then the open field where the trail cut into the woods.

"Headlamps on here," Jess said. "Rocks and roots will take you down faster than a man if you let them."

"How many of his people are out?" Ashlynn asked, voice low.

"Enough," Jess said. "Eyes like gnats. You can't feel them, but they're there."

They paused to let a pair of riders ease by, horses wearing glow collars like small moons. In the valley, the temperature dropped a degree, maybe two; every exhale made little clouds. The river sounded close, then far, weaving around the land's shape. The trail rolled through oak and the last threadbare savanna, dropped toward a wet meadow, then skated along the edge of a swamp that would take a boot without apology. Somewhere out in the dark, a fox barked once; something small crashed away through the cattails. Their headlamps caught a thousand eyes, the glitter of spiders, the brief coins of raccoons.

At park lots, Jess saw silhouettes in windshields and the quick blink of radio lights. She didn't wave. She didn't need to. Ashlynn's breath steadied in the second mile, evened in the third. In the fourth, Jess felt the knot in her own shoulders begin to loosen, anger sweating out along with the day.

They looped back when the sky stopped pretending it wasn't night. Back near the amphitheater south of the highway, the lamps along the path cast pools of dull gold. Teenagers laughed too loudly near the picnic shelter; a dog pulled a man sideways across the grass. Twice Jess clocked Casey's SUV rolling slowly, a shadow within, a hand on the wheel.

No cobalt eyes glowed from a car window.

No silver sedan idled at the curb. No red bulldog flashed in the dark.

At Ashlynn's door, the patrolman stepped out and tipped his hat. Ashlynn fumbled the keys; Jess took them gently and slid the locks home.

"You did it," Jess said. "You ran."

"I did." Ashlynn's mouth trembled into something that might have been pride. "Thank you."

Jess backed off the stoop and looked out across the court. Trailer windows lit yellow squares. Somewhere a TV laughed, canned and bright. The wind shifted and brought the casino's distant music, a thump, a shimmer, a promise to someone else. She clipped her radio back to her jacket and started the walk toward the road where Casey would be waiting, the night wide and watchful and not finished with any of them yet.

8

A Prism of Nightmares

Stone found Borgreve already in her chair, elbows parked on the desk, the blue of her monitor washing his face the color of aquarium glass. He didn't look up when the door sighed shut.

"Casey?"

He flinched like he'd surfaced too fast. "Oh, my god—Jess. You scared me."

"We need to talk about yesterday. I know I—"

"We've got a bigger problem." He jabbed a key, and the wall display flickered alive. Grainy footage bloomed, two women, different rooms, the same nightmare: a stuttering overlay of mirrored panes and prism-flare, as if the camera were seeing through a carnival illusion.

"Who is this?" Stone stepped closer. Her reflection fractured with theirs in the screen's gloss. "Did someone come in?"

"No." His voice had the brittle edge of sleep lost. "These were posted overnight to a burner site. We don't know who they are. We don't know if anyone's found them yet."

In the first video, a hand, his, ghosted into frame with a glass. In the second, a red mark flashed, then smudged away under the kaleidoscope filter while a straw touched a cup. The women's heads lolled; their mouths formed slow questions the microphone didn't catch.

"Both raped," Stone said, flat.

"And we can see him dosing the second." Casey's jaw clicked. He rewound a second, froze. "There. That red. At first I thought cloth, but—"

"A tattoo," Stone said. The frame held a left hand, fingers square, a wash of blood-colored ink like a splash of wine across the back.

"I've got a search going for left-hand, blood-red ink on prior bookings." He tapped to another pane: a grid of washed-out driver's license photos filling in slowly as a tide. "And we're scraping the effect to fish for clear frames."

"Why didn't you call me? When did these drop?"

"Minutes before I walked in. I figured you were right behind me."

"Track the IP?"

"Bounced through five countries and a VPN we know too well," he said. "We'll get there. Later. We need to find the women now."

Stone leaned into the screen's light, trying to will eyes open in faces that swam in and out of reach. "They look familiar, but it's all blur and drug."

"I started a match against Minnesota licenses."

"That's too small. Ashlynn came in from Montana. The rez is a river; people move down it."

He gave a tight nod. "Nationwide, then."

"And print me the cleanest stills," she said, backing toward the door. "I'm taking them to Agnes. If they're new, they've touched the Center for EAP, food shelf referrals, furniture vouchers, something."

"Jess." He stopped her. The apology came without theater, quiet and square. "About yesterday. I'm—"

"I know," she said, not unkind. "So am I. I'll call you."

The Community Center wasn't awake enough yet to smell like coffee and crayons, but the lights were warm behind the glass of the second-floor conference room. Agnes, Bernice, and Vaneeta sat with steaming mugs, calendars open, pens like little spears. Stone slid the stills into the center like a tarot fan.

"This is sealed," she said. "Two women. Raped. Maybe worse. The footage is distorted. We don't have much."

Agnes squinted, mouth downturned. "I haven't seen either, honey." Bernice shook her head, regret softening her face.

Vaneeta tilted one photo until the fluorescent glare hopped off the paper. She didn't speak for a count of three, then, "Maybe." Her finger tapped the right-hand image. "She came last week for a basic household set-up. I sent her to House Start for furniture and linens, and to River Basket for food and toiletries. She had a housekeeping job starting at the casino."

"What's her name? Address?"

"I'll get the file." She was gone on quiet flats and back in a minute with a manila folder. "We scan IDs. Here." She handed over a crisp copy: **THIBAUT, DAUPHINE**. Twenty-seven. Washington State. The second page carried a tidy block-lettered address of a duplex near the trailer court.

"Thank you," Stone said. Bernice touched her sleeve; Agnes squeezed her hand. It felt like a send-off and a blessing.

The duplex smelled like cold linoleum and someone else's cooking. No answer to their knock. The neighbor's door opened a crack; a man in sweatpants peered out and, after some worry, called the landlord. An older guy arrived with a ring of keys that could have anchored a boat.

"Just to look," Stone promised. "No damage."

Inside: neat, spare. A mug by the sink, a dish towel folded with the care of someone newly careful. No party scuffs, no broken lamp, no overturned chair. The bed was made with the exactness of a hotel room. It looked like absence.

Stone stepped out on the small stoop to call the housekeeping supervisor. "She never clocked in," she said when she came back. "Phone goes straight to voicemail."

"I'll ping it." Casey's thumbs were already moving. He listened to something only he could hear. "Dead. Last ping across the river."

He looked at the landlord. "We'll lock up. Thank you."

They dropped Stone's SUV and crossed the bridge in Casey's with flyers on the console, the suspect's face staring in charcoal from the dashboard. They hung sketches in gas stations that smelled of warm tires and cheap jerky; managers shook their heads and pointed to news stories on their phones. They pushed into fast-food places where fryers hissed like angry rain and teenagers tried not to meet their eyes. Faces blurred, hours slid.

South, the river cut a brown-black line through endless stands of cottonwood. "Bloomington Ferry," Stone said. "Out-and-back. If he dumped her, he didn't drag her far."

They took the hard-pack down under the bridge where graffiti bloomed like winter flowers. The trail changed its mind every hundred yards: sand giving to rock, giving back to mud. A rope-ferry spanned a side channel, and they pulled themselves across, palms burning on wet hemp, breath coming in steamy bursts. The sun made a weak attempt at brightness; the air smelled of iron and damp leaves.

Casey's radio cracked. "We found a body," an agent said, breathless.

He went rigid.

"She's alive," the voice rushed to add. "Hypothermic. Bruised up badly. Under the bridge."

They ran hard enough to feel it. Back at the SUV, they drove with their shoulders, as if leaning could hurry the air. At the hospital, sterile light flattened everything: hope, fear, time. The woman they'd hauled from the river had a name—**Dauphine**—and a coma and a skull that had been struck hard enough to make surgeons sigh. Stone stood in the corridor staring at her own shoes while Casey signed something that needed signing.

On the way out, Stone pointed to a squat brick building where a line of people moved in and moved out with modest bags. "River Basket," she said. "If the other woman's local, they've seen her."

The lobby air was warm with coffee and canned pears. A manager led them to a back office with a bulletin board of success stories and a fake ficus that had done an admirable job not accumulating dust.

"We need your help," Stone said, placing the second still on his desk. No preamble. No badge flex. "This woman may be in danger. Do you recognize her?"

His face was trained to be neutral, but grief broke through as if the paper had teeth. "She was here. Yesterday, I think. Food box, grocery vouchers." He blinked. "Is she—?"

"We don't know," Stone said. "We hope. Can you give us her name and address? We won't put you in it. Confidential stays confidential."

He hesitated, ethics and fear wrestling. "I can call her," he tried.

"She might not answer," Casey said, gently. "Time matters."

A long breath. "All right. But this is not how we do things."

The file yielded **DULCY ABADIE** and an address that made Casey lift his eyebrows as they pulled away from the curb. The streets shifted from cracked to cobbled, ranch to custom. The house they turned toward was a coastal daydream transported to the prairie: pale siding, tiered stone walls, a front lawn that rolled like surf. Inside, through those generous panes, they could see white-on-white warmed with honeyed beams, a cleanliness that felt curated rather than cold.

A woman answered the bell in a sweater the color of wet sand. "Betty Toussant," she said. "Can I help you?"

"Sorry for the surprise," Stone said. "We're looking for a tenant—Dulcy Abadie?"

Betty's hand flew to her throat. "She rents our guest house. Is she all right? Did she... is this about her fall? She slipped down the front slope yesterday, a terrible tumble. Said it wasn't our fault. I told her to at least ice her ankle."

"This isn't insurance," Stone said, and

introduced them properly. "May we speak with her?"

Betty led them through an interior that made even Casey's shoulders relax, brick and stone fireplaces, a pub room with iron stools, a fitness center that smelled faintly of lemon oil and effort. Past a retractable screen, the yard opened like a postcard: winterized pool under a tarp, a guest house beyond like a tidy thought.

Dulcy opened the door in a long-sleeved tee and leggings. The bruises around her throat were the purples and greens of a storm coming and going; the cuts on her knuckles were raw commas. Fear shrouded her eyes.

"Can I help you?"

"I'm Detective Stone. This is Special Agent Borgreve." Jess softened her voice. "Can we come in?"

She stepped back, arms crossing not with attitude but to hold herself together.

"What happened to you?" Jess asked, though she knew.

"I fell." The word landed flat. "Down the Toussants' hill. I'm not making a claim. Please don't—does Ms. Toussant know you're here?"

Jess put the still on the counter between a stack of mail and a bowl of clementines. Dulcy looked down, then away, then back. When the sob hit, it bent her at the waist.

"It's online?" she choked. "People can see it?"

"We need you to make a report," Casey

said quietly. "We need to stop him."

"No." Dulcy's eyes flew to the window that framed the main house. "If the Toussants know there's trouble, I'll be out. I can't lose this place."

"He's hurt other women," Stone said. "Some didn't crawl free. How did you get away?"

Dulcy swallowed like it hurt. "I woke up in a plastic—like painter's tarp. Couldn't breathe. Everything spun. He was wrapping, tugging. There was a hammer on the floor. He grabbed for it, and I kicked free. I ran. Vomited, ran. Trees, rocks, and a river. He followed at first. I could hear him. Then I heard cars, and I kept going till I saw lights. I walked to the casino at three in the morning. Hid in the big bathroom until I could stop shaking. Left at six-thirty out the employee's door. Came home the back way."

Casey unfolded the sketch and laid it beside the still. Dulcy's hand flew to her mouth; she nodded hard enough to hurt.

"It's him."

She staggered to the sink and was sick with the faucets running full, as if water could wash sound away.

When she came back, she was already closing, already shaking her head. "Please go. Please."

"We'll leave our cards," Stone said. "You can call anytime. Day or night."

They gave the pool a wide berth on their way out. The winter cover held a shallow lake of rainwater, perfectly still, an eye without a pupil.

In the SUV, Casey stared through the windshield for a long beat. "He's getting bolder. But he keeps finding fighters." He exhaled. "Until he doesn't."

"We gave her a way to reach us," Stone said. "Sometimes that's the start."

"Where does that leave us?" he asked, not expecting magic.

"Exactly where we were at dawn." Jess rubbed at the tight place between her eyes. "Try again."

Back at HQ, the tip line had bred like rabbits. They chewed through the ones with teeth and set the pranks aside. The glass walls turned late-morning light into something that looked like hope if you didn't stare too long.

"I'm going to the casino," Jess said, pushing away from her chair. "Surveillance. I want to see when Dulcy came in."

"I'll keep sifting," Casey said, phone already up again. "Call me if anything breathes."

The surveillance room was a constellation of monitors, each cycling its own small universe. Through a manager and a security supervisor with very straight ties, Stone got a chair and control of a joystick. Time became a long ribbon. She sped through it, then stopped, reversed, inched. There, Dulcy, head ducked, hoodie up, posture all angles.

She slipped along the wall like a shadow trying to outrun itself, vanished into the huge restroom off the main floor, reappeared hours later paler but upright, took the staff elevator down, exited by the employee gate as dawn turned the parking lot silver.

Jess rewound, slowed, widened the view. A clown, full paint, wig, a suit the exact color of wrong, sat at a slot machine, feeding tokens with methodical fingers. For a second, her stomach dropped the way it did in childhood when someone said "boo" too close to the dark. She zoomed. Foam nose. Painted smile. She made herself breathe and tagged the time stamp anyway.

Her phone vibrated against her thigh. **CASEY.**

"Dauphine Thibaut's out of the coma," he said as soon as she answered. She could hear the relief he was trying to sit on. "CSI is en route for the kit, but she's refusing visitors and her head wound is too fragile; the hospital's backing her play."

Stone's eyes stayed on the clown as it cashed out and wandered toward the high-limit room like a bad dream changing rooms. "Text me when they clear us to talk," she said. She let the video roll ten seconds more, then flagged the file and rose. The casino's hum bled through the door, a thousand small hopes clattering toward nothing. Somewhere in it, a man with a red tattoo on his left hand was learning to be careful with cameras and not careful enough with women.

9

The Other Side of Sanity

The CSI tech rapped lightly on the glass and poked his head into Stone's office. "Twenty-seven-year-old Washington State native, Dauphine Thibaut, is out of ICU. She's asking to talk to the FBI."

"We're on our way," Borgreve said, already up, a hand slicing the air toward the door. Stone fell in beside him.

They climbed the main highway as it unspooled north, past the casino's glitter and the soft-lit billboards selling luck to the day shift. Frost still clung in thin veils across the low meadows; the river ran pewter under a sky the color of a lost nickel.

"I feel out of place here," Stone said as subdivisions turned expensive with curated prairie grasses, tasteful stone, and mailboxes with their own foundations.

"You're doing it for her," Casey said.

"I know." She watched a runner in a neon windbreaker ghost across a cul-de-sac. "Just remember this the next time you suggest I move off the rez."

He smiled without looking. "What does Megan say? People aren't thinking about you. They've got their own storms. Breathe, Jess."

The elevator hummed them up through a hospital that smelled like antiseptic and oranges. On the neuro floor, a sliding glass door was open, the curtain mostly drawn. Machines whispered. Past the curtain, Dauphine lay propped with pillows, head swaddled in white, face a map of stiffening colors—yellowed edges, livid centers. The blinds were half-open to a winter sun that made everything look colder.

"Ms. Thibaut?" Casey kept his voice soft.

"Come in."

Her eyes were glass-bright, animal-wary. Stone introduced them and took the chair, angling herself so her body blocked the worst reflections in the window.

"Have you found him?" Dauphine asked, and the question made a small tremor in the IV line.

"We're trying," Casey said. "We're hoping you can help."

She shook her head a fraction, winced. "They said I was under the ferry bridge. I remember my front door, the click of it, and then... nothing. It's all fog. Why didn't anyone see? Did—did he—" Her breath caught, the trailing question collapsing.

Stone didn't answer with words. Casey slid his phone across, the video cued. Prism blur. The red smear of a tattoo. The low, wrong soundtrack of a man breathing like he owned the air.

Dauphine made a sound that was almost not a sound. "Is— is my name on that?"

"No," Casey said. "It's posted anonymously. We traced it as far as we could this morning—bounced through half the world. We'll get there."

"How did you find me?" she asked, panic turning the whites of her eyes wide. "How do you even know it's me?"

"We have a source," Stone said. "We haven't shared your name."

"But the news—"

"They don't have your identity," Casey said.

"So, if I can't remember anything..." Her voice thinned, frayed. "Does he get away with it?"

"Dauphine, he's done this to others," Stone said. "Two women survived. We're not starting at zero."

"And the others?" She already knew. Stone laid a hand over the thin blanket and didn't lie. Dauphine turned her face away and cried silent, tearing little sobs until the nurse came with something clear in a syringe and a voice that knew how to be steady.

They left their cards and stepped back into the corridor's fluorescent quiet. On the elevator, the boxy mirror gave them both a washed-out look, like they'd been rattled in a jar.

On the river road back, the dilapidated house and its red-peeled barn hunched against the gray like bad thoughts you couldn't quite outrun. They passed the turnoff and doubled back into the mini-mall lot, where the natural foods store steamed up its windows with soup and warm bread. Lunch rush clattered gently: carts, glass bottles, the whisper of bulk bins.

"We're looking for Charity and Savanna Harris," Stone told the manager. He glanced across aisle two to two young women stocking chickpeas and coconut milk, then waved them toward the breakroom behind the deli.

"Charity? Savanna?"

"Yeah?" They said it together, twin voices, twin faces softened by nerves.

"We're here about a friend of yours—Chardonnay Jolie."

The worry was instant and loud on Charity's face. "You didn't tell our manager, did you?"

"No," Stone said. "Why not tell him?"

"Leftovers," Savanna said, quick and small. "End of day deli stuff. It's against policy, but she'd starve."

"And comps," Charity added, braver now. "When we do good work, we get restaurant vouchers. We pass them on."

"It's getting cold," Stone said. "Warm today, but that's a lie this time of year. Snow will come on a Tuesday and stay till April. She won't make it out there."

"We know." Savanna's fingers worried the hem of her apron. "We tried to bring her in.

She's scared."

"Of what?" Casey asked from the doorway, leaning on a soda machine that hummed amiably.

Charity's eyes flicked to the hallway. "She says a clown will kill her if she talks."

The word hung there, sour-silly and terrible.

"She did go to the thrift store with a voucher," Savanna said. "Got coats, boots, blankets. People put together a 'lost and found' box for her. We emptied it into her arms."

"We need your help," Stone said. "We can get Agnes and the team to set her up with a bed, food, and counseling. But we have to get her to come out."

Casey's phone buzzed hard against the doorjamb. He stepped out, listened, and stiffened. "Jess. We need to go."

"What happened?" she asked as they jogged for the exit.

"Seventeen-year-old," he said, siren already finding its voice. "Snatched near her house, raped, and a strangulation attempt behind the elementary school. A teacher on a day off heard screaming and scared him off."

The adjacent town's little downtown was all brick and cold shadow, the kind of place that looks kind in summer festivals and mean in November. Patrol cars bracketed the school like bookends; crime scene tape fluttered in the low wind. A woman in a camel coat and sneakers stood with a patrol officer, both of them too upright, like collapse would be easy.

"She's a good kid," the teacher said, voice anchoring itself. "Honor roll. We've done plays together."

"Did you see him?" Casey asked.

"I saw enough," she said, shuddering. "Red—something—here." She touched the back of her left hand. "Like a phoenix. And those eyes that were blue, like marbles. His face was soft. Boyish. Maybe twenty-eight? Thirty?"

Casey showed her the sketch. She didn't even blink before nodding. "That's him."

"Name?" Stone asked gently.

"Madison. Madison Mills. She lives down the block with her grandma, Mary." The teacher's face wobbled. "I called Mary. She's meeting the ambulance."

At the hospital, the ER was its usual symphony of urgency: monitors, rubber soles, the tromp of necessity. Mary Mills' grief cut through all of it. She clutched at Stone like the younger woman was a pier. "They said he nearly killed her."

"They're with her," Stone said. "They're working."

Mary pressed her mouth to Stone's ear, voice suddenly granite. "Don't put him in jail." A breath. "Kill him."

A doctor came, precise and kind, explaining the kit, the need, the why. Casey added two sentences that landed like nails: evidence stands when memory shakes. Mary searched Stone's eyes and found the nod she needed. The older woman squeezed her hand like a vow.

They left Mary with her rage and grief and went hunting ink.

The first tattoo shop sat on a sleepy side street, bell jingling as they pushed in. Sterile smell, flash art on the walls like skulls, roses, the usual myths. At the counter, a clerk with a nose ring looked up with a careful, curious neutrality.

"We're looking for a bright red phoenix design," Casey said, sketch out, badge flashed, and put away. "Specifically placed on the **back** of the **left** hand."

"I just schedule and keep books," she said, already turning for a row of binders. Plastic sleeves flipped with a plasticky slap. "Here." The phoenix glowed off the page with its wings to the sides, a lick of tail.

She ran a finger down margin notes. "We've done this exact art... upper arms, three of them. One back piece, one lower back, three ankles. Nothing on the hand."

"If someone asked where else to get this done," Stone said, "where would you send them?"

"Cross the river," she said. "A mile from the community college. Cheaper, younger crowd, three artists. We get their spillover."

The second shop was louder with a buzz of guns behind curtains, a bassline from a speaker set somewhere in the dark. The clerk was a kid in a flat-brim with a freshly healing forearm. He squinted at the sketch, shrugged. "Manager," he said, and went to fetch him.

The manager arrived like a storm cloud full of color with tattoos up his neck, rings that could do damage. He took the sketch with delicate hands.

"Might've seen him," he said. "Red phoenix, huh? We did one on the back of a left hand last year. Not me, but Gio did the work. Most folks put it on the shoulder. This guy wanted to see it every time he reached for something."

"Is Gio in?" Casey asked, already lifting his phone to photograph the exact stencil.

"Six p.m. to close. I'll have him call." The manager snapped the binder shut. "What'd he do?"

"Rapes. Murders," Casey said without inflection.

The manager's eyes went flat for a second. "I'll make sure Gio calls."

Back at HQ, Stone ducked into the breakroom. Janine was there with tea, voice pitched low and hot with the gossip grief gives people who care. "I heard about Madison. They said Mary went hysterical. Who wouldn't?"

"Mary's steel," Stone said. "She bent but didn't break."

"And Charity told me you're trying to get CJ out of the barn," Janine added, searching Stone's face. "People say she's making up clown stories."

"People said a lot of things about me,"

Stone said, as gently as she could. "And we've got a rapist who wears jokes like skin. I'm not laughing."

"You're thorough," Janine said, squeezing Stone's forearm. "I mean that as a compliment."

Casey met her in the hall, coffee accepted, a quick, grateful nod. "CSI ran the phoenix placement—no direct hits in criminal files. Too many private artists, too many cash jobs."

"Then we do it the slow way," Stone said, shouldering the weight of the evening slump. "Tips?"

He lifted the stack: hand-scribbled, printed, anonymous, brave. Outside the glass, the afternoon leaned toward the blue hour where details blur and some men get bolder. Inside, they began again with phone to ear, pen to paper, one thread at a time pulled from the snarl.

10

Oath and Burden

The day arrived rimmed in pewter. Snow sifted down in dry, whispering threads that turned the casino lawn into a soft blur and erased the sharp edges of the parking lot stripes. Inside Stone's glass-walled office, the fluorescents hummed and coffee steamed, and the whole building felt like a ship battened down before a blow.

"Agnes just called with clown referrals," Jessica said, rid of her coat but still haloed with melting flakes. "Birthday parties, daycare gigs, the occasional charity thing. Three names."

"Let's roll the dice," Casey said, settling at her keyboard. The snowlight caught the new tiredness around his eyes and made it look clean. "Bachelor Number One is cleaner than a choirboy." Click, scroll, sip. "Number Two is also clean." He tried a smile. "Don't worry. Our luck's just fashionably late."

"Make it fashionably armed," Jess said, leaning over his shoulder.

The third name opened like a trapdoor.

Casey's face changed first—humor gone, posture sharpening. "We've got a prior," he said, voice flat to keep from rushing. "Sexual assault of a minor. But the clown alias is his stage name. Real name is Jackson Cottler."

"Identifying marks?" Jess scanned the rap sheet. "No tattoos listed."

"Conviction's old enough he didn't have the ink then," Casey said, already thumbing his phone for the road team. "If our phoenix is new, it never made his file. Let's not give him time to grow new wings."

They were on the highway two minutes later, siren strobing pale in the falling white. The river looked like hammered pewter under the bridge, ice shingled against the banks. On the far side, a suburb unspooled in quiet repetition with muted yellow fourplexes with timber decks, SUVs wearing snow beards, children making quick, jubilant use of the first true powder of winter.

"There," Jess said, pointing. They eased past a woman coaxing a toddler from a car seat and nosed into a driveway, fishtailing just enough to make the snow hiss.

"Ma'am," Casey called, badge up. "Does a Jackson Cottler live here?"

She hugged the child closer, startled, then composed. "We bought this place three months ago. I think it sat empty for half a year before that."

"From whom?"

"Landlord next door," she said, chin flicking toward the adjoining unit.

The next door opened on the first knock. An elderly woman with careful hair and the soft, skeptical eyes of someone who has outlived several disappointments peered out. "You're looking for my boys," she said before they asked. "Shannon and Jackson. Good neighbors. Helped me with groceries. They moved into an apartment not far away when our landlord sold a few units."

Casey's pen paused at "good." "Do you know which complex?"

"No. Only that it was close," she said, retreating to fetch the landlord's card. "What did they do?"

"I can't discuss that," Casey said softly. "Thank you."

The landlord answered on the second ring, confirmed the sale, and shrugged audibly about forwarding addresses. "They ghosted," he said. "Even the post office couldn't catch them."

By the time they'd circled the block twice, the snow had thickened, big flakes now, slow and theatrical. Inside the SUV, the heater clicked and the radio muttered. Casey's phone chirped from the console; he stabbed the green icon.

"Say that again," he said, and fell suddenly very still. He put it on speaker.

"Special Agent Borgreve, we ID'd the motel from the bed with a custom headboard, twin sconces, and a house phone. The night clerk recognized it. We pulled guest manifests for Jackson or Shannon

Cottler."

"And?"

"Old address on file. Pre-sale. No current card on record."

They ended up back at HQ, the glass walls now a watercolor wash of white and motion. Sleet ticked at the upper windows; the parking lot became a rumor. Stone stood a long moment watching the storm, her breath lifting the coffee's steam.

"What about his old accomplice?" she said finally. "The minor case. If he's upright, he can lead us. If he's not, he can try to run."

Ten minutes later, they were across the river again, staring at another townhouse where Christmas lights pulsed bravely under a new icing of snow. No answer. A parole officer's number yielded a sigh and an old address. A ping request put the accomplice's phone near the casino hours ago, and then nothing. Turned off, or tossed.

By midafternoon, the world outside had narrowed to the width of a plow blade. The casino's night shift began arriving early, their cars leaving soft wakes. Patrols inched through the property, radios crackling, security cameras blinking away sleet. In Stone's office, tip lines lit up, cooled, lit again. Casey's patience wore thin enough to show wires beneath.

"Where is he?" he said, palms flat, eyes hot.

Stone didn't answer. Her phone buzzed with a text from Agnes: **Have you checked the barn? Storm's bad. Worried about CJ.**

She could picture the volunteer coordinator's worry like a shawl.

"Casey," she said, pocketing the phone. "I'm going to the barn."

He didn't look up, and she didn't insist. She paused to tell Janine at the front desk, then braced the wind and shouldered through the tried-and-true ritual of Minnesota winter of a hat, gloves, breath frosting, and boots sinking.

The highway was a white corridor. Plows roared past in contrails of grit, and fields lay like sleeping things under quilts. The old driveway to the derelict farm was half-swallowed, the SUV's four-wheel drive climbing it in a slow, steady crawl. The house looked like a memory with its windows open to nothing, walls splayed, the last of the red paint flayed off by seasons. The barn hunched close by, roofline sagging, a slit of light showing at the loft window, strobing when the snow gusted.

"Finally," Jess breathed, and felt the old prickle that comes before walking into a place that wants to keep its secrets.

She radioed dispatch and stepped into the wind.

The barn door hung like a broken tooth. It protested when she pushed, and a mound of drifted snow tumbled inward, cold fog blowing off it. From above came the clatter of something hurriedly knocked over and boxes skidding, a bottle rattling against wood. She cursed herself for not clearing the main floor first, but kept her voice level and audible.

"CJ? It's Detective Sergeant Stone." She climbed the stairs, complaining beneath her, taser out and down, beam cutting the gray. "I'm here to get you someplace warm."

The loft smelled of cold hay, old oil, and the sour residue of too many meals eaten out of paper. Candlelight shivered in a tin, casting nervous shadows. CJ sat on her bed of blankets and flattened cardboard, bundled in a men's parka two sizes too big, eyes wide and shining in a face made younger by fear. The corners were piled with thrift bags, a hand-lettered box that read **LOST + FOUND**, a nest of quart bottles near the furthest window, and the little neat stack of cigarette butts by the sill where someone had stood and stood and stood and stood.

"It's just a taser," Jess said, easing it back into its holster and opening both hands. "See? No guns. We've been looking for you for months. We can get you food. A bed. Heat."

CJ shook her head once, fast, like a flick. Behind her, something shifted in the stacked boxes along the wall, just a sigh of weight, then the world broke.

The two-by-four came from the side: rotten, but heavy enough, and the blow turned Jess's sight into white static and a flood of noise. She went down hard, breath knocked out of her, taser skittering. The clown loomed where shadows had been: red wig damp with snowmelt, greasepaint streaked, mouth grinning too wide over a blur of flesh. Behind him, a man in a navy hoodie that was thicker, square around the shoulders, stepped into the candlelight, eyes bright and empty.

"I heard her come in," the man said, Jackson's voice, flat and pleased. "Taking a shit behind the tractor paid off. She didn't clear this room." He knelt and yanked Jess back from the loft's edge by the boots, a casual strength. Twine rasped across her wrists. "Don't get noble," he told CJ without looking up. "Shut up and stay put."

Downstairs, the wind combed the door, and the rafters creaked like old ships. The clown tore the shoulder mic off Jess's harness and punted her phone into a dark corner, then clattered down the steps with Jackson. The main door banged open under a gust, flinging snow into the shadows. Their voices rose and fell as they rummaged and argued in the blue light: metal scraped, wood thumped. Somewhere beneath the floorboards, the old tractor sulked.

Jess surfaced from the ringing in her head into a pocket of stillness. CJ had slid closer on her knees, eyes darting between the stairs and Jess's hands. On the nail-crate beside the bed, a switchblade stuck open, blade reflecting candle tremors. Jess flicked her chin toward it; CJ nodded once, a little yes that felt huge.

The cutting was delicate work, not fast enough. The twine tightened when Jess flexed, snapped in two sharp pulls. Blood rushed back into her fingers with pins and fire. She finished the rest herself, motion small, breath shallow. CJ belly-crawled to where Jess's phone had landed, hissed softly when she found it, and did exactly the right thing and dialed 911 and left the line open on the floorboards.

"We should run," the clown said below, voice too big in the cold space. "My car's at the casino. We go now."

"Shut up," Jackson snapped. "Hear that? Engine. Somebody's stuck." The sound came then, faint through the wind with the high whine of tires in snow, the steady groan of a plow farther off. "I'm not going back to prison."

Outside, the storm flexed, a solid wall of white beating at the seams. Inside the barn, time forked.

Casey's SUV slid to a stop at the base of the drifted door. The wind punched him when he stepped out, with ice needles in the beard he didn't have. He jammed his shoulder against the wood and shoveled with his hands, swearing at the cold and at everything that wasn't yielding fast enough. Through the crack he opened, he could see the clown and Jackson pacing behind the tractor like caged things, and above, in the shiver of candlelight, Jess, who was alive, on her knees, already scanning for angles. He let the relief hit his ribs and then moved.

Upstairs, Jess was already moving, too. She scooted to the two-by-four and hefted it; rot crumbled under her grip, but it had weight. The floor groaned, and Jackson spun and hit the stairs two at a time, face set in a hard boy's dare. He crested the top step, and Jess swung. He caught the timber, snarled, and yanked it away. He lifted the taser he'd scooped off the floor earlier, and she crashed into him like a tackle, driving them both toward the stairs. They tumbled. The taser clattered into the gloom.

"Shit, shit—" Casey grunted, hauling the door high enough to crawl. Snow poured into his sleeves, found every seam.

Jackson staggered to his feet below with a hand to his nose, blood bright in the gray. Jess had the switchblade now. He saw the blade, saw the door shift again, and hesitated. It was enough. She slashed and drew a red smile across his cheek, then lost her balance on the slick boards and skidded toward the loft's edge. Her hands found the broken lip and held. The fall below was a cathedral of rust— tractor, spikes of old iron, angles that had no forgiveness.

CJ lunged for her, small hands braced, and in the scramble, a candle went over. For one stunned second, the little flame was beautiful, a coin thrown into the dark. Then the hay caught with a sound like a sigh, then a roar.

"Out the back!" the clown yelled, shoving at the rear door. It was drifted shut. He grabbed a shovel and hacked at the snow, breath gusting, greasepaint breaking into sweat. He looked up once and saw lights at the base of the hill with headlamps snow-furred, blue strobes stuttering. "They're coming."

The front door finally gave under Casey's leverage and flopped outward like a loose tooth, slamming into the drift. He rolled under and came up in the main room as smoke thickened, his light searing through it in a clean beam. Above, Jess found the stair lip with her boots, swung her weight, and climbed. CJ grabbed her arm, pulling, soot streaking her scared face.

"Down!" Jess coughed. They ran for it, the two of them, as the heat lifted the hair on their arms and a part of the loft let go with a sick crack, collapsing onto the tractor in a brief, appalling shower of sparks.

"I've got her," Casey yelled through the smoke at the backup officer who slid in behind him. "Get CJ outside. Everyone's out—go!" He didn't wait to see if the order landed; the clown's red wig flashed at the back door like a bad flag. Jess peeled right, after that blur, snow exploding under her boots as she cleared the jamb.

She saw the patrol car at the hill's base, lights rolling the color of urgency across the white. She saw two figures staggering toward it: the clown and a dark shape that could only be Jackson. She lifted her weapon. Wind knifed sideways, snow ramped into her eyes, and for half a second, the clown's head was the only true thing in the world.

She breathed in fierce, cold air, steadied,

and then lowered the gun and moved.

She killed the passenger-side tires with two fast shots when they reached the car; the rounds thumped in the snow-tamped air. The men swore, veered, and ran. The clown slipped and went down hard. Jess ran past him, trusting Casey to scoop, and cut after Jackson, who was already angling away toward the mini-mall lights and, beyond them, the dark shoulder of the community center.

Casey went to ground with the clown in the snow by the patrol unit, knee in back, cuffs clean and cold. "Hands," he said, breath steaming. "Don't test me." He jerked his chin at backup. "We've got one in custody, and Stone went after the other. Send units to cover the community center and the memorial garden. Move."

The storm had softened to fat flakes by the time Jess hit the frontage road. The world narrowed to white breath and the drum of her heart. Jackson had a head start and desperation; she had anger and lungs that refused to quit. He crossed the highway in a slash of blaring horns and dashed over the berm into the mini-mall lot, then toward the darker, unplowed scrim of the community center grounds. She followed his slide marks around the north corner of the building, boots chewing through drifted powder, past the black skeletons of shrubs and the blank faces of office windows that reflected the white world back at itself.

They broke into the memorial garden at the same time from opposite ends. Snow had turned the plant beds into gentle mounds and put soft shoulders on the granite markers. The new two-foot-wide, four-foot-tall upright meant for the murdered women leaned against a sawhorse, waiting for a thaw to anchor it. Beyond, a pair of bare cottonwoods sounded like old paper.

Jackson turned hard and swung, fist catching Jess on the cheekbone. Pain flared hot and stupid. She answered with a kick that took him in the groin, and he folded, then surged, hands finding her throat and squeezing with the last he had. The world tunneled and beat against her with snow and blood; she clawed for his eyes and found them. He cursed and rolled off, scrabbling for leverage. She stumbled back to her feet. He lunged again, the blunt intent of it like a bad dream you've had too often, and this time she stepped aside and let momentum do the work.

He hit the upright granite slab with a sound that was both stone and bone, face-first. The snow received him without pity.

Jess cuffed him while his breath still sounded human, knees in the snow, hands both shaking and precise. When Casey skidded around the corner seconds later, she was sitting back, panting, blood dripping in a patient line from her nostril to the lip of her glove.

"Hey," he said, breath ragged. "Hey. You

good?"

Jess looked up, eyes bright and glassy in a face smudged with smoke and blood and snowmelt. She looked over his shoulder at the memorial, at the way the storm had gentled in the last few minutes, flakes big as feathers. "Look," she said. "It's letting up."

Behind her, the sirens converged with their tribe of sound, and beyond them, the barn's fire was already losing its hunger to the snow. In the quiet between the wails and the wind, you could almost hear the small tin prayer of heat ticking down in the metal of the ruined tractor, and the brave, thin chorus of tires on wet pavement as the plows passed, and the breath of a town that would sleep a little differently that night.

Casey helped her up with a hand at her elbow that was gentler than she'd ever admit she needed. "Oath and burden," he said softly.

"Oath and burden," she answered, and watched the breath they made vanish into the cold.

Children's laughter rose faintly from the playground behind the community center, drifting thin and fragile through the frost-bitten dusk. Snow lay in bruised heaps where plows had pushed it aside, and the memorial stones stood like dark teeth waiting for names. On the road beyond, a single cruiser rolled slowly into the thinning storm, its red taillights bleeding across the drifts before vanishing into silence and leaving behind only the hush of winter and the echo of what could never be fully buried.

The End

A Soul Darker than Midnight: start of Novella #4

Bonus Chapter

A Prayer for the Unseen

The tribal police headquarters buzzed faintly with the hum of fluorescent lights, their glow turning the glass walls of Jessica Stone's office into cold mirrors. Outside, a November wind clawed against the siding, and the last tatters of autumn leaves scraped along the pavement like restless spirits.

Inside, Stone stood stiff at her desk, shoulders squared, fists pressed white-knuckled against a stack of case files. Her voice cut the air like a blade: **"What the hell is a white woman doing as the poster child for Missing and Murdered Indigenous Women & Girls?"**

She was thirty-two, taller than most of her colleagues, built from years of training and running trails at dusk, her long dark hair falling into her eyes now as she snapped. Her gaze burned into the man across from her—FBI Special Agent Casey Borgreve, who leaned with practiced ease against the doorframe, all six-foot-two of him, muscular arms crossed, blue-green eyes steady but edged with fatigue.

"She's gone missing from the casino," he said evenly, though the corner of his jaw tightened. "And she's not just anybody. Elizabeth Henry is 17/32 Dakota Sioux. So what if she looks white? Be grateful it shines a light on our cause."

Stone's laugh was sharp, joyless. "Why? Because her skin makes the posters palatable for the public? Because she doesn't carry the scars we carry as in the trauma that dogs us through generations, that brands us with addiction, abuse, violence, arrest records?" Her words hung in the air, jagged as broken glass.

"Jess, nobody is saying those things," Borgreve countered, though he shifted his weight, restless.

"Then why not use one of our actual missing sisters—our murdered daughters—for those posters?" Her voice cracked at the edges, anger curdling with exhaustion. "Why Elizabeth Henry?"

"She *is* one of yours," he pressed, stepping closer, lowering his voice. "It doesn't matter if she looks like a square peg. I didn't choose her. Washington did. My higher-ups told me more resources are coming—more agents. That's what matters."

Stone's teeth ground together. The fluorescent lights buzzed louder in the silence that followed. "Elizabeth Henry," she spat, "is going to be the face of our crisis. You don't live here, Casey. You don't hear the whispers. It won't be you they turn their mistrust on. It'll be me."

Before Borgreve could answer, Janine, the tribal police clerk, popped her head around the glass partition, voice hesitant. "Jessica, the tribal council wants to talk to you. About the news reports. The chief says you're the one to go. Immediately."

Stone exhaled hard, the sound like a slammed door. She shot Borgreve a glare that carried both fury and something unspoken. "You really piss me off sometimes."

"Jess, it's not my fault either," he said softly. "Let me come with you."

She shook her head. "They know you're here. If they wanted your voice in that room, they'd have asked for it."

His mouth curved in the faintest grin, an attempt at levity that fell flat. "I can be awfully persuasive."

Stone was already moving toward the door. "Not this time. The tribe isn't about to hang your damn poster."

The council chambers smelled of cedar and old tobacco, smoke woven into the beams from years of ceremonies and debates. A carved drum sat in the corner like a sentinel, its hide stretched tight, as if listening. Fluorescent light hummed above, but the room felt dim with shadows clinging stubbornly in the corners, as though unwilling to leave.

Jessica Stone stepped inside, her boots echoing on the worn wood floor. The seven council members sat at the long oak table like judges, their faces carved with history and hard miles. The air was thick with unspoken disapproval, the kind that didn't need words to wound.

"Detective Sergeant Stone," Chairman Red Elk greeted her with a nod that was more command than courtesy. His silver hair gleamed under the harsh lights, his eyes sharp as obsidian. "We've all seen the news. We've all seen the poster."

Jessica drew in a breath, steadying herself. Her voice came out low, controlled. "Elizabeth Henry is being used as the national face of Missing and Murdered Indigenous Women & Girls. That wasn't my choice. It came from the FBI."

Councilwoman Dora Two Hearts leaned forward, bracelets clinking. "Then you should have stopped them. A white girl on our posters? The whole community is laughing, Jessica. They're saying we can't even protect our own, that we need outsiders to stand in for us."

Stone's jaw tightened. "She isn't an outsider. She's Dakota Sioux—"

"On paper," Councilman Wapasha snapped, his voice gravelly with age and cigarettes. "But the public sees pale skin and blue eyes. They see one of them, not one of us."

The words stung, but Jessica held her

ground. "She's missing from *our* casino, on *our* land. That makes her one of ours, no matter what she looks like. And if her face forces the FBI to send more agents, then I'll use every resource they give me."

A murmur rippled through the chamber. Some leaned back, thoughtful. Others shook their heads.

Chairman Red Elk drummed his fingers against the oak, slow and deliberate, like a heartbeat. "Do you understand what this looks like, Stone? Do you understand the message it sends to the families of the women we've already lost?"

"I do," Jessica admitted, her voice softening, though her spine stayed rigid. "But I also know what it's like to have no attention, no help, no backup. If this girl's face on a poster gets us the manpower we need, then maybe—just maybe—we find *all* our women faster."

For a long moment, silence settled like dust. The hum of the lights seemed louder.

Finally, Red Elk leaned back, exhaling. "You're walking a knife's edge, Jessica. If this backfires, it's your name they'll spit on in the community, not mine. You want the weight of that? Then carry it. But don't expect us to shield you from the fallout."

Jessica bowed her head, just slightly. "Understood."

She turned to leave, the sound of her boots again cutting the silence. As she reached the door, Dora Two Hearts' voice followed her, sharp as flint:

"Pray you find her before they decide she never belonged to us at all."

Jessica pushed through the heavy doors of the council building into the brittle afternoon light. The cold cut through her coat like needles, the kind of wind that scours a person's spirit as much as their skin. She walked fast, boots crunching salt and ice, each breath sharp in her chest. The council's words clung to her, heavy as chains, every echo of "not one of us" gnawing at her bones.

By the time she reached the Community Center, dusk had begun to creep in. The building stood like a lantern on the edge of the reservation, its windows glowing warm against the slate-gray sky. Inside, the air smelled faintly of coffee and frybread, of cedar boughs hung to dry near the entrance. Children's laughter spilled faintly from the gymnasium, muffled by thick doors; the sound of life carried against the shadows of grief.

Agnes GreyEagle was at her desk upstairs, framed against the wide window that overlooked the casino lights beyond. She turned as Jessica entered, her eyes kind but unflinching, as if she'd already read the storm written on Stone's face.

"Jessica," Agnes said softly, rising to pour a second cup of coffee without asking. "The council?"

Jessica sank into the chair opposite her, setting her gloves on the desk like discarded armor. She didn't answer at first, only exhaled a ragged breath that trembled in the quiet.

"They tore into me," Jessica finally said, her voice low, thick. "Called her an outsider. Said I'm betraying our own dead by letting her face stand for theirs."

Agnes slid the steaming mug across the desk, her rings catching the lamplight. She sat, folding her hands over her own cup, waiting.

"I fought back," Jessica added, her voice sharper now, as though confessing. "Told them she belongs to us. That if her face gets us more agents, more eyes, more pressure—it's worth it. But it didn't matter. They don't trust me. They never will."

Agnes leaned forward, her gaze steady as stone. "Trust isn't given, child. It's carried, like fire in your hands. Burns you some days. Lights the way on others." She paused, letting the words breathe. "And sometimes, it's both at once."

Jessica stared down into the dark swirl of her coffee, her reflection warped in its surface. "They said it'll be my name they spit on, if this goes wrong."

"And if it goes right?" Agnes asked gently.

Jessica looked up, the faintest flicker of hope surfacing beneath the exhaustion in her eyes.

"Then it will be your name they remember," Agnes said. "Not for failing. For standing."

The hum of the casino neon pulsed beyond the window, casting faint colors across the glass like restless ghosts. Inside, the warmth of the room pressed close, Agnes's presence anchoring Jessica against the cold weight of the world outside. For the first time all day, Stone felt herself breathe.

Jessica wrapped her palms around the mug as if the ceramic could steady the tremor inside her. Steam curled upward and fogged her lashes. She stared into the swirl of it, voice breaking low.

"She doesn't fit, Agnes. Elizabeth Henry—this girl they plaster across posters and newsfeeds, but she doesn't carry the scars. No foster homes. No DUI arrests. No mugshots. No one whispering about who her father was or whether her mother stayed sober long enough to make it through a parent-teacher conference. She looks like she belongs in a glossy brochure. And because of that, people care."

Agnes didn't flinch, only watched her with the stillness of a stone face carved by centuries.

Jessica's words quickened, sharper now, the storm spilling from her chest. "What about the others? The ones who vanish from the back roads, from trailer courts, from bus stations? Where are their headlines? Their faces don't 'sell the cause.' So, the FBI lets her stand in for all of them, and I'm left choking on the bitterness of it. Because the community sees me, sees me letting her be their symbol, and they call it betrayal."

The room seemed to tighten around her confession, the hum of the heating vents a soft pulse against the silence.

Agnes leaned forward, resting her elbows on the desk. Her voice came slowly, deliberately. "You're right, Jessica. It isn't fair. It isn't equal. The world notices beauty and passes over the faces carved by hardship. But listen to me: Elizabeth Henry *is* one of ours. Blood doesn't lie, no matter how pale her skin. And if her face pulls open doors long locked to us... maybe that is her offering, her burden to carry."

Jessica blinked hard, her throat thick. "But why do I feel like I'm betraying the others every time I let her name cross my lips?"

Agnes's gaze softened, and she reached across the desk to cover Jessica's hand with her own. The touch was warm, steady, a counterweight to Jessica's turbulence. "Because you carry them, too. Every missing sister, every silenced girl, every mother who never came home. Their names are carved into your bones, Jessica. That's not betrayal. That's love."

The words hung in the air, heavy and luminous.

Jessica swallowed, her shoulders loosening, though her eyes still burned. "Then how do I keep walking into those rooms? How do I face council, community, the mothers, and not feel like I've already failed them?"

Agnes squeezed her hand gently. "One step at a time. You remind yourself: every poster, every case, every night you don't sleep, those aren't failures. They're prayers for the unseen. And prayers don't always look pretty. Sometimes they look like you: bloodied, angry, still standing."

Jessica let out a ragged breath, the kind that carried both defeat and renewal. Beyond the window, casino lights shimmered like false stars, and in the glass her reflection stared back at her that was not polished, not perfect, but resolute.

Jessica finished the last of the coffee, lukewarm now, bitter on her tongue. Agnes didn't press her further as she never did. The older woman knew when silence could do more work than words, and the hush between them was thick with understanding.

When Jessica finally stood, the chair legs scraped softly against the wood. Agnes rose, too, and they embraced. Jessica felt the press of bones, the steady heartbeat against her own chest, and for a moment it was like her grandmother again: someone older, wiser, carrying the weight for her when her own shoulders sagged.

"Go on," Agnes murmured near her ear. "The storm's waiting."

Outside the office, the center buzzed with small, ordinary life: kids shrieking from the gym, someone rolling a cart of folding chairs across tile, Bernice laughing too loudly in the corridor. The warmth of it contrasted cruelly with what Jessica knew she was walking back into, the headlines, the missing girl, the whispers from her own people that she'd let herself become an arm of the Bureau instead of their defender.

She tugged her coat close and stepped out into the parking lot. The air slapped her, cold and metallic, carrying the faint throb of bass from the casino down the road. Neon light reflected on the wet asphalt like smeared paint. She pulled her keys from her pocket, eyes drifting skyward. No stars. Just cloud and electric haze.

By the time she slid into her SUV and turned the ignition, she'd locked her face back into its mask. Agnes's words still lingered in her chest, but out there was no room for softness: only work, only cases, only the grinding machinery of what came next.

The radio crackled alive with dispatch chatter. Another sighting, maybe. Another name to add to the list. Jessica gripped the wheel tight, the leather cold against her palms, and drove back toward headquarters, the casino lights winking behind her like false constellations.

The drive back was a blur of wet pavement and half-frozen drizzle streaking the windshield. Jessica barely registered the casino traffic or the way the neon bled into the dark like veins of false daylight. Her mind was already at the station, already bracing.

Inside tribal police headquarters, the warmth was stale, heavy with burnt coffee and the hum of fluorescent lights. Janine glanced up from the front desk with something unsaid in her eyes, but Jessica didn't stop. She pushed down the hall, boots clicking against tile until she reached her office.

Borgreve was already there, perched at the edge of her desk with a file open, his tie loosened, shoulders taut with restless energy. He looked up the second she entered.

"You're late," he said, but his voice wasn't sharp; instead, more relief than reprimand.

"I went to see Agnes," Jessica replied, tossing her coat over the chair. "Needed a dose of clarity before I drowned."

"Well," Borgreve tapped the file, "hope she gave you some, because we've got a fresh lead." He slid a grainy photo across the desk. It was a screenshot from casino surveillance. A van, pale and nondescript, parked behind the hotel's loading docks. The timestamp was Halloween night.

Jessica leaned in, studying the blurred figures near the back doors. Her throat tightened. "That's the same type Wynter Stewart described—the one she said had young girls inside."

Borgreve nodded. "We cross-checked every van registered to staff and contractors. This one doesn't match any of them. Plate's obscured, but my techs are trying enhancements."

Her pulse ticked faster. "So, either Elizabeth was taken in that van or she saw what she wasn't supposed to see."

"Exactly. And the kicker?" He flipped the page. Another shot, this time of a man half-shadowed in the van's headlights. Chubby face. Blue eyes caught in the glare, unnaturally bright.

Jessica exhaled sharply, her jaw locking. "It's him."

The office felt colder suddenly, as if the building itself was holding its breath.

Borgreve closed the file with a snap. "We've got a vehicle, a timeframe, and maybe even a route if the highway cams caught him. We need to move fast before this trail goes cold."

Jessica nodded, but her hand lingered on the photo. Agnes's words were still there in the back of her head, whispering about belief, about conviction. But here, staring at those blurred blue eyes, all she felt was the weight of the hunt.

"Let's go," she said.

And together, they walked out into the hum of headquarters, the walls already vibrating with the ripple of a case about to break open.

By the time they reached the monitoring suite, the room was thick with the glow of screens and the low murmur of techs sipping cold coffee. The casino's security office had given them full access, but it was the state highway cams Borgreve was after.

Jessica stood behind a young analyst whose workstation bristled with feeds. The traffic footage was a blur of headlights and streaked rain, timestamped Halloween night. The analyst scrubbed backward until the grainy frame of the pale van appeared, rolling out from the casino's rear service road.

"There," Jessica said, her hand tightening on the back of the chair.

The analyst zoomed, tried to sharpen, but the plate was smeared with mud or purposefully obscured. The silhouette of the driver was no clearer than a ghost.

"Timestamp?" Borgreve asked.

"2:37 a.m.," the analyst replied, fingers clattering over keys. "Headed eastbound."

Another tech pulled up the next junction. The van slipped past a gas station lot, headlights flashing across wet concrete. For a moment, a passenger's arm hung out the window, pale against the night, before it pulled back in.

"Freeze that," Jessica ordered. The arm was slender, wrong against the burly shape of the driver. Her stomach sank.

"Elizabeth," Borgreve said under his breath.

They followed the van hopscotch-style through cameras like the casino access road, frontage lanes, then onto the main highway where traffic thinned to long-haul trucks and stragglers. Each frame was worse than the last, the van slipping deeper into anonymity.

Finally, at the ferry bridge, the trail broke. The van vanished into darkness, either taking an exit beyond the cam's reach or cutting into the service roads along the river.

"Pull up the riverside cameras," Jessica pressed. "If he dumped her like Dauphine..."

The analyst shook his head. "The closest working cam is two miles downstream. Nothing shows."

The room was quiet except for the hum of electronics.

Jessica stepped back, rubbing her temples, eyes burning from the flicker of screens. "He knew where the blind spots were. This isn't sloppy. This is rehearsed."

Borgreve's jaw flexed. "Which means he's done it before." He tapped the table, leaning into the analyst. "Flag every vehicle matching that van's make and color in the last thirty days. I don't care if it's two a.m. or two p.m. We need a list."

Jessica's gaze returned to the frozen frame and the pale arm in the night, a fleeting fragment of a life swallowed whole. Her throat tightened, but she forced her voice to be steady.

"Casey," she said softly, "he's still out there. Hunting."

Borgreve didn't look away from the screens. "Then so are we."

The river roads were little more than ribbons of wet gravel, swallowed by trees and the hiss of the current below. Borgreve's SUV crunched along the shoulder, headlights cutting through fog that curled low across the banks. The casino's glow was long behind them now, replaced by patches of black woods and the occasional glint of water through the trees.

Jessica cracked her window, letting in the night air sharp with mud, cedar, and gasoline fumes that seemed to cling to every pull-off. She kept her flashlight balanced across her knees, fingers tapping against its metal grip.

"He could've cut down any one of these service roads," she said, eyes scanning for ruts in the gravel, fresh tire tracks, anything that didn't belong.

Borgreve slowed at a turnout where the brush opened into a rough path leading to the riverbank. The SUV idled as he killed the headlights, leaving them in a darkness that pressed close, broken only by the silver shimmer of water.

"Boots on the ground," he muttered, slipping into his parka.

The river roared louder here, swollen from recent rains, chewing at the banks in frothy swells. Their flashlights sliced across the mud, catching beer cans, broken fishing line, cigarette packs gone soggy in the drizzle. Jessica crouched low, running her hand across tire grooves still sharp in the clay.

"Fresh," she said. "Within the last twenty-four hours."

Borgreve angled his beam toward the reeds. There, trampled stalks bent toward the water, as though something heavy had been dragged through. He crouched, pulling a latex glove from his pocket, and lifted a scrap of fabric half-buried in the mud.

Scarlet. Thin. Torn.

Jessica's chest tightened. "Not river trash."

"No," Borgreve agreed, slipping the scrap into an evidence bag. "Looks like clothing."

They pressed deeper toward the waterline. The mud grew slick, nearly sucking the boots from their feet, until the river itself came into view as a black, heaving expanse lit only by their beams and the dull reflection of the ferry bridge lights downstream.

Jessica froze. Across the ripples, a shape bobbed and drifted against a snag of driftwood, too pale, too human.

Her breath hitched. "Casey."

But when his light found it, the thing slumped and turned, revealing not flesh but a mannequin's head, its painted grin grotesque beneath the beam. The current pulled it under, and it vanished into the dark sweep of the river.

Silence held between them, broken only by the churn of water.

"This isn't random," Jessica said finally. Her voice was low, almost a growl. "He's leaving us messages."

Borgreve's jaw tightened as he glanced upriver, scanning the endless shadowed bends. "Then we'd better start reading them before he writes another."

They pressed farther downstream, boots crunching over pebbles, sinking into black mud that reeked of algae and rot. The beam of Jessica's flashlight jittered across low branches, snagged on tangles of driftwood, and then fixed on something pale caught high in the reeds.

She waded closer, the ground sucking at her boots, until the shape resolved. A shoe. Women's, sequined, waterlogged, the glitter dulled to a sickly gray. She lifted it with two fingers, mud dripping from the heel like blood.

"Same size as Elizabeth's," she murmured.

Borgreve bagged it without a word, scanning the river's edge with a hunter's gaze. A few yards farther, his light caught another anomaly in a rope hanging from a branch, frayed at the end, fibers stiff with silt. The knot looked deliberate, practiced.

Jessica ran her gloved hand along the rope. "Somebody tethered something here. Weighted it." She looked up at the current, then downriver toward the ferry bridge, its red hazard lights flickering through the fog. "This is a dumping ground."

They kept moving. The path narrowed to a wash of sharp stones, slick as glass. Jessica slipped once, catching herself on Borgreve's arm. He steadied her, then pointed ahead with his chin.

"Jess. There."

Half-buried in a drift of wet leaves was a crumpled paper mask, a clown face, the cheap Halloween-store kind, its paint running in the damp. One eyehole torn, the mouth warped into a twisted leer. Jessica stared at it, bile rising in her throat.

"He's taunting us," she said, voice flat. "Leaving familiar ghosts in plain sight."

Borgreve crouched, bagging the mask. His jaw flexed. "Or staging a trail he wants us to follow."

The current below heaved against the banks, carrying branches and debris, but Jessica swore she saw something else in the foam like a scrap of red cloth swirling, vanishing, reappearing just long enough to suggest a sleeve, an arm, a phantom that refused to surface fully.

She turned away, pulse hammering. "Casey... he's been here. And recently."

The wind shifted, carrying the sharp tang of gasoline from upriver. Borgreve's eyes narrowed. "He's not just discarding. He's burning. Cleansing."

They stood for a moment in the dim, the river's roar swallowing everything else, both knowing they were walking inside the perimeter of someone's ritual.

The river narrowed, choked with fallen branches and mats of cattails that rattled in the dark like bones. Their boots sloshed, the mud clinging heavier, pulling at them as though the land itself wanted them to turn back.

Jessica's light picked out more fragments: a hair tie snagged on a twig, strands of blonde woven through its elastic. A crushed Styrofoam cup. A scarf half-buried in muck, soaked and stiff as parchment. Each scrap whispered of presence, of lives funneled into this gullet of the river.

"Jess," Borgreve muttered, his beam sweeping wide. "There."

At first, it looked like a log jammed against the roots of an overturned willow. Then the shape shifted with the current, pale flesh showing between rags of clothing.

Jessica's stomach clenched. She waded forward, icy water seeping over the tops of her boots. The body rolled just enough to reveal a face, swollen, mottled, unrecognizable, and yet unmistakably human.

Her throat tightened. "Female. Young. Goddammit."

Borgreve already had his phone out, calling it in, his voice clipped, professional. But Jessica barely heard him. Her eyes were on the hands. One palm was splayed in the current, fingers curled as if reaching. On the back, faint but visible under the water's distortion, was a smear of crimson ink.

Not a tattoo. Not paint. A mark, drawn hastily, bleeding into the skin in the outline of wings.

Jessica staggered back, the reeds thrashing against her legs. "He marked her. He's escalating."

They stayed with the body until the patrol unit's lights pulsed faintly through the fog upriver. Jessica forced herself to look away, scanning the opposite bank.

And froze.

A figure was standing there, just beyond

the glare of her beam, broad-shouldered, still, watching. For a breathless second, she thought it was Borgreve's reflection, but the eyes caught the light: bright, cold, unnatural.

The figure melted back into the trees without a sound.

"Casey," Jessica hissed, voice cracking, "he's here."

But by the time Borgreve swung his light across the far bank, there was only the empty hush of the woods, and the river carrying its secrets downstream.

End of Chapter

AUTHOR NOTES

Domestic abuse, sexual assault, and running away are very real experiences that can leave lasting scars. Without proper intervention, they can lead to serious mental health struggles, suicidal thoughts, or even death. If you or someone you know is experiencing this, please know you are not alone — and help is available. Below is a list of organizations that can offer support and resources:

Rape, Abuse & Incest National Network
1-800-656-HOPE (4673)
http://www.rainn.org/

National Suicide Prevention Hotline
Dial or Text 988 or 1-800-273-TALK (8255)
www.suicidepreventionlifeline.org

National Alliance on Mental Illness (NAMI)
1-800-950-NAMI
Or text "NAMI" to 741741
www.NAMI.org

National Domestic Abuse Hotline
Text START to 88788
1-800-799-SAFE (7233)
www.thehotline.org/

National Runaway Safeline
1-800-RUNAWAY
www.1800runaway.org/

ABOUT THE AUTHOR

Angela Grey is an Indigenous novelist, poet, and painter whose work explores the intersections of memory, identity, and healing. She studied creative writing, as well as spirituality and healing, at the University of Minnesota, where she deepened her commitment to storytelling as both an art and a form of medicine. Alongside her writing, Angela finds balance in yoga and mindfulness practices, particularly Mindfulness-Based Stress Reduction (MBSR), which shape the reflective quality of her work. She lives in Eden Prairie, Minnesota, with her husband, one spirited pup, and four cats. When she's not writing, she enjoys camping, budget travel to places like Maine, Oregon, and the coastal Carolinas, and gathering with family around a BBQ grill.

Website: angelagrey.com
Website: ShadyOakPress.com
Instagram: angelaellengrey
Facebook: angellaellengrey
Twitter: @AngelaEllenGrey
Tiktok: @authorAngelaGrey